This book dedicated to family members.
The story is fiction, with the help of Mississippi family history
Special thanks to members who shared and did not discourage
The names are many; you know who you are, God bless you

IT'S ALL RELEVANT

by

Jerry J. Powell

This book is a work of fiction. Names, characters, places and incidents are products of the author's imagination or are used fictitiously. Any resemblance to actual events or locales or persons, living or dead, is entirely coincidental.

ISBN: 978-1-7366387-5-0

Cover Design: Brittany Jackson

Published by G Publishing, LLC

Printed in the United States of America

FOREWORDS

More and more, when I single out the person out who inspired me most, I go back to my grandfather."
—James Earl Jones

I was searching through my mind for a singular moment from my grandfather that inspired me, but I could not find one because his existing in my life is inspiration enough.

Even though my father has always been in my life, my grandfather, or "Poppa" as I affectionately call him, has always been a big presence in my life. The lessons my Poppa taught me allowed me to grow into the man I am today. The confidence I have walking into a room knowing that I am enough no matter who else is in that room, the pride I have in where I come from, and the lineage of my family, all come from my Poppa, Jerry Powell. So, it is exciting to see him write about his grandfather and the stories he was told as a child. For me, it just opens the door to see what shaped him as a man, and what he has passed down to me will be what I pass down to my children. It is important to me to have insight into what shaped your predecessors. Every conversation I have with my Poppa imparts knowledge inside of me from something I did not know. Whether we are talking about the plight of Black people in America, or the importance of being a man, the value of how to treat a woman, all the lessons I learned through him are what he learned through his father and grandfather or through his journey in life.

It is an honor to write this foreword for my Poppa because I want to not only show the readers his importance to me, and how this book should touch you after you read it but it's also my way of telling him Thank You. Thanks for the long talks and sound advice. Thanks for always being dependable and thank you for teaching me how to be a man. I am aware that not all black men are blessed with individuals like my Poppa so I am extremely grateful for him being in my life, and I'm even more grateful that the world will get to read his words and see how majestic he is. Hopefully, this book gives you a glimpse of how special he is and where that seed was planted.

– Jerrod Berry

My name is Zetta, at least that's what my family calls me. I was born the first girl after three older brothers, and I guess I am the closest to this big brother because he was at home during most of the time that I was. He was the youngest of my three big brothers. He used to tease me and my sister by making us wait until he felt like giving us some of his ice cream and cookies as he ate it in front of us. He's always been a good artist and has a passion for writing poems. He saved me on the playground when needed and encouraged me not to give up on assignments when failing multiple times, he helps me in my house with repairs and remodeling since my husband died. We've done some dumb things together and through God's grace made it through. Stepping up when we had to was automatic. How can I not be proud and ecstatic when reading his writings? I'm so grateful to God for my mother who supported us with love and togetherness in any type of weather. Read this book and know how love, family, and life's experiences go hand-in-hand. Enjoy! from his oldest little sister.......

–Rosie **Withers**

TABLE OF CONTENTS

INTRODUCTION

Studd starts looking in different directions, new avenues to travel. Ones that will show favor as he treks through his life's journey. One favor Studd is seeking is that of fining and marrying a magnificent woman, one that he can grow old together with, one lady to become his wife. The woman Studd has in mind must be a good housekeeper, a mentally strong and physically good-looking woman. A mate that he thinks he can begin a large family with to help oversee the farmland, and other family business acquisitions that they would acquire. In addition, his wish is to become a generous person, a person helping those folks in need . . . indeed, family's matters especially.

Education, the gaining of information that will equals success. One of the models Studd has decided to integrate into his life, "knowledge is power."

CHAPTER 1 . . . Situations to ponder

A person sure has time to think when there is no one in his or her ear. On this hot morning in June 1911 it is a relief, knowing that the loud sound of singing voices and music blasting has come to a halt. This was a rough Friday night I tell you, Studd said thinking out-loud. Too many fights and broken bottles for sure was Studd continued reflection. Old man Jeff getting into fights with every young buck that looked toward his woman Sue who is a lot younger than he is. He is more like a Sugar Daddy, a withdraw teller for Sues pleasure is what most of the population view him as. Sue is pictured as being the kind of woman that likes to see men exchange punches; she acts as if she is the gift that every man seeks. Jeff must know he is not the only one she permits to enter into her private cavity, which is not that private anymore. Believe me I; George "Studd" Freeman has been entertained there a time or two myself. As Studd continued his recollection, he recalled the first time being with Sue. He remembers becoming one with her a couple of times that occasion. Not that I chased after her, she offered herself and I had nothing else to do. We got busy right in here, after the other customers had left Studd recalled. Beside they are not husband and wife anyway Studd reasons with himself. Further recalling actions taken with Sue, Studd now knows not to touch her with a ten-foot pole, too much drama. Once Sue saw Studd with another woman and she did not know how to act. She started to act a fool out in public cussing and fussing as if he was not supposed to see any other woman, although she has Jeff on the side whenever she wanted him. Now whenever Sue comes around the Juke Joint it means it is time to set out the tin cup no glass anything, nothing that can be easily broken. Sue would make it her business to flirt with as many men as possible. Any amount of attention from a man seen to validate her. Fact of the matter, Sue is a shapely mighty fine good-looking woman. Enough about that Studd thought that is the past, time to move toward the future. Situations to ponder, new directions to explore, more hats to wear in future business ventures is what I suppose to be focusing on Studd said aloud to remind himself.

Finish with the cleaning of the Joint, Studd sends the waiter help home. As he began to lock-up, it came to him that maybe if a dress code was in place on Friday Nights that would limit the dangerous incidents. Maybe that would slow down the violent acts between customers while dressed to impress. After all, most of the farm hands had only a couple of sets of church attire. Wrapped up locking-up the joint Studd walked down the dirt path to the main road. While walking; he decided that he would talk over his ideal with his brother Man. His most trusted business partner would give him an honest opinion of the ideal. Studd started to look forward to reopening the Juke Joint later that night. In a hurry to see what his brothers sense on the matter would be. Together they would explore the possibility of local advertising for the Juke Joint.

I am so glad this Friday night is over Studd said to himself aloud. We have closed again this morning, thank you Jesus, the Juke Joint was rocking with folks, we made a few dollars, and no one got seriously hurt. Now it is time to make that long track back to my apartment. During Studds walk down the dirt road heading home, he could hear the sound of a rooster crowing. Being a country farm boy himself he could picture the roosters spreading their wings as it made boastful alarming sounds. That unique sound reminds people that it was time for them to rise and begin their day. Saturday morning rooster crow was a reminder his Friday night had ended as Studd made his way on down the road. During the course of Studds trip home, several thought crosses his mind. Should he invest some of his saving into transportation, knowing time is money, and his feet and legs get awful, tired stand on them hour after hour daily. On the other hand, investing the saving he had built up into some other venture wasn't a bad ideal either; he knew today, that wealth is power. Power in this communality was something he longed for, to make a difference for his family.

While working the stocking job for Mr. Charles at the Warehouse and managing the Juke Joint on weekends Studd had accumulates a good amount of cash. Now the decision is what does he do with the money rather than just let it sit in the glass jar under the sink. Knowing it take money to makes more money Studd decided to look toward expand his operations. Acquired land he knew would be a very good investment, so looking to procure some was his next mission for sure. Now that he has a few inside connections with the county authority and knows money talks Studd is certain he will be able to acquire his desire acquisition.

After going around and through many channels, Studd was able to purchase thirty acres of land about an eighth of a mile off the main thoroughfare with a limited access road to his property. With the help of his Warehouse associates, Mr. Charles, and his son Jay in particularly as well as a couple of the County administrator, Studd was finally able to purchase land in the region, however many hands had to be fed before success was met " payment under the table that is ". Studd on-going vision for the land was that he would be able to raise crops to feed a family as well as to sell to wholesale distributer. Selling retail to the public as a street vendor at county markets was also envision; this is what he foreseen in his future clear as day, this belief would become true Studd knew. Being the thinker that he is, Studd knew he needed someone's help. Someone he could trust to watch his back when he was not around. A person to oversee construction of the home he someday plans to build. No one would be a better fit then his brother Man to staff a crew of builders. Man had done such a great job on the completion of the Juke Joint that Studd knew without a doubt Man was the man for this task as well. While Studd was thinking, he realized that Man, his brother, his friend, and partner needed security too. Studd decided he would look into acquiring land for him as well. He wanted never to forget the person that helped him to become the operator, owner of the Juke Joint, his big brother never lets him down.

Studd only had a second-grade education; was not able to read very well. Therefore he had to rely on other to translate paperwork and contracts for purchases. Because of his inability to read, a number of Studd transactions left him indenture to other after liability fabricated paperwork appeared. However, Studd was a man of his word, "words on papers not always understood" he so honored papers that were misquoted with his supposedly signature on them. Studd knew that this reading issue he has, had become a big problem. He made a promise to himself that one dilemma he would be triumph over, come hook, or crook. That he would learn to read and take care of his own business paper trail within the next few months. Thinking some more, Studd decided it would not hurt to check with Miss Elisabeth for counsel. She works as a teacher in the Negro school perhaps I can get instruction from her Studd contemplates. Hoping that for a modest fee, she would work with him during her free time schedule. Reading with self-assurance would make thing a lot easier, easier in general Studd imagine. If Miss Elisabeth would accept an hourly pay rate, it would be great. After all fair exchange is not robbery Studd had come to realize. But! For the time being he will have to have faith in the relationship he shares will Jay. After all Jay did help get him started with the land purchase and supply for the Juke Joint. In the very beginning, Jay was the one person that invested in his dream. Jay had been a trusted partner so far in their business association. No operation alarms or signs of misuse had Studd witnesses from Jay. So soon, Studd thought Jay would get another chance to prove his trustfulness. So! Far trustworthiness has been Jay's middle name.

'Getting together and talking about a new business venture Studd envision would be the focus for tomorrow meeting with Man and how other people would play a part. Right now it is time to relax the mind get into the apartment and rest.

CHAPTER 2 . . . Reflection

With the air standing still and the temperature near 100 degree Studd is awaken around 1 o'clock in the afternoon. He sat-up on the side of his bed and began patting moister off his forehead with a dry towel. With his body wet from perspiration Studd could not take it anymore, he disrobed from the rest of his sleepwear. Studd walked into the kitchen undressed went straight to the Ice Box open the door and just stood there. More ice will be needed soon Studd sees in his mind's eye as he enjoys the coolest. After a few minutes of great pleasure and watching the ice melt, Studd decided to close the door. Not able to get away from the heat Studd thought a shower would be the next best thing. No, better yet he could go out to the family pond and position himself in it for as long as he liked. At the same time gets a chance to talk with Brother Man of the upcoming business situations he'd envision. After quickly washing his face, brushing his teeth Studd puts on his over-all, shoes and made it out the door he went. He would grab a ham sandwich and soft drink from the Bar-BQ joint down the road Studd decides as he hit the first steps exiting out of the apartment building door.

This is one of those times, when the transportation reflection would come to Studd mind. Getting a vehicle was a future event, something else to look forward to. That too being kelp in Studd's rational concept also. As he picked-up his walking pace, he notices not many folks out on the boulevard today. Usually on Saturday afternoons, the town and its business district are as busy as can be with all kinds of commerce going on. It must be the weather that has people staying still was Studd's conclusion. One thing about this town however, its growth has been non-stop the last few years. The construction of new buildings and shops opening on a weekly basics, how cool was that. Those actions can only help the community with job opportunities for skill and un-skill labor, white and black citizens alike. Problem is the pay scales always favor the white people. That is just the way it has been, with no changes anticipated in the fore see able future. The pay scale and hiring practice look as if it would stay forever, Studd shed tears within just thinking about the injustice. Someday we as Negro's will overcome the short pay for the same amount of work as White has and get equal compensation Studd thought anticipates the future. Continuing his walk, he thought, back in the day he knew almost all the people in the county. Now with the new growth of the county during a walk many people pass without, "a how you do" or wave of the hand. Things are changing for sure; the town has sidewalks and streetlight installation. No more walking in the roads, while in town, too much automobile traffic now. In addition, there are louder noises than before. People seem to be rushing here and there most of the time. Was all of the transition good or bad for the town Studd was not sure?

After clearing the road traffic in town, Studd notice there was still no cool gentle breeze as he walked down the empty section of the southern Route 55 road. Suddenly the sound of a nearby truck engine catches Studd attention. An old red damage pick-up truck pulls over to the side of the road and stops. A voice shouts-out Hey! Studd, what you are doing out here, in all this heat. I am traveling down the road a few miles, would you like to get a lift, the man inside the truck Marty Thomas inquires. Marty just happened to be a down stair acquaintance living in the same apartment building, which Studd was glad to see this scorching heated afternoon. Marty, my main man, Studd happily replies. Yeah! I can use a ride I am going down the road to my folk's farm, right off Route 55 just a few miles from here. Studd continue his greeting by calling Marty by his whole name Mr. Marty Thomas. You traveling this way is a blessing to me Marty! Mart, Studd said just to acknowledge their friendship standing. Studd wipes his forehead with his favorite hanky during his sharing of small talk with his neighbor. So glad to see you out here today you are a lifesaver Studd ramble on. Get on in then! Marty said in his deep baritone voice. I am on my way to the market in

Georgetown. I got things to do and people to see Marty said all the while smiling showing that a couple front teeth were missing. I got to pick-up a few ears of corn for this fried corn my old lady is making for us this evening Marty inform his new passenger. Studd hurriedly cross the road and goes around to the truck's passenger side opens the truck door and slide into the rip seat. Sound like you got it made Dude, with a woman that is good in the kitchen cooking for you Studd alleged aloud. That is something I am seriously thinking about finding for myself, a wife Studd shared honestly. Listen! My man, shoot, believe this or not, it ain't always a bed of rose's Marty said with a frown appearing on his face. Don't get me wrong Marty continues as he put his truck into low gear and started off. After pulling, the teeth pick from between his lips Marty declare. My old lady is a treasure for sure. Most men would not be able to get away with the things I do. Her loving me unconditionally is mostly a thrill for me. I would come in late or the next morning wasted from drinking all night, but she still helps undress me as I try to get into the bed. Now that is one of the advantages for me. Although the loving is good, we just cannot sleep together, when it is time to close our eyes for real, we do not share sleeping quarter, she snores like a train coming down the track. Then too sometimes, a married woman mouth just won't stop Marty said finally ended his rave. Well! In my humble opinion Studd states, marriage is not a 50/50 relationship anyway. Someone has to have the final say or make the ultimate decision when things get rough and tough. For better or worst that the plan I intend to keep Studd said with his attitude voice that became a little deeper. Without catching his breath, Studd passionately continues to expose his belief. I think each spouse be it man or woman whoever has the better intellect for sustain situation, should be the one to make the call that benefit the couple.

Yeah! Okay, my man was Marty responds. Then added I guess you will make some woman a find catch, do you do window too Marty jokingly asked. Studd, believe me, if you are serious about finding a good marriage candidate. You should go to a church Marty boastfully suggested. What do you know about that Studd inquired? When was the last time you put your head into a church building Studd added to his questioning? Look my man I do not spend all my time at work or at the Juke Joints. At church is how I meet my wife Henrietta, as a child we were forced to attend church on Sunday and some of it stuck, know what I mean Marty asked. Listen Studd, most churchwomen are faithful women and hard workers. I might be clowning around a bit from time to time but believe me I am not going to blow this good lady that's in my corner for anyone. We go to church on a regular basic and you are welcome to attend with us if you like. We are Christians that attend Mountain High Baptist Church; service begins at 8:30am Sunday morning bible school, Worship service at 10am you can ride with us anytime. Matter of fact I have a couple of sisters that go there, nice women that are looking for a good decent respectable man Marty let it be known as his smile got bigger the more, he talked. Studd finally cut in intruding Marty to ask a very important question that would make all different. Marty, check this out no disrespect to you or your wife, the way I see it Henrietta's a fine-looking woman and that one of the requirements I am seeking. Is there any more Henrietta's at Mountain High, Studd asked with his hands up just to be on the safe side? He was hoping Marty would not take his question the wrong way, which it appears he did not. Look, I am still a man so I see a lot that looks good to me; your intellect and favor might be a lot different from mine. Just come to a service, see, and meet for yourself Marty strongly suggests. Yeah! Right, listen, one Sunday soon, I will take you up on your offer I will definitely keep that in mind Studd volunteers. You can let me out around the next bend and thank you very much for the ride and conversation Studd said no longer whispering. A short time later, the truck start to slow down and finally come to a halt. Studd open the door thanking Marty again as well as leaving him with a couple of dollars on the seat for gas. Big time, I did not stop and pick you up for a fare Marty said while waving his hand left to right in a manner that says no, put those in the collection box at church for some needy family, I am good. Helping-out this is what we do, one neighbor looking out for another. Studd gave Marty a hand salute, closed the truck door as he responded with see you later then, my man.

CHAPTER 3 . . . Not the same

Studd step to the side of the road, watched Marty drive away in his old beat-up Ford and thought, maybe it is time. As quick as that thought came to him, another vision kicks in. Stay the course, obtaining some homeland for his future family, is the next acquisition on his list of things to accomplish he remembers. Studd snapped back to the presence task and began his walk down the over-grown weeded entrance road to his sharecropping family farm. As he looked about Studd wonders if Poppa, has continue his saving for the pull-tractor. And, if so, how much more would be needed to make the purchase. Just a thought Studd said in his head, knowing Poppa was a very private man. Matter of fact, secretive is more like the truth Studd surmised. I hope that I will get a chance to discuss the tractor issue with Poppa, Studd stated aloud in an eager but low voice to himself. After a couple of minutes, Studd is able to recognize the house he grew-up in. In sight of the farmhouse Studd, see several children out in the front yard playing. Each one not quite old enough to be field hand help yet, this was visible to all that knew anything about Mississippi Negro farm life. Thinking, that he had not been out to the farm for a while, things still looked the same came into Studd's mind. Within shouting distance, the children saw him and began to holler out his real name "George! George" while running toward him. Did you bring us something was the first question? Wait, wait a minute, you little people. You guys know better, a proper greeting is what's expected from each one of you Studd said in a forceful responding voice. The children did not seem to pay attention to Studd first commanding order, so he had to repeat his stipulations louder. I know, you all heard me, so! What you going to do, I need my hugs and kisses before I give out anything "fair exchange is not robbery" Studd reminds them of his one of his life lesson teachings. With that being said all of them started to jump onto Studd with their hugs. Okay! Okay, Studd said while surrendering the hard candy out of his pockets to the more than excited children. All of a sudden, a high pitch sounding voice was heard, it was his Mama, what's the commotion all about out here, she asked with that distinguish southern drawl. Most folks around the county that knew the Freemans called her Big Mama or Mama Viola. Hey! Ma was Studd's quick reply, as he walked up the pouch steps to greet her formally. After rapping his arms around her and planting a long kiss on her cheek, Studd asked how are you feeling, how you doing Ma? Before she could answer him, he started asking another question, Studd had forgotten his manner. Got any cornbread made, he said while opening the screen door to enter into the house. Boy! Have you lost your mind or what? You asked, how I am doing, and then walked away. I do not think you really wanted to know about me, you just here to get some of my cornbread Mama Viola smilingly told Studd. Ah! Sorry about that, Studd told his mother while still on the quest to the kitchen. You know you're number one in my world, Ma, how are you doing? It's just that you always say I'm fine, so I guess I take it for granted, that would be your responds. I do not say that all the time Mama Viola said while slapping Studd upside his head playfully. Ma, why you hit on me, Studd said. As he, continues his search into the icebox cabinets. Move out of the way, Mama Viola tells George pushing him out of her way. I will get it for you. I know what you want, cornbread and buttermilk right? Right you are, you know me to well Mama, Studd answers. Get a bowl, here your food she said putting in on the table. Thanks Ma, you are better than the best Studd said loud enough for all in the house to hear. Mama, I have something for you too, as he pulls out an envelope from his right rear pocket. Since his mother back was facing him, Studd had to reach around her waist and place it into the pocket of the apron she was wearing. Son! Each time you come home; you do not have to bring me a gift Studd mother assures him. Ma, these gifts are a pleasure for me to give to you, there a small token of appreciation, for the love you show us on a daily basic Studd said reassuring her. Not taking no for an answer Studd said to encourage his mother to keep the present. Furthermore, he wanted to share with his family and knew if she had, the rest of the family will benefit as well. That's one of the secrets he kept to himself. Mama Viola took Studds right hand and rubbed it gently as she thanked him for helping with the monetary packets. Now! Sit down and eat your food, we do not want any flies to get into it, Mama Viola said ordering Studd to the table. Home, no place like home Studd said aloud while starting to sit in a chair at the kitchen table. When visiting the farm, he sometime would reminisce about his past behaviors and activities. Just thinking about the good and bad times, so many lessons learn out here in the back woods of Copiah County, Mississippi.

It did not take Studd long to eat his delicious bowl of buttermilk and cornbread. Afterward the cleaning-up of his mess was his obligation, a habit he learned while growing-up here at home. Cleaning right after you make a mess was the way to go, that way no bulging number of dirty dishes mounted-up. Noticing how quiet it had become Studd wondered where everyone disappeared. He quickly decided to go and investigate the surrounding area, first inside the four other rooms then outback. A quick look indoor found no one in the house so they must be outside Studd concluded. Out the front door he went, to his surprise the whole family stood silently right be on the porches steps. What! What is going on Studd said to the group all puzzled. Poppa and Mama, steps forward with a decorated basket full of canned fruit and vegetable. This is for you son; we the family wanted to come together and thank you for all the generous contribution you have given us. Each offering you shared has extended and enhanced our way of life. Still, we do not have a whole lot, but we want you to know that we as a family recognize your help, Poppa says as a tear ran down his cheeks. Suddenly as if on command applause of appreciation from all of them began. Having not witness anything like this before Studd become overwhelmed himself. Turning his lowered head away from the other, he began to wipe away the crocodile tear that came from his eyes. Shocked, Studd had no words he just began to hug those nearest. You, my family is all I have, I am nothing without you on my side. So! Thank you, especially for the directions that you gave to me during my young impressionable years Studd said with a shaky voice, while still rubbing his eyes. This was so unexpected; you folks are something else totally Studd express to the family. I will remember this, the rest of my life thanks, now go, back to doing what you were doing, and get those crop out of the field before their ruined Studd continued as if he was giving order. Poppa, Mama, I have something I want to discuss with you, as soon as possible Studd inform them as he waves his hand, requesting for them to join him on the porch. Both parents looked at each other, with baffled expression on their faces, wondering what this talk could be about. Before walking up the stair steps Poppa pull Mama a bit closer to him and told Mama that he thinks George was going to say that he is moving up north. Both had heard that the northern city hires Negro's into the automobile plant and pay them the same as they pay the Whites per hour. Once arriving on the pouch Studd, invited them to sit, then he began to express that he was considering buying, buying some flatland himself down by the riverside. That the site would be parallel to their and the property he currently own. About fifty-five square miles of land to develop. A big task for any man and that he would need their knowledge to transform it into profitable real estate. Wow! Son that is a massive amount of land to clear Poppa said as he rubs his head in disbelief. What are you saying George, just how do you figure to pull this land grabbing out from under those barons that are sitting in the county clerk's office? Well Poppa, you see knowledge is power too. I know a few things about many powerful peoples that they do not want to be making public. Some of which I have share with them; the paper trail I have would truly hurt quite a few of their bank accounts. If it became awareness to all of the state the economy would take a nosedive, which would take years to recover from Studd said informing his parent. George, this is! This George is the kind of actions that could get you lynched. Beside get the land is one thing but keeping it is another. The Klan will be on you, as if flies were on cow dump Poppa said calling himself advising his son of the risk. Yes, I know Poppa, I have given all of that the attention it warrants. Know that you did not rise a fool. Ever since you place me into Mr. Charles care, I have been sitting on the side just listening as the good old boys talked as if I was invisible. Keeping my mouth shut while listening and watching every transaction. Soon, well I could say after a while, I was able to decipher good deal from the shaded one. Now translating their codes, I can do rather easily Studd shared with his parents. Much of the information I received actualizes read to me by Jay Charles. He said that he's cut out of a lot of valuable deal. So! With that being, told to me, I just removed the carbon copy from the files. No one has notice anything missing to this day Studd enlighten his trusted parent. In the midst of Studd's story both Poppa and Mama Viola sat still in one position, with eyes bulging and mouth open. I know, sorry Studd said I believe I have giving you more information than needed for this venture to be successful. I did not mean to overwhelm you; I just been holding it to myself for so long. Trust me, I am not working on this project alone, I have a couple Lawyers in place for legal matter Studd said hoping to assure his parent of his safety. This undertaking is quite a bit more. Thought through than a northern carpet-baggers scheme he vowed with a smile. The negative possibility of this endeavor has been considered. For any ugly contingence, Studd attest. However, Poppa being from the old school of thought and knowing the method of the mad white man, men that kill Negros' for whatever their want and keep it moving. So! Poppa request that he accompany George whenever he plans to inspect the real estate property before the acquisition. Not a problem Studd said which comforted his father; fact was, I was going to ask you to accompany me anyway, I need you, for your land culture expertise. Things will never be the same for this family once I get a hold of this land with river access Studd proudly said.

Successfully obtaining 63-acre plot of flat black bottomland with Pearl River access from the Copiah County, Mississippi Land Authority would be an important conquest. A magnificent success that, no other Negro in this territory, has ever accomplished. These tough and challenging real estate actions should definitely take and allow the family members out of bondage from the sharecropping landowner and their overseer forever. Southern white men still follow the practices of the past, a family never gets from under the landowner debt Studd came to believe. As he watches, his father and other Negro families barely survive. Year after year, sharecroppers would be in the hole owning the landowner for seed or money to make it through the winter months. This purchase of land would have a mile and a half of river access. Adequate shoreline that both, commerce shipping and recreation actives can survive. A people of color place to enjoy swimming and family fun, etc..... Private beach access for a small fee would bring in a nice bit of change too. The river water is deep enough in the area that large containerships could easily dock, that is after a dock was built for service to them Studd envision also. Suddenly Poppa stood-up from his seat, walking toward Studd with right arm extends and hand open, as if to shake his son hand. With a broad smile, Studd greeted his father hand with his. Both gave a long hug to one another as well as strong solid handshakes. After a few moments pass Studd attention went toward his Mama. Ma, you sat there without asking any question, nor did you talk about any concerns, Studd put to his mother. Sweetheart during my lifetime any outside business of our family been cared for by the man of the house. Your Father knows what's best, I have trusted him with our livelihood before you were born. I thank you for including me; however, the decision has to be that of your and Poppa's. My expertise is those of the kitchen and home making, if you need a quilt, I am the person to see Big Mama proudly voiced. Well, thanks for your listening ear, Studd said informing his Mama as he reaches down to hug her as she sat. I believe everything planned is going to become reality and GODs on our side Studd pledge.

During Studd, declaration of the truth as he knows it, Man just happens to walk through the front door. Hey! What's going on, I saw everybody walking back to the fields away from the house? What happen, is everything all right Man asked with a worried look on his face? We had a little celebration, to honor your brother, for his continued help around the farm Big Mama whispered as if; it was for Man ears only. Well! My brother must have some long arms if he has helped around here Man whispered in responds to be sarcastic. Man, you know we had planned this, but again, we could not find you to participate in the presentation Mama continue looking unsatisfied. Look George does not need me around for him to feel his worth Man interrupt. He and we all know how much he contribute to this family, Man said in a smart attitude voice. Turning away from George and starting to talk toward his oldest son Poppa bellows out wait! Wait a damm' minute here Poppa interrupts not liking the tone Man was using with his wife. Only one man is going to raise their voice in disagreement around here Poppa said, as he looked straight into Man's face. Man, knowing big hands Poppa was not one to be challenge quickly put a smile on his face. Hey! "Hands up, don't shoot" Man said as he acted out the gesture. Sorry if I was out of order, I did not mean any disrespect toward Mama or you Poppa, Man acknowledged. While Poppa was talking to Man, Studd ease his way between the two men in case stiffer words exchanged. Poppa was not taking any backtalk from a child he raised at any time both Studd and Man knew that. There only one alpha male in this house and all knew in what order they start.

Abruptly Studd barge into the conversation with a suggestion, now that we three are together, I want to get Man's perspective on my decision too. What! What decision are you talking about Man asked, while patting his Poppa shoulder? Just have some ideals for the convenience of the property. I think the future is what we have to look forward to. We have been discussing the value of river front real estate for our family. Whatever riverfront properties purchased you will be a big part of Studd continues. All of the investments will have your name on the contracts as well. So! Get ready to roll-up your pant legs. Causes we are about to wade into water that has never been explored by Negros, Studd said hoping to sway the other. We do not want anyone to take advantage of us, so we have to make sure all gates are close, Poppa introduce to the conversation. Sure, your right, Man said agreeing with his father. Now, we have to take this in a different direction, make them the County Clerk Office think that this property is worthless.

Studd comes up with an ideal, Guys, I will commission Jay Charles to get the assessment papers, have the land survey, and throw a party. Throw a party; I think that would be a bit premature Man swiftly cut in. The party is not to celebrate it is to get the assessment paper signed and Notary stamped. I know, you know when men, women, and booze come together, no telling what can take place Studd confesses. We will have the party at the Juke Joint, which mean no Clerks will have a woman with them. Right, we know they will not bring their Southern Belles to a Negro joint, Studd said continue with his plan. Jay will come, deliver the County Clerks and the paperwork, after a few strong drinks, I will have a couple of my lady friends entertain them. Before you know it, Grace and the girls will have the paperwork signed, sealed, and delivered to us Studd assured the fellows. Grace that is my girl, Man makes it known. I hope she do not have to service them to much at the party Man interrupt to say. It is business, Poppa said reminding Man of the reason for the activity. Just doing what they do was Grace and the crew. Servicing men for a profit, fair exchange not robbery Poppa concluded.

So! With just a few more detail to be worked out, we will be equipped to start the process, Studd said with a huge smile. I think, we are finish with all we can plan for now Studd suggested. We will get together again right after I recruit Jay. I am sure for a fee or commission he will join us and accommodate our plans. It should not take long after getting him aboard, and then we can see our earlier preparations moving into action, Studd tentatively ensuring the other. Afterward with arms up and fingers crossed on both hands Studd, turn his body, facing the door, he proceeds to walk and exit the house. Once on the porch, he calls for Man to come out and join him. Wait a minute I have to get me something cool to drink Man replied. Do you want a glass of water or something before you take that track back into town Man question Studd? Matter of fact will have some cool water Studd said acknowledging Man's inquiry. After coming out of the house door with two Mason Jars full of cool lemon-aid, Man sat down on the top step next to Studd and hands his brother one. Before a word is said, both men hastily consume the contents of the jars. Behind a loud bulgur from Studd, he quoted "better out then in," and then afterward informs his brother that he wanted him to walk back into town with him. Look, here, I have to get some rest George, Man said in a no non-sense voice, I been up all-night and day. In a few hours we will be back at the Juke Joint waiting on crazy acting people, so we can talk more later at the club, Man enlighten Studd as he got up from the steps. Matter fact we need some transportation brother, doing all this running back and forward, Man goes on to tell his brother.

It was obvious to Studd that this conversation over, it was a discussion he was not going to entertain. Okay! I am out of here, see you later Bro, maybe we will have time, maybe not Studd tells Man. Off the steps Studd went, walking in a fast pace he soon exits the family sharecropping farm. Once entering into Route 55, he notices that the highway leaving back to town again was empty of automobile traffic. Looks as if he would be walking back into town he thought. Studd however was thankful that the sun had gone down a bit; and that the humidity was lighter. The air was much cooler than his morning journey. From the look of the sun direction, it had to be about 7 o'clock this evening Studd thought. After traveling a while, Studd figured he had only a few hours before he had to be back at the Juke Joint to unlock the doors. Knowing only Man and himself were people with keys, he had no choice but to be on time to welcome customers. Man has completed his part of the bargain after all. Opening the joint on Thursday and Friday nights Studd had to bear that in mind. This arrangement was good business for both parties Studd was convinced. Because he never knew, what time of day would be the closing time for him at the Mill Warehouse? Besides, once he gets into town, he hopes he would run into Miss Elisabeth it should still be daylight. Miss Elisabeth is a good-looking woman as well as an educated one Studd thought with a smile on his face. Perhaps one day soon, she may allow me to take her out for dinner and a movie Studd thought, continuing his daydreaming. Suddenly an automobile horn sounds, making Studd jump to the side of the road. As the automobile passes Studd notice it was Commissioner Kelly. One of the men he knew he would soon have to do business among. John Kelly was one of those nighttime-hooded riders. He let it be, known that he did not care for people of color and tried to keep a boot upon their necks whenever possible. After seeing the driver Studd thought, John must be in a good mood. After all, he blew the horn not run over him. Thinking back, Studd remembers when that redneck used to play in the river with him. Also, time to time they would hire themselves out to nearby farmer to work the fields for extra change. Johns known as a redneck because the back of his neck would turn red after the sunrays beat down on it as he bends down to picked cotton or soybeans. Studd remembered they often had good time together until both reached the age of fourteen. That is when John was, told he was a man and that White men do not play with Niggers. After that he was prohibit from befriending people of color. Shortly after his sixteenth birthday Kelly was send off to college, when he returned, he showed only hatred toward the Negro population. I often wondered what happen to him during his stay at college. The days of us sitting at Mama table eating milk and cornbread is long over Studd says aloud ending those through of their past. Now, it is

Mr. Kelly if I am addressing John, Studd said to himself having to remember. Almost there Studd thinks after hearing then seeing more automobile traffic. Just over the horizon is the town, a collection of high-rise and low-rise brick building. Many of the wooden frame structures have been cover-over with bricks, which makes the area looks uniform. Also, this is tornado country, and the bricks help the structures withstand stronger winds Studd realizes.

Entering the town, out of the road, onto the sidewalk Studd adjust to. Speaking and tilting his hat as he greets others as he walks, sometime stopping to window shop. Quickly approaching his apartment Studd observes the different in the upkeep on the streets. As he approaches the Negro community, he notices that more debris covered the area. Thinking again, it came to his mind that the storeowner did not live in this neighborhood so outside of their business doors things did not matter as much Studd accepts as true. Only the windows being clean was important, to see who and how many customers would be coming into their business. He recalls never seeing any business proprietor out cleaning the front area or near their stores. Each closes the doors at a selected hour, locked-up, and never worry about the outside surrounding. Things just got to change, was Studd opinion. Owning not just buying from others ethnic group is the future Studd keeps reminding himself of. Private enterprise and education are ways he visualizes improving his people position. Needs are, to overcome racial injustices in the country that is what Studd has come to recognize.

Just as he began to collect, his thoughts back to his present occurrence. She appears, Miss Elisabeth in all her glory. Elisabeth walks tall showing off those magnificent curves in her bright yellow and orange sundress. Slow down heart Studd thinks as he places his hand upon his chest. Looking at her as she walks down the sidewalk with her head held high, eyes straight forward is all Studd could surmise from this distance. Hastily Studd rushes by other people walking in the opposite direction. Once at the corner he then began to cross the busy street traffic contrary to the red light. The beeping of several automobile horns sounded as Studd continues his mission to reach Miss Elisabeth. Because of the ducking of his head as he successfully dodged automotive traffic Studd lost track of Miss Elisabeth's whereabout. Looking in the direction in which she was walking Studd no longer saw her. Perhaps she went into one of the shops Studd deduced. So! Quickly, Studd approached the next store, a shoe store window and to no avail, was Miss Elisabeth observed. Continuing down the sidewalk, he looked into each store window until finally his dream came true. He was witnessing Miss Elisabeth checking-out a multi-color feather hat with the cash register clerk. Not realizing his sweated face was on the window until, a white man with an apron on come within reach of him and said can I help you with something boy! Studd, without hesitation responds with I am waiting on my lady friend. I just did not want to go into you all fine business with these dirty clothes on. Well you can wait out here that is fine; just keep your face off the window glass the white man said in an unmerciful tone. Studd stepped away from the window pulled out his hanky and began to clean and dry off the area in which his face touches the glass. Boy! Just get away from the window the man with the apron shout; we do not need the help of your kind to do anything around here. Studd, looked at the individual for a few seconds, put his hanky away, and walked several feet pass the borders end of this store. All the while feeling the stare of eyeballs on his back from this guy. As if he was unworthy to be on the same street. Studd definitely did not want to cause a disturbance, so he continues to walk away slowly. After every few steps, he would turn around hoping that Miss Elisabeth was finish with her business transaction in the store. Since the verbal exchange with the store handy man Studd notice, that he was a bit dusky. He surely did not want to give Miss Elisabeth the wrong ideal. That he was an ordinary field hand without any ambitions, just wanting to get under her petticoat. But! He knew if he passes up this opportunity, no telling when he might see her again. This is the time Studd said to himself,

I got to go for it as he continues to dusk himself off with both hands. As he lifts his head up, he notices Miss Elisabeth coming out of the store. She stops once out of the door, adjusts the packages in her arms, and began to walk in the direction of Studd. Studd decided to walk toward her, once in arm reach of her he greets her in the southern tradition, a bow, and tip of the hat. After a swift polite exchange, Studd asked in a trembling voice if he could be of any assistance, it would be his pleasure to help her with her packages. Miss Elisabeth looked at Studd then said thanks but no thanks, she has to refuse his offer, that she did not know him well enough. Quickly Studd interrupt saying he knows that she a lady and assure her that he has nothing but honorable notion in mind. Matter of fact Miss Elisabeth I want to discuss reading lesson with you. Again, my name is George Freeman; I work with Mr. Charles at the product warehouse on Main Street. I also own and run a small juke joint on the weekends. I really need your help more than you need my Studd voiced effortlessly. That the truth Studd said as he reaches for one of Miss Elisabeth bags. As Studd touch the bag with his hand, he locked into her eye with his, after a second or two both heads turn away. With a big smile on his face, Studd asked again verbally if he could assist. This time a gentle yes respond given. Slowly off they went into the sunset, both smiling and talking as if they had known each other for years. During their conversation it was agree upon that, they would meet at the church on Wednesday after bible study for an hour. That the reading lesson fee would be set depending on the work required. Miss Elisabeth was as excited as Studd for the lesson, to know that a grow man wants to better himself. One thing for sure that Studd had insisted upon, was that these lessons did not become public knowledge. Therefore, the preacher, Miss Elisabeth, and he would be the only ones with knowledge of these transactions. Reaching Miss Elisabeth house, she thanks Studd for his assistance and acknowledged she enjoy their conversations. Agreeing to meet next Wednesday should be finalize after talking with the preacher on Sunday Miss Elisabeth assured Studd. Fact is, you should join me when I talk to the Reverent, Miss Elisabeth strongly suggested. Well! Wednesday is busy at the warehouse day and night Studd replied after her request. See what you can do George, let them know you have other important opportunity as well Miss Elisabeth said as the sound of her voice echoes as her front door closes. What a woman Studd thinks, it is going to be very nice seeing and learning from her on a regular basis. That woman sure is pretty and smart Studd said aloud, then remembering the time, he shouted oh! My LORD, I have to get a move on. Studd hastily made it to his home, change into his Juke Joint work attire, and open the Joint all within an hour and forty-five minutes. Thanks to the Johnnie Bourns' taxis service that he hired to run him to both places. What a Saturday and all is well Studd thinks, what an interesting day.

CHAPTER 4 . . . More than you know

Changed quickly and made it to the joint within an hour, how about that Studd said patting himself on the back. Markus, look like you have gotten started without me Studd said in a playful deep sounding voice. Yeah! You were taking too long Markus replied. I needed a taste before you arrived, so I brought one with me Markus said as he lifted his bottle from his coat pocket. You know, we sale that brand in here Markus so you cannot bring it into this Joint Studd reminds his dear old friend. Markus takes your drink out to the woods and finish it, then come back for some fun and entertainment Studd said with a smile as he unlocks the Juke Joint security door. Once inside Studd turn the jukebox on to some good old down-home blues. The color lights were next, then the grease for the chicken to be fried, a must for any well-equipped booze-offering establishment. Not as hot as last night Studd deduced as he placed some more beer into the icebox. Inventory taken this morning so we should be good on the booze stock for the rest of the night Studd remembered. Next thing you know, several voices heard coming from across the road. Lets get this party started, I am here, ready to sing and shout all night long. That was Big Franks claim to fame, his entry introduction. One thing about Frank, he always brings a group with him, he likes to show off with the money he works hard to accumulate. Frank like for all those around to have a good time, he will share his drinks to the end. If you are out of cash Frank got you covered. He is the high roller around town, although, most of the time he would pass out before mid-night, his head on the table, with drink still in hand, go figure. Frank, hey Chief, Big Frank, Studd shout-out back to him. I got what you need, right here, just waiting for that big paw Studd continues to rib Frank. That being the case make mine a double Frank said without hesitation. George, make that a double for all my friends Frank added. Just then another noticeable voice sounds off, count me in on those double Grace said coming in showing off her big, long legs. Grace appears out of the ordinary one of those fine as wine looking color girls that knew she had it going on. His stature was magnificent, her facial features were beautiful, body built like a cola bottle, waist length hair, caramel color skin and hazel eyes. Most men in the county colored and white have tried to monopolize her time to no avail. Grace shares the knowledge that her time went to the highest bidder, hours, or days at a time. Many times, after the close of business, Grace and Studd would sit and discuss about their ideals for the future. Grace has a plan, a plan to save money for a clothing boutique to be open in New Orleans that would specializes in women undergarments. Grace came to the joint at least one night during the weekends Friday or Saturday. Not too often both nights, Studd's and Grace had a special relationship, their deal went into effect whenever she comes to the Juke Joint. Each time a customer buys her a drink, she would quickly turn it up emptying the contents. The reason for that was only colored water would be the drink she received. Grace had a reputation for drinking men under the table that is the secret to why she was able to outlast them all.

More than you know, is a covert saying Studd and Grace would say to one another throughout the night. Lot of people thought the saying was a romantic signal that they shared. All the while, not knowing that it was a reminder for each of the hush-hush' secrets they carried. No one knew the better until after a few weeks Man added to the mix. After all, he also is a business associate that would share in the 60/40 split. As with most things, the house gets the largest end of the pie. For sure, the Ownership was taking the largest chance. If it got out that watered down, drinks are served. The customers would think each been cheated on. The perceptive would never change, that Studd and them was crooks feeding off the labor of hard-working field hands mostly. Therefore, a system put into place, that Grace would only drink the best dark liquor in the house. Crown Royal, a Canadian Whisky turns out that her drink of choice. So, a private stock was set aside for Grace's enjoyment always. Studd carried an additional secret as well, whenever someone bought him a drink. He would act as if he drank the beverage. Studd would put the substance into his mouth. Then, spit it out into an empty dark brown color beer bottle. That was his trick for not getting intoxicated while working the Joints bar.

At the beginning of the Joints daily door opening, to get the party going Studd or Man would place a dollar in change into the jukebox. Four quarters would allow twenty songs to be select and played. This action would allow any of the first customers, to decide what kind of music their wanted to hear, on the house. It seems to set the tone for the rest of the night. Always the Rhythm and Blues music at the beginning, lots of baby, baby please or some kind of love done me wrong songs. Swing tunes later on, ones that you can jump-up and down while swinging your dance partner. Once they have exhausted themselves from the dancing, it is time for the Blues. This is the life, as they know it songs, the for-real everyday type of melodies all can relate to. During this time of the night, it shows, you are either happy or sad about some kind of situation. Now, that is when the sing along songs never stops. People become really compassionate and sensitive during this time of night. Most of the disagreements between customers happen during that slow dancing period of patrons. Dancing too closely, rubbing bellies with someone else's significant other can cause trouble. It is best to know with whom to dance with as the night is goes on. History has revealed that whenever Grace is in the house, things seem to go smoothly. No fights have happened, not one person has been hurt. Nothing, which would cause the law that, is the Sheriff's Department to come and investigate. Substantial physical damage to a person usually came from a customer using a knife or razor. That behavior would shut the place down for about four or five business nights. There is usually no difficulties, no physical altercations in the Juke Joint with only the regular client.

Let a new guys come into the Joint and all hell might break loose after a while. One of the regulars will want to try him. More likely than not, it would be Markus getting into the new person face for one reason or another. Markus's physique was not big as a minute, yet always wants to provide evidence that he can handle himself. Markus has missing teeth, a scar over his right eye as well as two missing fingers from earlier exchanges of blows to his body. He was the kind of person that wants to defend others that he considers friends. Putting his nose into fights often times that he has no business involved in. That was Markus Hines day or night, wanting to be the big fish in the little pond. For some reason Markus had the ideal he was the King, King of the Breast. A premature baby boy, born in September under the zodiac sign is Leo the Lion. Markus once he is influence with that alcoholic brew would often proclaims, I am the King up in here then begin to roar. Studd then would remind Markus with his own shout-out, snap out of it, there are no animal in here. You need to take that noise outside Studd continues with a loud southern accent. By chance, it just happens that no other regular male customer of the Juke Joint celebrates a birthday under the sign of Leo. Markus is totally the opposite of being the loudmouth when he is not under the influence of alcohol. More like a quiet church mouse if anything. Despite the facts of his ludicrousness the bunch of regulars at Studd's Joint liked Markus most of the time.

As more and more patrons, enter the brightly colored wood and tin shack, the louder it became. Because the customer continually stomped their feet with excitement while dancing to the beats of the various musical selection. The floor and walls of the joint would shake and rattle. To the point that the floor planks as well as the wall panels sometime becomes loose in and on the shack. Causing at least once, a month them to have to be fastening back down. Appearances mattered to Studd, so he had recruited his friend Walter Jenkins to paint the interior of the Joint; on one wall was a mural of folks dancing. On the other side of the room, was what Studd called his rainbow wall. That wall been painted in various shades of color. From a dark brown shade that gets lighter and lighter until it becomes a pale yellow in tint. This symbolizes the skin colors of his heritage and that which his customers represent. During Studd's travels around the county delivering supply to many fine white owned establishments. He notices that the successful business has one thing in common, continue improvement. Always repairing, making the place look more attractive. Old and broken furniture is changing out, with newly constructed things. Important to a business also, is how the outhouse was kept clean. Tissue for inside of the facility, hand soap, and water right outside would be a main stay to help keep customers comfortable.

Studd also noticed how each person enters their business establishment was greeted. Each welcomed with a cheerful voice recognition and smile. Those acts where some of the things Studd wanted to incorporate into his establishment. Making sure that the customer thinks that they are unique as well as it being a special place for them to attend. The Joint had to provide for its customers something that they could not fine away from this place. Atmosphere, Studd knew was the most important aspect of the Juke Joint success or failure. The Juke Joint had to always look ahead, staying current was only a beginning. Appearance matters changing furniture around from time-to-time counts. Studd had what he called, his spotter, people that travel often around the Tri-state region as well as the country. People he would hire on the side to be on the lookout for new and unusual articles. Picture catalogs from Sears and Roebucks was a big help in keeping up with interior furniture ideals including lighting fixtures alignment. Do not get it twisted, make no mistake Studd was not alone in the upkeep of this entertainment venture. Man took pride in the operation of their business endeavor as well; he made sure that the booze, appliance, and all fixtures are in the place where they correctly belonged.

Since the opening of the Juke Joint, Man, became the fashion master. He never seems to wear the same outfit of clothing twice. Man, believe to be successful you had to look the part. That was something introduce to him at the start of his business relationship with George. After all George was the one to first share his thought values of looking successful? Positive behavior is the way to suggest flourishing achievement in the business community. Let others know that you are, the man that you and success go hand in hand. This mind-set had become both brothers signature approach when out in public. This kind of person needed in a businessman. He is the kind of guy that gets along with most people. He just seems to have a soothing natural appeal that draws people. His gift for verbal communication has been a blessing that benefits himself and the Juke Joint constantly. So many times, he has talked and walked out of tight squeezes. From annoyed and upset customers wanting to fight, to stopping possible homicide. That big body yet gentle manner he demonstrates just seems to defuse most dilemmas before the county deputies are involved. What an advantage he is, Man has saved the Juke Joint so much money and time away from the courts. The plus side is Man loves what he does, dressing smartly and communicating with associate. A debate on any subject Man will always rise to the occasion. Whenever the opportunity occurs, he will continually try to fine the positive to sidetrack violent. Understand, Man is no coward he has had to stand his ground and fist fights a few times himself. After all, he is from a family that refuses to be bully. If someone, for whatever reasons wants or try to challenge Studd, Man is the first to offer his assistance. Be it in the form of words or a hand-to-hand struggle, an encounter with big brother assured. There is a saying "never underestimate the recourse of a Freeman" in which both brothers apply their decision-making options. Man, has the notion that you just do not step to his little brother with some dump-ass stuff. That if someone needs his or her head disciplined; he would handle that obligation. He believes that if either of them had to go to jail he could handle it better. He had seen the inside of the so call County Correctional Facility that was hard labor. The correctional part was being a part of a chain gang. Doing labor out of the roads and in some, cases on private own cotton or bean fields rain or shine. In the south singing during hard labor, which is how the

Blues began. Where singing mostly about the misery in one's life made it a bit easier during tough times. Knowing one is not alone during their hardship seems to make the suffering tolerable.

Man has come to terms that George is more business minded then he. Also, he bears in mind that the Juke Joints main backer were George's associates. George incarcerated for any season would look very poorly in any instance. It would prove without a shadow of a doubt to certain whites that colored are unqualified, to run any sort of sociable business. More so important than that, Man thought how would he explain to his parents if their Golden Boy George lands in jail, and him not intervening? Those were just some of the considerations Man has visualized each weekend since the Juke Joint has been open for business. More than people know, this weekend show is hard busy work. Trying to satisfy customer yet not taken advantage of is an ongoing process. From first to distance cousins wanting handouts, child-hood friend let's not forget the problem sometime caused by the White Deputies. Thinking they can feel on color women breast and butts without consequents. The latter offence quite often leads to more tense moments. Resolve of the Juke Joints owner, ability to play down individual situations. Problem solving, is a big part of any solution process, finding results, something that all party can live with. Changes of perspectives often have to happen when trying to smooth over hot tempers. White men for generation have taken advantage of women of color. However, in this Joint the brothers of color are not having it. When seeing an injustice happening to one of their sisters they speak-up. Because of this, some out-spoken brothers have lost their lives, other thrown into jail for challenging Deputies. If a Negro man finds themselves behind bars, it is a no-win situation. All of the court officials are white and go along with whatever the arresting Deputy say. On many occasions colored women have said nothing after being, molested, knowing that the action of a loved one may cause them death. On the other hand, placed into a system that would make them wish they were dead. Because nothing said, most Deputies think it is okay to continue this behavior. They seem to have an attitude of "if white you're right, if black stay back." As if skin pigments relate to being a superior being, that GOD favor them over all others. The NAACP clashes continually with the justice system in this region, to no avail, however.

The Juke Joint social gathering has begun, and all of the patrons are in high form. Dancing to the soulful sounds of Big Richard Smith's blues jams, kicking up their heels dressed to the nine. Big Dick Smith is what the women call him, the reason only the women knew for sure. The style of dance did not matter, most just got on the dance floor, and started shaking what the Lord had blessed them with. What a sight to see, however some people show the sign of African rhythm instill in them, moving with grace and precision. While other just jump-around looking a clown with happy feet. Hats flying off heads, dresses swing overheads; as well, it did not matter. Fun and contentment was the agenda for the evening. Very few people really came to the joint to start a violent commotion.

When out of town patrons come to the Joint; that is when it was most likely to be an argument or fight. Territories seek to be a big issue for a lot of the men folk back in the back wood area. They think that only the women in the area should only be entertaining them. However, the women know of the regular guys that came to the weekly affair. So, they felt charmed when unfamiliar men approach them. After all this was the place to meet unmarried and available suitor, other than church. Rejections had a lot to do with the attitude of men not wanted by the women they were pursuing. When seeing the women delight in another guy that is not from the area. It is hard for the pursuer to envision the women he is interested in abandoning his advances. Often that leads to the unfamiliar males in attendance being challenge. Man, being a Freeman male always see themselves as the Alpha male; he is not one to back down. If so, he would then be considered a punk and pushover, which is not a good thing to be regard as in this region. So! That is when a good counselor in behavior management needed. Man's the peacemaker is then that person to supply the sense in the non-sense. Man is the guy that tries to avoid a fight. But will not run if he sees no way out and his life seems to be in danger. Life in the Tavern business is something else night to night.

To cut reduce violent at their juke joint Studd and Man set-up tighter security. Men and women alike would be body search before entrance to the joint. Large signs will be post at the front door entrance. Women search ladies' and men search men that will be the norm. Most agree that this action is a good ideal one that would curve down aggressive activity. At the early opening nightly, all the drinks are served at a discount price. These value drinks describe as happy hours special apply the first couple of hours after the door open. Usually, fifty percent is the rate taken off local brands of spirited drinks. Therefore, customer will come early to get what they call their money worth. Studd knows a customer needs to feed the alcohol, so not to get intoxicated. Smashed patrons mean lost revenue, customers with heads on the table not a good sign. Hands should be going into their pockets to bring out dollars, not a pillow for heads. Food's given out complementary during happy hours. Smother potatoes with onions, fried chicken, and cornbread are standards dishes. In addition, Studd's Juke Joint has an extended menu of foods that are available for its customers. Mostly a lot of very hot spice seasoned dishes that would help sober - up the patrons. A hot mouth means, something cool needed for relief. Cold beer satisfies most people's dilemma. Patron's needs means more profit and the cycle continue night after night.

CHAPTER 5 . . . And the beat goes on

As the night continues this seems to be a special night at the Juke Joint. Everything is going smoothly, no problems with any of the customers, old or new. However, a strange thing does happen a little after 9 o'clock that night. Grace, the finest woman in the joint asked Studd if she could sing a song. Studd uses to hearing people calling themselves singing said sure knock themselves out. Grace asked that the music on the jukebox stopped. That was a big surprise to Studd that kind of request. Studd told Grace to hold on a minute, he had to clear it with the customers. Before getting a clearance Studd asked Grace was she sure this was something she wanted to do. Without hesitation, Grace boldly answers make it happen, I want to sing to the world tonight. Okay then, here goes Studd answered. Man, Studd shouted out, cut the music for a minute. At first Man did not understand what said. Therefore, he placed his hand up to his ear as to signal Studd to repeat what said. Studd tried to make his voice louder but with the music playing and the customer singing and talking it was impossible to be heard from across the room. The next best thing was hand signals. Studd act as if he was playing the guitar and like a throat cut. Man, finally got the message and shut down the music all the while wondering why. With the sudden stop of the music the patron began to shout aloud, hey what is going on, what is happening, put the music back on. Again, Studd tried to raise his voice over the cries of the unhappy customers. Studd repeatedly shouted, Ladies and Gentlemen quiet please I need your attention. Little by little the noise subsides. He then is able to convey to the entire listening crowd that Grace wants to sing a song unaccompanied. And! If it's all right with them she would begin to perform her song now. After a few people mumbles about a non-professional was entertaining, mostly women hating. People started to clap to encourage Grace as she walked into the middle of the dance floor to do her thing. Graces name really serves her well; that is in which the manner she carries herself. It is an act in itself just watching her start to sing. And! After the first few note the whole joint is silence. Only heard was that of the clear unadulterated sound of a magnificent southern Blues singer. The original song she sings talks about the hardship of a southern black woman in the back woods of Mississippi. She sang with such passion that the whole joint became quiet and still after she deliver that powerful stirring message in song. Claps and congratulation followed her for the rest of the night. Grace had again shown she was and still a classy act. That no one in these regions can outshine her. It was not something she would say, it was just something that she displays daily.

While making her way back to her table Man meets Grace before she halfway there. He takes her right hand in his hand then kisses it gently before accompanies her the finally few feet. What a fine performance Man said as he helps Grace into her seat. One day you are going to make a hell of a wife and companion for some lucky stiff. Grace do not get me wrong when I say stiff, a men would have to be straight and secure in himself. With all the attention, you will be receiving. Lady if you have not heard it today let me be the first to say, "You got it going on." If you need a manager to go out and get futures singing dates, I am available to make that happen. Listen Man, I did that song for the women in here that daily caught hell with their man and for others that have a hard time working for people families that do not appreciate them, if you know what I mean. A woman work is never done, always there servicing somebody. Grace, I know that might be true but with a voice like you got, you can have them servicing your needs. More people should have the opportunity to hear and feel the sincerity you have to share Man responded. Look here Man, you can go on with that talk, and I am not interested in performing. So, you can go and blow smoke up some other woman dress, thank you very much Grace said with a straight face as she downs her drink. What a waste, Man was heard saying as he walked away.

Turn the jukebox back on, was the sound Man heard as he walks away from Graces table into the direction to plug the machine back up. Man still thinking what a waste of fine talent. As he bends down to plug the jukebox wire back into the electric socket. What can I do to get Grace to change her mind about singing in public Man mumbles to himself, then a light went off in his head? Knowing how tight Grace is with Studd maybe he can get Studd to talk to her. Think; think Man said to himself as he walks in the direction of the bar where Studd is working serving drinks. Those are some pipes Grace have Man said to start a conversation with Studd. Yeah! That was one hell of a song; I did not know she had that in her Studd answers back. Brother, what if we could use that voice to our advantage Man questions. Our advantage, just what are you talking about, our advantage. Grace working for us is that what you mean Studd asked. Right, Brother, you and I are on the same page. Maybe we can get her to come in one night a weekend and be our hostess that sings every now and then Man said as he put an inch of whiskey into a jar for himself. Did you hear and see what she did Man said continuing to try and sale Studd into the ideal? The customers really enjoyed the entertainment I agree Studd said after a short interruption due to customer needing service. It defiantly is something to think about Man, we need to discuss it more in detail Studd said ending the conversation for now. Man, I need a little help here I need more ice put into the cooler Studd instructs. Yes Sir, Mr. Boss right away Mister Sir, Man said in a displeasing tone in his voice. Studd, tilted his head a little to the right while giving Man a disapproval look himself, wondering what that was all about. I just asked for some help with ice is that a problem Studd question Man. Not a problem Brother, it just seems to me that you put my ideal off quite a bit. Man, you are missing the point, we here working tonight, now is not the time to make business decision about the future of this establishment.

Man, listen here there are pro and con to all new suggestion. It takes time to weed out the good from the bad.

We are in the moneymaking business not the giveaway store. So, bear with me, I am for continue improvement as well. It is mandatory that we sit down together and figure out what is best for our future profits Studd said passionately to his brother. I want us to continue the smooth transition we share here. We both have duty that we are very good at. This Monday evening after I get finish working for Mr. Charles at his scale warehouse, I will be available to sit with you and come up with a solution to this ideal. Man, know that I value your opinion; none of them overlooked. Studd, I understand procedure I just jumping the gun, forgot about the process. I was looking at cash possibility and not the negative odd. My fault Studd for causing the misunderstanding, I will try not to let it happen again Man alleged as he reached out his hand for a handshake. Studd smile and slapped Man's hand away, while saying, "we cool." You are still my main man even if you got no sense Studd jokingly response. Man, I need you to cover the bar for a few; I want to run back into town. I need to check on a couple of things Studd said to Man requesting his service. No problem, Brother, I will hold it down as I do most night anyway. It is nothing new for me to do Men boastfully replied. Without saying another word, Studd exited the joint quickly without looking back. The truth be known Man was not thrilled about Studd leaving, it seems it was becoming a habit. On Friday nights he is mostly there running the joint, now on Saturday's nights Studd been disappearing. My pay grade is going to have to be elevated Man said aloud to himself. This kind of bull crab I did not sign up to, Man said continuing his talk to himself.

CHAPTER 6 . . . Liberated Position

Since leaving the joint so hastily, Studd realized he did not tell Man about what his plans are for returning. I will have to emphasize to Man the important of me leaving the operation so early regularly. I need to let him know those absence hours from the business is not for pleasure Studd said in a low voice as to make a mental note to himself. Sharing is caring also, one of the lessons taught to the Freeman family, taught at early age. Caring about Man mental disposition has always been one of Studd's concerns. Therefore, reiterating his near future plans would set Mans mind to ease Studd contemplated. A understand is the best way to keep a good business relationship together, Studd found that out while working with his employer the Charles at the Mill Scales. Many times, he had heard the Charles clash over issues such as business authority, money, even hours worked, or not worked. The Charles is a father and son business that had many underhanded dealings going on between them. Studd knew he did not want any backstabbing between him and his brother. Studd try to be a righteous kind of person, knowing it is a blessing when he can give to other. A person can only give because of GOD grace, which allows them abundant, the blessing is from the Highest. To share with family first is the only way to be successful Studd believed. As Studd continue his fast pace of walking, he also knows he has to do something about his mean of transportation. Time is money and it is taking up too much of his being on foot. Therefore, a new method has to be incorporate into his lifestyle Studd realized as he walked down the dark dirty road

Resulting from his fast pace Studd arrive at the church before the bible study class had ended. Ahead of schedule, he knew this because of the loud Amen going on as he approaches the building. Rather than wait out on the church steps Studd decided to go into the building. As he enters the house of worship, he notices all of the devotee heads and eyes had become fit upon him... Without hesitation, Studd started to walk toward the front row of pews, where most of the congregation sat. After nodding his head up and down in a greeting manner, he sat down. While looking around to see if the person he came to meet was there. Studd observe a big smile that had come onto Miss Elisabeth face. Seeing Miss Elisabeth, Studd began to envision the possibility of him and her getting together as more than business associate get. Wow! Studd thought, look at her she has all the attributes any man would hope for woman. Miss Elisabeth looks gorgeous to him each time he would see her. Even in the dim, low light surrounding Miss Elisabeth seem to light-up the room with what appears a sanctify glow. Knowing that appearances matter, Studd could only imagine what thought she might have toward his appearance. Studd hope that with him trying to improve himself she might consider becoming a willing companion for life. Miss Elisabeth did not know it yet, but she was about to meet a person that prepare to wear her down with kindness.

A short while later, the music choir rehearsal was over and Studd gathers up his audacity to approach what he considers to be his future wife. Saying good night to most of the church people Studd finally made physical contact with his dream girl. With her back turn away from him, Studd reaches out and touches Miss Elizabeth's shoulder as he called her name. Miss Elisabeth responded right away, turns, and faced Studd with a delightful smile. George, she replied Miss Elisabeth you do not have to call me, Elisabeth will do just nicely. After all, we have known each other for some time now she continues. Whatever you say Studd replied as he extends his hand out to hold open the door so that they could exit the church. Elisabeth then asked why you are opening the door. It seems a bit hot in there to me and I could use the fresh air. Beside there a big light in the sky tonight in which I can study in, that is if you do not mine Studd said. Elisabeth smiles as she thinks this is a bit romance for studying, but she agrees to the suggestion. Okay! This time Elisabeth said in no nonsense pitch in her voice. Still smiling Studd guides her to a bench on the church porch.

During the course of their practice reading section, Studd made it known to Elisabeth that he would like to see more of her. Elisabeth tries not to seem surprised response with a question to Studd, George if I was not your reading instructor would you still be interested in courting me. If the sun did not come out in thirty days seeing you on a regular basic would still light-up my world Studd assured Elisabeth. So overcome from George's remark Elisabeth face turn a beet red. As red as she was that is how hot she had become. She had to use the practice notebook to fan herself. Studd noticing the change in her behavior had to question her if she was all right, as he presented her with his clean handkerchief. Thanks Elisabeth replied after exhaling the last breath she had taken. George, I need you to complete two tasks before I agree to your request Elisabeth answered. Studd looking a bit surprise, and a little suspicious of the task she might have in mind. Turning to look at her face-to-face Studd said what! What is the two tasks that I will have to consider? Then I will judge if I want to move forward, this better be good Studd instructed her. Nothing real difficult Elisabeth said as she pulls a book from her carryall bag. To assure Studd, that the task is easy to duplicate Elisabeth opens the book and starts to read a couple pages. George all I want is for you to be able to read this short story to me. Secondly, I want you to attend at least one church service a week for two months. Hey! Girl was Studd immediate reaction. With his face all twisted-up he continues are you crazy or what? What makes you think I want to spend my time up in a church, know what I am saying Studd exclaim. The book, yes, I am down for that, I am sure after a few more session I will be ready to read every word, right Studd said ending his verbal outburst. Look here Mr. Freeman, the choice is yours, and we can continue as usual or move forward in an adult couple relationship. I just want to be sure, that I be with a man that shows resolve and discipline Elisabeth informs George. I did not think asking you for those tasks would be complicated, not too much for you to handle Elisabeth said delivering with a gentle yet firm voice.

Let's go, it is getting late, and I had planned to walk you home Studd said voicing his concerns. Before we leave, can you tell me of your decision Elisabeth humbly asked. Shoot! It is still hot out here and right now; I have not decided yet Studd said answering her question. To cool himself off Studd took off his shirt; he did have on an undershirt so he had the mindset that Elisabeth would not be offended. What are you doing, Elisabeth asked as she watches Studd start to remove his upper garment of clothing? Trying to stay cool that is all, take it easy, no need to be alarm. Your virgin station in life will not be compromised by me Studd said to assure her. George! What the hell you are talking about, where the hell is that coming from Elisabeth voice fully question Studd. It was that look you had, with those eyes of your opening all-wide I just wanted to make sure you, knew with me my plan with you would always be courteous. If I said something to make you uncomfortable, I apologize, Studd confess. But! Then again, those reactions you displayed showed me a different side of your personality Studd added to his remarks. Listen George, you do not know me, or what I am capable of so please do not try and judge me Elisabeth declares. Therefore, you can keep those smart-ass remarks to yourself Elisabeth said giving Studd the riot act. Studd just listen quietly with a straight face, during the time he placed his fold shirt under his left arm. Once Elisabeth had finished her proclamation, she asked Studd if they were good. Let's be on the same page going forward she continue as she reaches out her hand to give George the book he needs to read. Smart lady, Studd thinks to himself, she one of a kind and I have to make her mine is in his though, in his mind eye. No problem are we going to have Studd swear as he reaches to receive the book. Miss Elisabeth, I really like your company however, we need to pick-up the pace to get you home. There are two reasons I am hurrying; I need to get back to the club as well as your reputation. You know being, seen with me late at night might just give people the wrong ideal

Studd admit. There you go; again, Elisabeth said starting to fuss about George statement about her reputation. I can take care of me, thank you very much Elisabeth informed Studd. I beg your pardon Miss, it just important to me how we are looked-at, appearance matter to me Studd said interjecting his believes.

Realizing George was truly trying to be chevalier, Elisabeth smiles and said OKAY let's pick up the tempo then. From that, point on the rest of their conversation was nothing but pleasant chatter and laugher. Once Studd and Elisabeth reach the front steps to Elisabeth home, it became a bit uncomfortable. Each of them stood there silent and motionless for a few second. Realizing the uneasy calm Studd breaks the silence by saying, how he looks forward to seeing and studying with Elisabeth again next week. Well! Until then George you will be in my thoughts, I pray for your health and safety Miss Elisabeth replies. Studd, who had been carrying the books extend his arm and hand to return the books back to Miss Elisabeth. Smiling with that gorgeous smile, she takes the books and says good night. Studd turns around after watching her enter her house, when suddenly he hears the soft gentle sound of Elisabeth voice again. George thanks for seeing me home and carrying the books, she said as she sticks her head out the door. No problem, my pleasure Studd replies as he starts to grin while waving his hand to say goodbye again. Feeling as good as a child with a dime to spend in the candy store Studd started the pathway back to the Juke Joint. Smiling, singing, and kicking rocks as he marches down the road with the thought of being with Elisabeth again Studd repeatedly envision. What a woman, what a woman, what a mighty good woman Studd sings aloud for any to hear.

CHAPTER 7 . . . Not alone

From about, half mile away dim lighting of the Juke Joint seen. Knowing soon on the back burner his pleasant thought of Elisabeth would have to be. He inhales a big breath of fresh air hoping that would help clear his head of Elisabeth thoughts. Studd knew it was time, to put his person in charge hat back on. No more kicking rocks, hoping no ass kicking would be required either Studd thinks as he walks pass several horse and buggies, some peoples way of transportation. Arriving at the joint, he heard a loud cheer as he reaches for the front door. What! What in the world Studd thinks, as he enters the celebration? Trying to catch his bearing Studd looks around to see if he can spot the cause of such an up-roar. He then realized that each of the patrons was looking in his direction. As Studd threw up his arms and said, WHAT! The place became silence. Only the sound from the jukebox heard. What! Again, Studd inquires. That is went Man steps forward from around the bar, hands clapping and inform Studd of the small wagers the regular customers had made about him. Betting on me, now I am the game Studd asked in a non-friendly manner. What the HELL! I am not the horse in you peoples race Studd assure them. You folks want to bet, bet on who can get their ass thrown out of this spot Studd went on continuing his unusual rage. He then just stood there with his face all turned-up as Man request that he relax, take it easy. George, we did not mean any harm; it was not about putting you down. I had started talking about you leaving out for a few hours each Saturday evening to Ralph at the bar. That when he said he had seen you and Miss Elisabeth together talking a couple times.

You and Ralph talking about me, and my business Studd interrupts. George, it was meant as a little friendly bet between a couple guys. That all we just got caught-up talking and other heard about are bet and wanted in. It was not to put you down, believe that Man said as he presented his hand together as if praying. So, you see; others notice your absence as well Man interjected into the conversation. George the bet was about the time you would return if at all Man quickly added. Matter of fact, what time is it anyway Man asked as he saw Studd face expression relaxing. Time to mine you own darn business Studd said in a firm voice. All come on now younger brother it was just a bit of fun we were having, is this not the place to have fun, am I right Man went on to ask. Studd then turn his head a bit to the right, right you are my brother. If I can give it, I should be able to take it as well Studd said as he apologist to all for his behavior. It is ten forty-three Studd said loudly, who won the bet and for me acting so foul the drinks are on the house. One drink per customer that is free Studd said as he looked in the direction of Ralph. Why are you looking at me like that, what for Ralph asked? Cause you and Man are costing me, cash, and aggravation mouthing off about me Studd informs his old buddy. Ralph laughs a little for a few seconds then whispers to Studd, did you get it man. Although knowing what Ralph was talking about Studd decides to answer him with a question, did you win the bet? Ralph threw his hands-up in the air as he sat back in his seat while saying fair exchange is not robbery. Studd look at him with a frown before saying mind you own blasted business, I have to get back to work, now what are you drinking? The night went smoothly for all in the joint, drinking, talking loud, dancing, and sweating a good enjoyable time everyone was having.

During a break in serving the customers that night Man, approach Studd saying I got a question to ask, you do not have to answer if you do not want to. Sure, what is it brother Studd replies. George, I need to know, while you were away and being with Miss Elisabeth were you able to get into the honey spot. Man! Come on now, a gentleman never tells Studd answers, while shaking his head as in disbelief. This is brother to brother; it will be a secret that not revealed by me for any reason Man swears to Studd. Why, why are you so concern about what I am doing with my penis Studd smartly answer with a question? Look, between you and me, I try to get with that fine ass women myself a year a so ago, to no avail. She shot me down quicker that fleas will mump a dog. That's funny Studd tell his brother as he snickers, you use the same old tried line on all the women Studd added. Yeah! Yeah, that is beside the point Man alleges, did you or not I want to know. No, to answer your question no, I did not even try. For now, it a business, however I did ask her out Studd shared with his brother. I am hoping, there is a possibility that our relationship can develop further, into something everlasting Studd said with a beam in his eyes. Okay! I see, you rather fancy this worldly women Man said swiftly speaking up. Worldly, worldly just how well you think you know this woman anyway Studd cut into Man's statement. Not like that, I used the wrong combination of words to speak about her worldly knowledge. I am not trying to scandalize her name I like her too. One thing about me Man adds, if I cannot score. I will be dam pleased to know you have the right stuff to succeed with Miss Elisabeth knowing her educational and intellectual background and all. Matter of fact I think she would be a real good addition to our family, Man said with a smile as he walked away to serve another customer at the other end of the bar. Hey man, when you finish with your customer I want to talk, it something I am contemplating. Sure, be right back, I know what she wants, one short dog coming up Sue, Man shouts heading in her direction.

Studd initial perception after hearing Elisabeth request is she is too, much work for him to handle. Still not able to get Elisabeth proposition from his thoughts, he wonders about the Joint woozy. Not able to pay full concentrate to the orders, he informs Connie the barmaid he is going out back to get some air. Man seeing Studd leave the area shout-out I will be there in a few minutes, anticipating his brotherly conversation. As Studd steps out of the door into the humid clammy no breeze night air he notices a shooting star in the sky, is that a sign. Now that thought is another thing, he has to consider. Next thing you know "LORD have mercy" comes from Studds mouth. To his surprise Studd said aloud; where did that come from? After which a profound revelation came into his mind.

With Elisabeth to share, the rest of this life is she the right woman. For better or worst in GOD he will trust is now his considered thinking. The message seems clear his questions had been answered, and the task ask of him will be completed.

Next thing you know Man comes walking out the door. What you want to say, I am here for you, you are not alone brother Man assure Studd. Sure, you are right Studd said acknowledged his brother caring comment. However, I have this figure out the decision I was wresting with, I am going all out to gain favor from the woman of my dream. Tonight, I know we are destiny to be together. That's right Miss Elisabeth and me Studd shares. I just have to demonstrate an ability to commit to certain things that Elisabeth thinks is important, Studd shares with his brother. Demonstrate, commit what the hell, George are you allowing her to castrate you, cut you balls off right in the prime of your life Man quickly question Studd. You have to be kidding; Studd said forcefully questioning his brother. Then added come take a walk with me Man. No! It is not like that, it just that Elisabeth wants to see the moral character of her future companion Studd interject into the conversation as they both step slowly down the dark dirt road. Man, suddenly stops to light-up a cigarette, after taking a couple puffs, he addresses George; that the kinds of bull crap that makes a dude like me. Not ever, want to be in a relationship with just a single woman. Just what kind of request is it that she requires you to complete Man asked as he exhales a large amount of smoke from his mouth? Studd stand there for a few seconds; contemplating how to inform his brother about this demand. He put his right hand into his vest pocket and pulled out a pocket watch as he begins to explain the situation. She, Elisabeth wants me to go to church service. At least one service a week for four straight weeks and read a complete book. After which I reported to her the contents of which I've read. While looking and pointing at my watch Studd joyfully said, it seems the time is right for me to begin that journey. Man, shoot I may never fine a strong, wise, and sensitive woman again. One that thinks an uneducated man such as me is worthy of their hand in jumping the broom. Brother, it is a pleasure that I am looking forward to, to have Miss Elisabeth Smith come into our family. I sense inspiring possibility for us all Studd said as if confessing to Man. Well! A sorry mole has only one hole to run into, remember that Man advises. But! If your mind is made-up, I can, not happily support this insanity Man said in a whisper.

For now, let us just keep the decision between us Studd order with a passionate voice. It is your thing George, Man said as if he was unaffected. I am on the outside of that muddle up situation, and not trying to look into the madness that you got yourself into Man enlightens Studd. George, that plan just don't seem kosher to me Man confesses. Studd listen intently before following with, I am happy, knowing the lady I desire is giving me a chance. A chance to change my life for what I consider a no brainer Studd declares. Be happy for me Man, if you see me totally acting out of character then jump in, because you have to remember some things require alteration before life gets better Studd sincerely tells his older brother. After taking a final draw from his cigarette Man responds by saying whatever, do your thing man, I am in your corner regardless.

Back to the Juke Joint both brothers enter the front door. Standing at the door for a few seconds, the brothers gather their thoughts. As they look around at their Juke Joints successful accomplishment before going back to their prospective job stations. Once again, Studd is feeling refresh with loads of confident. He thinks, after this night he can begin another part of his pursuit. The land acquisition and a wife are just parts of the vision. Something's are worth the wait, Studd rationalize as he begins to help serve the patrons their liquid refreshments.

CHAPTER 8 . . . Holy Smoke

After another successful night at the Juke Joint Studd and Man says farewell to each other as they head in opposite direction toward their homes. Man, is out of sight quickly after jumping upon his mule to lighten the load off his tired feet. Studd starts to realize that his saving is interfering with progress, time is money, and money does not wait on anyone, Studd deduces. The time has come, these long walks back and forward has taken its toll. This will be the last foot travel Studd will entertain, that a promise he made to himself as the sun start to reveal itself from over the horizon. The sound of an automobile is heard and Studd steps over to the side of the road. As he turns his body to the side to see the oncoming traffic, notice the red siren on the top of the vehicle. It was one of the sheriff deputies of Copiah County on patrol. It seems to be slowing down, matter of fact; this kind of action was not surprising to Studd. Once alongside of Studd the patrol car comes to a halt. Studd standstill, waits on the officer to speak, hey there George the Deputy shouts out from the driver seat. From across the road Studd recognizes the officer as Deputy Jeff Simpson.

Simpson's one of the racist sons of a bitch in the county. That was a statement of fact, which this deputy was please to identify as, no shame in his game. His Confederate State of America flag was always on display. Hello Deputy Simpson, good morning Studd said after clearing his throat. George, come on over here I want to have a few words. Yes Sir, Deputy Simpson was Studd response as he starts to cross the road. Standing in the middle of the road with his head, tilted downward Studd asked how I can help you Sir. George, you know, we know that you have been running that Joint in the back woods with unlicensed liquor. We have given you some time to build up a customer base and notice the success. It seems that place packed every weekend. So! With that being said, we strongly suggest you guys donate to our benevolent fund. Ah! Deputy Simpson I am certain I do not know of that organization is it a new social order in the area Studd asked all the while knowing the funds the Deputy was talking about was bogus, more like a personal fund. Listen George I just know the funds committee has pencil your Clubs contribution in for let say five dollar a month. We will be expecting that payment from now on at the end of the month, let say the last Sunday morning of each month Simpson inform Studd as he strokes the handle of his 38 Special Revolver. Deputy Simpson I do not carry cash down these roads, it somewhat dangerous out here. Our shipping and receiving business hour for the Joint is one hour prior and one hour following customers operation. If you would be so kind as to see us during those hours, we are sure to be able to address any concern Studd said as he slowly backed away from the patrol car. Deputy Simpson position a half smile onto his face, as he points his finger toward Studd. You got a point there boy, I will see you next Friday before the jungle music start. You be careful out here and stay out of trouble Simpson said as he presses his foot down hard on the patrol cars gas pedal causing, a large cloud of dust to fill the air near Studd.

Wow! Damm, another financial issue that I will have to address as soon as possible Studd instantly recognizes. At the farmhouse, no phone service so I cannot talk to Man for quite a while Studd say aloud to himself. Distinguishing a threat is one of the things Studd has become very good at recognizing. Deputy Simpson is patting of his gun while talking is one of those situations not taken lightly. Studd's concern, however, is Simpson talking just for himself or is that demand a requirement from the whole department. If the threat is just for Simpsons pockets, other demands are surely to follow. This problem with need helps from people of the opposite skin color, Jay where are you my friend Studd thinks as he walks into the town. He knows White business associate can discover the circumstance much easier and faster. Why, when and what caused this episode to show it ugly face. For managing this kind of incident Jay is the go-to person that Studd trust, to help secure the right method of clearing up this situation. Run-in with the law in these regions is definitely a no brainer. It is never a good outcome for people of color when dealing with southern Sheriff Deputies and the so-called justice system. The County Justice Departments' will look for large quantity of cash in exchanged for favorable decision for people of color. To avert negative possibilities padding the sheriff's pockets are the best way to prevent chain-gang confinement. What disturb Studd mostly is that Simpson came alone to request the payoff. He was very comfortable in stating what he expects to receive on a monthly basis. Entering the front door to his apartment, Studd heads directly to the booze cabinet. Pulls a glass from the countertop and pour two fingers of whiskey. Studd down the drink, in a matter of seconds, wanting to be relieve of his thinking as soon as possible. He then opens the windows before pulled all the shades down, trying to darken the place as much as achievable. Then off came his boots and clothing before collapsing face down into his bed with the goose feather mattress. Sunday, Studd thought, then says aloud, supposedly a day of rest, but not for the weary. There are always trying to keep you down, regardless to what you do a boot is put into the back of color folk. It seems so easy for the white folks to grasp that perception. Sleep is what I need; I need to rest my mind. This Sheriff Deputy situation got to be addressed as soon as possible, this cannot be put off for later, Studd surmise while releasing a loud smelly fart.

Lying in bed trying to get some sleep to no avail is Studd next dilemma. Hour after hour his mind would not shut down. He continues to think of possibility that would affectively solve the different situation in his life. With no electric fan to help keep him cool, he wet a towel to rap around his head. As he sat in the chair next to the open window no breeze did, he receive? So, he decides to stick his head into the icebox for a few minutes. To him the only cool place available at this time of morning. Relief if only for a few minutes feels so good. Before you know it, the roosters are sounding off crowing, waking all within hearing distance. Suddenly, a light come on within Studd's mind. Sunday morning and church service will begin soon. Why not, Studd thinks why not initiate the proposition Elisabeth presented to me. That first step toward her bonding stipulation surely would impress her Studd believes to be true. After turning on a lamp in the apartment he begins to race about the place to find some Sundays go to meeting clothes. He simply has to dress to make an impact. He wants all affiliate to know this sharecropping farm boy has grown and become a successful individual. Excited about seeing Elisabeth at church he forgot how hot he was. Hanging within the storage closet is a clean white shirt. A bit wrinkled but the moister from his back will take care of those. The denim trousers he has been wearing would be just fine. Quickly put a shine to his boots and all is well Studd deem as satisfactory. Hardly any time at all had passed, Studd had washed and cleaned himself, put on his clothes and out the door he went.

The churches' location was at the other side of town, the poor section of the city. Meaning Studd had a few miles to walk before reaching his destination. As Studd, travels pass a couple of the town open white only restaurant he smells the aroma of coffee and freshly baked biscuit. The smell seems to go straight down to his empty stomach. Keep going, keep going he thinks after hearing the sound of his stomach rumble. He was not about to go to the back of the building to give those rednecks his money. Another reason is he did not trust them; they just might put dropping into his purchase. While near the window of one of the restaurants a deep serious sounding voice from within shouts out; hey boy, if you want something come around to the back. And! Don't put your hands on the window. No way was Studd going to respond to that invitation, he simple threw his right hand up as if waving and walked away. Studd tries not to purchase goods from business that only service color folks from the back. Besides, knowing the older sisters that attend the church be putting their foot in the cooking, some of all kinds of food might be prepared. I heard tell that the sisters really take care of the men, breakfast with all the trimmings Studd remember hearing. For a fine breakfast plate, I don't mind placing a nice donation into the offering plate Studd thinks, as his smile gets broader. The closer he gets to the church the more run down the neighborhood appears. Wow! Studd thinks as he walks into what looks like a dumping ground for any unvalued item. Seeing color people sitting on their porch and steps surround with trash, make Studd feel terrible. The fact that some color folks don't mine and continue living in these dreadful conditions hurt Studd to the extreme. Dirty and disorderly conduct has become the norm for most of the area residents. While walking Studd envisions participating in social and political organizations to bring reform into the Negro community. Knowing, that if we do not transform our surrounding as people, no one else with care. Studd makes a pledge to his own self as he continues his walk dishearten from what he has observe.

After walking several more minutes, Studd is now in sight of the church. He notices other folks dress in clothes to celebrate God's Day also. A few of the other churchgoer arriving by means other than their feet he witnesses. Studd again identify the needs for daily reliable transportation. Thinking of buying a piece of motorized equipment as a business investment would make it a lot easier for Studd to. Not wanting to release, the purse strings Studd still has to fight within to convince his own self, that it is a necessary asset to purchase. Time is money, so getting around faster is worth the financial withdrawal he rationale. Studd finally arrive at the churches pathway and stood at the entrance for a while. Trying to gather his thoughts, what to say when he witnesses the gorgeous Miss Elisabeth this morning. After all it was less than twenty-four hours since they had discussed a courtship. Now, that he is attending church so soon, will it appear he is over eager? Will it appear he is trying extremely hard to satisfy her? Will this deed cause her to think her commands will always be achieved? Stop, you are over thinking, just go inside, and try to take pleasure in the service Studd thinks.

Once he enters the building, it seems as if all the church folk turned their heads to watch him come in. The parishioners are a talkative group, so before he came into the door word was out that George Freeman was outside. His entrance anticipated and most welcome it seems. Looking around Studd notice Miss Elisabeth getting up from her second-row seat, looking fine as ever. Wearing a yellow and red sundress, she walked down the center aisle to meet Studd as he stood at the doorway. Elisabeth reaches out her right hand to receive his, smiles broadly to show her gratitude. As they walked back down the aisle to a seat, tightly holding Studd's hand. Elisabeth tells him welcome glad to see you, in a soft and gentle voice. Studd replies good to see you too as they both reached the second row of seats to sit down.

The service was going along smoothly for Studd until the Preacher asked each parishioner to testify about the goodness of GOD. Not expecting to witness, Studd was undecided on what he would testify about. After hearing many amazing accounts, when it was his turn, Studd shares about the journeys he often takes down the dark cloud covered roads without harm becoming him. After Studd finished his acknowledgment of the goodness of GOD, many parishioners could be heard saying, thank you Jesus. Beside him still was the exquisitely dressed Miss Elisabeth. Who in turn share her gratefulness for GOD favor and that of allowing her friend to make his way to the service today? Wow! A public acknowledgement that we are special friends Studd thinks as he can only smile with satisfaction. The service is over a short time later and out the door into the bright hot sunlight, they went. Many of the churchgoers stick around outside the building and visit with one another, sharing their events of the last week. Studd share greeting with most of the people after service. In attendance were his friend Marty and his lovely wife also. Both acknowledge Studd and invited him to dinner for that evening. Studd gratefully decline the offer, telling them maybe some other time. He still has not been to sleep since yesterday and that he had to get some rest.

Elisabeth made her way to George, waited for his conversation to finish with Marty before asking him to walk with her home. Studd thinking how he could easily find himself back here in the near future. The attention he has been receiving seem to stimulate him. Acknowledging Elisabeth and agreeing to walk with her, he then excused himself from the group that had seemed to surround him. As the walk down the road with Elisabeth begins, she opens the umbrella she had been carrying. Come, Elisabeth tell Studd, it is enough room under here for both of us to stay out of the sun. Let the sun stay out if it means staying close to you Studd replies. As Studd, get closer Elisabeth raps her arm into his. Smiling, she than began to shed more light on how happy it had made her to see him attend church service today. Without a doubt she told Studd this Sunday morning has been the best way to start off her week. With that being said Studd inquires Miss Elisabeth, would you mind if I called you Liz, asking bravely as he pulls her arm closer to his body. Most of my friend do exactly that Elisabeth replies. We are becoming friendlier as the days go by, she said emphasizing friendlier. Okay then, Studd said just above a whisper, all of a sudden feeling a bit shy. Studd after a few minutes of quiet finally broke the silence. Elisabeth, can we talk, I mean talk about issues relevant to our private lives. George, with this relationship I want for us to become best of friends, meaning we can share concerns with each other Elisabeth replies as the walk came to a standstill. She goes on to say, one day I hope we will not have any concealed dealing from each other. That is something I too will look forward to Studd said agreeing before his next comment revealed. Elisabeth, I have a problem I would like to discuss with you, it is involving the County Sheriff. Oh! Lord, Elisabeth said followed by a shy. George anything I can help you with I will do she continue. Thanks I am sure I will need some advice, probably with the understanding of permit paper Studd instruct Elisabeth. Deputy Simpson stops me on the road this morning. He said the joint has to pay an assessment fee of five dollar per month, starting the last Saturday of each month. I do not recall any county documentation that states that requirement. In my opinion, this is just a stick-up ploy Simpson is doing to fill-up his own pockets, Studd said with a hostile sounding voice delivering his belief. When do you expect to see him again Elisabeth questions? Hard to say, may be tonight or it might not be until the end of the month, was his answer. Studd told Elisabeth he wanted her to know about the situation. I just need to be prepared for any circumstances. Right now, I do not know what my options are Studd hesitantly informs Liz. So, for me, it is important that I notify my brother Man too. What I have aired with you keep it to yourself Studd added to a sympathetic Elisabeth.

During their conversation, neither of them had notice the distance they had covered. Until brought to their attention by the sounds. Of an Ice, delivery wagons horse feet hitting the cobblestone road. We are almost there Elisabeth update Studd, only a few more minute and you can go get some rest she said as if her statement was a command. Yes! I am feeling a bit tired. Studd responds in a lower tone voice. During the final juncture of their walk the pace picked-up and not much was being said, each had things on their minds. Once arriving at Elisabeth's, both got-in a quick hug. During their farewells Elisabeth, throws Studd a kiss as she climbs the stairs. Studd watches as the magnificent view disappear. During his stroll home, he realizes how heavy his eyes lids had become. So, he set his mind on reaching the apartment; the beds calling.

CHAPTER 9 . . . Get it done

Upon his, arrive to his domain Studd notice a note pin to his door. Looking around the area for anybody his first thought. Seeing no one nearby he reaches for the note. After unfolding it he looks at the bottom for a signature. To his surprise it states Deputy Simpson's full name on it. A few seconds pass before Studd is able to reexamine the full content of the message, him being shocked to have received this note in the first place. In it is an announcement that a person of interest will be contacting him to collect funds due. Simpson again, Studd reflect on as he enters his front door. One name, only Simpson's no other leads to investigate Studd says aloud as he starts to disrobe while moving closer to his bed. With just his boxer on, again he plunges into bed, this time without a problem. Heat and all he quickly falls into a deep uninterrupted sleep.

Several hours pass as Studd sleeps; all the while Elisabeth is looking into the possibility that this Sheriff Deputy is a lone wolf. Elisabeth being an Eastern Star has connections that can look into places ordinary folks cannot. Right after leaving George, Elisabeth entered into her flat with her mind-set is on helping relieve George of that Deputy situation. She could only go by what George has shared. With that bit of information, she decided to seek help from an Eastern Star sister that works within the County Municipality Building. Without hesitation, Elisabeth is back out the door, going to seek out the specialist in legal and illegal arbitration that she knows. Elisabeth rushes to a near-by colored eating establishment. Once arriving she entered, and then closed the door, all the while attracting the attention of her mentor Millie. Who sits at a back table close to the kitchen door? Millie is a light skin, straight hair Indian looking woman that wears a lot of make-up. Who thinks she looks younger than she is? If you see Millie, you see painted lips, her signature brand if she wishes. She also is the owner and sometime hostess of the restaurant. More importantly, she is a Grand Madam of the Eastern Star in Copiah County.

After a brief but cheerful greeting Elisabeth with her hands out-reaches says to Millie, I need your help. Looking into Elisabeth sad eyes Millie inquires, baby girl, what's going on, you know I will do anything I can to help. As long as it, not against the law Millie whispered as she winks her eye. Signal for the server to come over Millie asked again, what's happening. While having a seat, Elisabeth begins to tell Millie about the circumstances her friend George Freemans in. George Freeman, that name has been in my ear quite a bit in the last few days. I get the understanding he has become a good businessperson as well as a women chaser Millie said reciting unknown truths. Well! I don't know where you get information from. All I know is George is a good man that I want to help stay out of trouble with the law Elisabeth reiterate. His situation sounds like a no brainer to me, Millie declares. Give the cop the change and keep it moving. Tell George to up his prices a few cents on each drink to cover the cost of doing business. Millie that parts understood, what he needs to know is, are there any outstanding county payments due on his properties. Probably isn't any money due those crooks; they just want a piece of the action Millie said with her know it all accent. What kind of concession will have to be made, for this infringement to go away is the dilemma Elisabeth is trying to separate George from. Millie, can you find documentation that shows George is clear, up to date on all tax matter. At least that way, they will know he cannot forfeit his property to the county Elisabeth states as a request. In general, the notion Elisabeth gets is that the Deputy is committing a crime too, a robbery by force. A mugging to deprive, take away earning George makes from the sale of illegitimate booze at the Juke Joint. So Studd's activities being observed, and for him to continue he has to pay the piper Elisabeth thinks. Fair exchange is not robbery she has heard many a men agree. Therefore, know that the Deputy, will not intrude the illegal cash flow from liquor as long as he gets a cut from the income she realizes too. The brutal fact of the matter is George will have to pay to play, another lesson taught Elisabeth knows George will discover and adjust too as a result. As Elisabeth sits sipping on her coffee she begins to think, Simpson is most likely blackmailing others as well. Deputy extortion, if it can be, substantiated would be a great safeguard tool to have for any person she contemplates.

Trying to dismiss the fallacious and colorful gossip being, passed around by Millie, Elisabeth excuses herself to go to the restroom. Once returning she informs Millie of another engagement she must attend. Before leaving Elisabeth tell Millie she would like to check back with her in a few days. To come back for any information that she might discovered at the County Building, pertaining to George's situation. I will do my best, although it probably will take more than a few days. Elisabeth you should check back next weekend, which will give me more time to confirm a few things Millie advises. Certainly, I will return then Elisabeth assures her mentor. Saying farewell to all in hearing distance Elisabeth exits the restaurant. Once out the door back onto the street she thinks, boy! Can Millie go; she seems to know something about everyone in the county. Did I ask Millie to keep the George matter confidential she ponders? Her being my sister a mentor, an Eastern Star Madam, I am sure it will go no further Elisabeth convinces herself. Damm, I had better go back inside the restaurant to make sure, that she understands. That we are of one accord on this issue that it be, kept secretly. Sticking her head back into the restaurant Elisabeth's unladylike like shout-out to Millie that talk we had; I want to go no further. Realizing its Elisabeth voice, without looking-up Millie shouts right back, girl please I got you. Satisfy with the words that she heard come out of Millies mouth Elisabeth departs from the shop again.

The sun seems to be at the high period, I cannot imagine it getting any hotter today Elisabeth thinks as she walks down the shady side of the street. That's about all I can do today to help George she thinks. The next move cannot happen until more information is revealed. Upon reaching her flat, rather than going indoors, Elisabeth decided to sit outside and read the newspaper that left on her porch steps in hopes of catching a gentle breeze at the same time. Still not able to get the issues with George out of her mind, getting it done is Elisabeth biggest concern; she definitely would like to have a future with George. Not able to concentrate while attempting to read the paper she starts to think again of other possibility. Elisabeth wonders if they can catch Simpson in a compromising situation. One that even the white folk would frond upon. Something like that would without a doubt stop him in his tracks Elisabeth speculates as she sits with head in hand. When I see Millie next weekend, I must be sure to ask more question about Simpson, Elisabeth said to herself to make a mental note.

As the day begins to come to an end it seems more and more people start to come out of their homes into the streets. Most are out trying to catch the same as Elisabeth. However, still no breeze to be found, even the leaves on the trees does not move. This happen to be one of the evenings that it is just too hot for romantic encounter too Elisabeth feels. That is probably why so many grown folks, and couples are out and about this evening. The hot stream condition indoors is just too must for touching one another, "no foreplay no sex, it's the rule" Elisabeth said, afterward lets out a little giggle. Elisabeth has never been married nor has she been sexually intimate with a man. So, she often guesss on how the feeling relate into action for two consenting partners. One day by and by, it will be my pleasure to become one with a man she says under her breath. It's said just loud enough that only her ears could hear the proclamation. Back to reality when a big burly men name Samuel come over wanting to court her. Elisabeth in the pass has let it be, known she was not interested. Romantic relationship of any kind with him she not interested. Still, repeatedly when he sees Elisabeth out in public alone, he will approach her with songs. "You are my sunshine, my only sunshine you make me happy everyday" He has a lovely voice that Elisabeth continually tells him to share with and on another young lady. To this day, you are the only lady I want to share for eternity with Samuel expresses to Elisabeth. Elisabeth, thank him for the compliment then share the story of her new interest. Samuel eyes then appear like those of a little puppy dog hurting. After a few shy he says he is sorry she feels that away about them but if it does not work out, know that his shoulder is there for comfort. Wow! She thinks to herself, I only hope George is as attentive as Samuel seems to be. Elisabeth stands up to say good-bye to Samuel and watches as he walks away out of sight. That man is going to be a good catch for some lucky woman, I just hope he not misused Elisabeth pleads out to the universe.

After being in a cool house a couple of hours now, Elisabeth begins to wonder if George has been able to get any snooze time in. Thinking; the inability he must be facing, not being able to adequately rest, He should have been down by the river; that would have been a perfect spot to catch-up on some rest. With the sound from streets becoming quieter, Elisabeth decides to call it a night herself. Tomorrow, Monday Elisabeth plans to try and catch-up with George and map out some strategy to take toward Deputy Simpson.

CHAPTER 10 . . . Circle the wagons

Awaken after several good hours of rest Studd feels replenish and ready to go. Putting his feet on the floor he heads straight to the bathroom for some relief. Why, oh why oh my Studd sings as he finishes the flow over the toilet bowl. Shaking off his private part, for any remain in his shaft he put it away and begins to run bath water into the tub. Much cooler now than when he first came into the house. Easier to get things done Studd reasons as he goes into the other room to prepare clothing for tonight episode at the Juke Joint. While deciding on what to wear tonight he figures he might as well clean his grimy looking boots. Estimating the time, it will take to fill the tub Studd knows he has time to complete the task. Still looking toward his closet he recognizes his choice of dress is very limited. Appearances matter in the customer service business Studd learned long ago while working in Mr. Charles warehouse. The checker shirt will have to do Studd thinks as he finishes with the boots and head toward the bathroom.

A rap on the door stops Studd in his tracks. Who could that be he thinks stopping to figure out what visitor it might be? Answering just a minute Studd says as he then continues to the bathroom. He needs to stop the water from running into the tub. Finish turning off the water he returns to the front door. With a forceful voice this time, he asks who it is. It is Grace was the unexpected answer. Grace, Studd said surprisingly, ah! Wait, just a minute I need to put something on. George opens the door Grace replies, you do not have anything I have not seen before Studd? He returns to the door with just a towel wrapped around his waist he opens the door. What! What is so important Studd question? Grace enters, seeing Studd in a towel she looks him down and back up. Eyes stop in the area of Studd's private mid-section before travelling up to his face. Nice looking body George, Grace say before Studd interrupts. What is going on, why are you here? You know it is time for me to get to the Joint, so again what's!

Going on? he questions her? Listen George, I do not have a problem, but it seems one is headed in your direction she shares. And that would be, what, Studd said as if pulling teeth. There talk, that the county is going to put you out of business. Shut you down because there is oil on the property Grace said talking fast. This information delivered a surprising blow to Studd already delicate mind-set. Just what I needed another situation to challenge me Studd says to make plain his resolve. Grace, you know how much I appreciate you, now tell me just how you came across this information Studd response. You know my john Ralph he works in the Land Office down at the County Building. After a few drinks and me making him feel good, you know stoking his ego his lips tell all kind of secret. Stoking his ego, what you mean Studd questioned Grace. Grace gave Studd a hand jester of pumping her clinch fist up and down. Oh, so that what you are implying Studd said while entering the bathroom. Make yourself at home he also instructs her. George, you have been living at this place for some time now. When are you going to invest in some furniture Grace inquires as she wipes the dust from the busted glass coffee table? She explores while waiting for Georges to return from the bathroom, looking into the cabinets and icebox. Because of the dust, covering most pieces of furniture Grace decided to stand. Not want the dirt to get on her freshly press linen suit. George, I am surprised you do not have digest problems inhaling this air Grace shouts. Wanting George to hear her concern through the closed door, she asked do you hear me. Suddenly the door opens with a reply from Studd. Woman, do you have to be in all my business. I care for your welfare that all, after all you are the only big brother, I have to protect me in case of an emergency Grace say in a gentle tone. Yeah right! Studd replies then following up with the question of and this john of yours. I need you to find out more of the particular from him so we can plan a challenge to fight their attack Studd said as he lace-up his boots. Okay, I will do what I can, know this is going to cost you Grace assure Studd. What's new about that Studd replies adding, and the price is? Not any monetary amounts with be sufficient Grace, interrupt, stop trying to be funny. You know what I mean George; you will not have to pay me anything. But! Information from others just may be a different matter she continues. Thanks Grace, I definitely owe you one Studd said testifying. I got to get out of here, and open the Juke Joint, are you going my way he asks Grace as he opens the door to exit. No, but I will see you a little later. Got too catch-up with our new best friend Samuel she said with a grin. As she crosses in front of Studd to leave the apartment. Do not get in trouble asking too many questions Studd warns her. I got this, Grace answers while doing the hand jester thing. Locking the door once they had departed, Studd checks his watch. He notices he has about half an hour to get to the joint. Studd thinks there been a couple of situations that still has to be address. There is a lot of information, he needs to share with Man, as well as listen to his input Studd said identifying necessity.

Once unlocking the several pad lock on the doors Studd enters. He then turns the open sign plat to notify customer. Then Studd starts to lift-up windows to let some fresh air in. During the hot muggy day, the place had become like a steam room. Next chore for Studd is to place peanut into bowls at each table. The short time after, Studd had arrived in the joint, he begins to get agitated. Where are the folks he is thinking, he had not seen anybody? That also includes during his journey to the juke joint as well. Looking at his watch, he realizes that the iceman has not arrived either. Suddenly, unexpectedly a rough deep baritone voice catches Studd by surprise. Turning around swiftly Studd discovers it his friend Markus. Hey Studd, yeah, I saw you earlier today. Ah! Slick, when did you convert, or does what's her name have your nose open Markus sounds off as if he knows what's he talking about. Oh! I see you done started early Studd answers. Now! What you trying to say, you think you know something about my activity outside this establishment Studd inquires. I just know what I saw, you come out of that A.M.E. church on Clay Street, arm in arm with Miss Elisabeth. It seems to me both of you guys where grinning and feeling on each other Markus says to inform Studd he knew of what he speaks. Do not entertain thoughts that you might know what I'm doing, hear me, Markus. My business has nothing to do with you, so what you think keep it to yourself Studd said responding to the reference that his old friend made. Matter of fact, are you here to drink or report on what you think you know, in other words gossip Studd question Markus? Satisfied his question was not answered Studd moved on to ask Markus where everybody at. I do not know but! Count me in, set me up with a double whiskey Markus request as he pulls four bits from his pocket. The first one is on me tonight Studd said as he takes two Mason Jars down from the shelf. Pouring a finger of liquor into each, they touched glasses said cheers and down the contents. Well, Markus looks like it's me and you so let's get this party started. Here put these four bits into the jukebox and play some Rhythm and Blues for us Studd said handing Markus the coins. As the music began to play others enter the establishment. It was like the pipe-piper affect, the more the music played the more people arrived. The night was going great, the iceman delivery was only a few minutes late. He even threw in an extra half a block of ice, for the inconvenient he said.

With most of the regulars in the house, Studd hopes it will be an uneventful night. All partied were being themselves, loud talking and singing along. When this unexpected visitor open and enters the door. It was no other than the Sheriff Deputy Simpson in the flesh. Once the customer notices his presents the place become quiet. Because of him, you now can clearly hear the lyric of the song played on the jukebox. During Simpson walk toward Studd, Studd places his right hand under the bar, to make sure their weapon is available. Studd waits for Simpson to reach the bar before saying if he can be of service. Deputy Simpson reacts with a shy grin before answering. There was a complaint about someone firing up a moonshine sill in the area. I am here to checkout if any illegal alcohol is being let us say made available, he says with a cold, bold southern drawl. Sheriff Deputy Simpson, no such thing is happening around these parts I can assure you Studd replies. The only thing cooked around here is chicken and fish, sometimes we get a coon to throw in the pot Studd add to his explanation. Simpson looks Studd eye-to-eye then turns in a clockwise motion, checking out all of the people in attendance. Deputy, I will absolutely let you know if any rumors of such an activity occur. With that said Simpson, turn back to face Studd before saying I will be back, trust me. To play it off Studd tell him with a smile of his own, you are always welcome at the Juke Joint, no reservation required. With a tipping of his hat as a farewell jester Simpson leaves the joint. As quickly as the place got quiet, it explodes with conversation when the Sheriff Deputy leaves. You never know who might pop up in here, shoot! He could have at least bought a drink Studd said as a joke to relieve the customer of any tension. At the same time Studd is no fool, he knows this appearance is a warning.

A short time late Man's happy go lucky butt walks through the door. Hey! Howdy, so this is where the high spirit folks reside, he yells for all to hear. Although his appearance is notice by some, others continue right-on doing what they were doing. Studd right away signal his brother to come over to the area of the bar that he has been holding down. Looking razor-sharp in his white shirt, gray vest, and powders blue linen trouser Man approaches. Hey, younger brother, how is your boat floating Man ask in a humorous accent. We, we need to talk, there some issues that needs addressing yesterday Studd said with a serious expression on his face. All shit what done hit the fan now Man asks relating to his brother words and facial expression. One of the Smokey was in here tonight, referring to the Sheriff Deputy, and he is coming back to extort money from us. Their threatening to shut us down if we do not comply with their demands Studd counsels. I will be John Brown, Man then recites, take, take, and take that's all they do. Get a step ahead and their want to push you back two Man echoes. With the understanding, Studd feels the same way. That is not our only concern Studd said to interrupts. Earlier this evening Grace Stops by, with news there is oil under our property. Heaven knows they are going to knock us out of that windfall Studd explains. You got anything else Man ask as he sat on a stool before resting his head into his hands. Those are the majors Studd assure his brother. Now we have to come-up with some alternative to stop any of this action for happening Studd said as if quoting an attorney. Okay! First thing first, we can afford to offer the Sheriff and them something. At lease, a small monetary donation to their bereavement fund. That should slow down their aggression for a while Studd suggest to Man. I can go talk to the Sheriff, sometime Monday or Tuesday and let him know of our intentions to donate to the worthy cause he too introduces into the conversation. That sounds well and good however we do not know if the Sheriff is a part of the extortion or not Man said to question the process. That's true of course, but if he does or does not, the money will be placed into his hands anyway. He will then have the opportunity to broadcast our donation to our Deputy. One way or another it will get back to Simpson Studd said to comfort Man. That sounds like a stopgap, for Simpson brothering us Man said agreeing with the preparation.

Now about the land situation, Man questions his brother. We can only wait to get more information about the possibility of oil being on our land. My county contact person Jay can view more in a day then they would allow me any day, I have to get him involve Studd shared. In the morning when I get to work at the warehouse, I will request his help. We just have to circle our wagons and seek the assistance from associate for now Studd emphasize.

CHAPTER 11... Transparency

After their short but informative conversation, both brothers when on with their bartending duty as if no problems during the day had transpired. Fact of the matter, this night it seems there's been a additional discovery made. During an interruption of the music, one of the customers starts to sing alone without the back up of any accompaniment. This person sang so sweet and mellow they're asked to sing a few other favorite tunes. The voice was so clear that you could see and feel each soulfully word delivered. As the voice continued to amaze the folks in attendance, only one thing said. That sound only compares to that of the great famous Ella Fitzgerald. Not knowing she had it in her Grace was belting out some high ass notes. As if she had fetched some church praise up in here, Studd thought. When she finally decided to call it off, stop the singing that is Studd quickly stepped to her. Seeing dollar signs Studd tells Grace, baby girl where you been hiding those amazing pipes? Why in the world you do not want your amazing voice shared with the world? he says as he holds out his arms to embrace her. Grace returned a strong hug after walking into his open arm. George, I do not know what came over me she whispers. Well all I know is that needs to be heard more often, those sounds. The rhythm, the words just seem to illuminate over the whole place Studd assured Grace. It's been twice now that you've displayed that talent. I want you to sing here on a regular basis. Grace listens, if it is about confident, use this place. After a little while, we can advertise you as the next Rhythm and Blues southern Bells. Come on girl, as you can see, the folks here loved what you bought. Work with me here, Grace, I see it being beneficial for both of us, no more hustling johns for you. With you as the headliner, cash money becomes hand in fist. Grace it a blessing that voice of your, needs to share do not be selfish Studd said testifying.

That was some kind of a sermon, George. Did you delivered all that for me Grace said with a bit of a smile crossing her face? Well, I'll tell you what; I will think about it a while. I will let you know by mid-week? promise. Leaning toward Studd, in a faint voice Grace remind him of her activity of get information from her Samuel. Oh! Shit, believe me I had not forgotten anything. What you have told me I plan to address first thing in the morning. So! Are you going to see Samuel anytime soon Studd said getting straight to the point? Can I tell you something, something that I need you to promise never to tell anyone? Grace, please you know what is said between us stay with us Studd replies. Samuel really treats me like a lady, open doors, and pull out chair the whole nine yard. He gives me more than the standard rate, whenever we spend time together. And most of the time it not sexual, he just wants to be with me. That has made me think more of him than just a john. I am starting to get feeling for this guy, and that could be trouble, know what I mean Grace asked in a tender soft exchange. Grace I am going to be straight with you. He's a white man in this small southern Mississippi town; he could easily turn on you. Remember business is business no personal feeling is how it goes. Or stop the whole damm relationship, I do not want to see my little sister hurt. This thing you are feeling, it cannot go any further; he will never take you out into any public place as his woman. Look Grace just go back to the business end, that way no harm will come to Samuel, or you. We just need his testimony about the property with oil, soon as possible Studd instructs. I got this; Grace reassure Studd. If any more information is available, I will make sure to pass it along; I guarantee you, Grace states with a straight face and right hand over her heart. Your friendship and trust have always been of value to me Studd tells Grace before he turns away to go back to his bartender post.

By it being a Sunday night the crowd at the Juke Joint is much smaller. But it does not stop some folks from still acting a fool. Sue had come in high as a kite, with the split on her skirt up well be on her knees, wanting attention as usual. Only this time it was without Jeff, each man she approaches and passed she had to touch. As well, as make sexual suggestive remark. Finally making her way to the bar, she only wants George to service her. George, she shouts out I need a double shot of Gin straight-up, chase with a Budweiser. Studd comes over with warm words. Sue, dear Sue, how did you get here he asked hesitating to get the drink. Forget how I got here; I am going home with you she recites while trying to sound enticing. Those other bitches are not going to have all the fun with you. I want my turn she demands as her head hits the bar counter face first. Her face hit so hard Studd became concern. Studd quickly calls out to Man I need your assistance over here. Man, stopped the conversation he was having. Looks around to see, that its Sue that needs attention. My, my, my, he recites as his approach her limp body. Wow! She really has a thing for you Man, tells Studd as he lifts her from the barstool. What the why would you say something like that anyway Studd comments. Cause, most drunks try to make their way home and she came to see you, that all I am saying as he continues to hold her up. Man, then picks her up into his arms then takes her to a nearby empty armchair. I am going to look outside and see if anybody waiting for her Man announces to Studd. Still concern Studd asks if one of the women would get a cool towel and place it upon her head.

Outside Man, see no one waiting in any type of transportation. He returns with the information, directing it to Studd. So! What you going to do with her Man question his brother. Let her sleep it off as long as we are here, we just need to keep an eye on her. And make sure none of these womanizing men done try to take advantage of her Studd emphasize. Behind this situation Studd, notice the caring of one woman for another. Every few minutes or so one woman or another would come with a fresh cool towel to apply to Sue forehead. How wonderful Studd thinks as he watches the rotation-taking place. Sue was in no shape to walk home in the morning. So, Studd had to figure-out a way to get her there safely. The only person that he trusts to get her there was

Grace. Grace never walks further than you can throw a stone. There always some form of transportation near that she has access to. Thinking as such, Studd ask Grace to give Sue a lift home when she gets ready to leave. Grace's reply was you know that out of my way, but! For you okay George. I, taking a broad home is not something I do. Besides her waking-up around you is what she really wants to achieve. She has been having the hottest for you for as long as I can remember Grace shared this unnecessary comment. Just let me know when you are ready, and I will get someone to assist getting her to the ride Studd said to assure Grace. He did not want her to leave without Sue.

A couple hour pass and Sue head still rest on the table in the same position. Then a shout-out to Studd heard, it is time to go. That the signal that the person assisting Sue should be lending a hand on. Okay Studd reply with a wave of his hand. Lionel, give Sue a hand to the ride waiting outside. Follow Grace, she will show you where to sit her. Out the door they went, not to see any more that day. During the travel to get Sue home, she reveals that George is the father of one of her children. It seems talking in her sleep was one trait she has that could easily be misinterpreted. Was it real talk coming to the light or outlandish drunk gin talk? The fact is it was heard plus too much other information about their relationship. Grace, listen all the while turning-up her nose as if smelling some unforgiving stinky shit. This is one of the reason George has the nickname in the first place. He slings that private part of his into any wet cavity a woman allows him into, Grace assumes. Her big brother seems to be the worst type of whoremonger. Word was out that a couple others have had George babies as well. One thing about Studd if he has had steady relations with a female, he does not refuse to acknowledge any newborns. So! Sue sleepy admission only verifies the possibility George's yet again has father an unwed mother. It is time Grace said loudly, getting the attention of Sue. Sue, half-asleep lifts her head up as to look around to get her bearing. Home I see, Sue murmurs as she helped to exit the carriage. Noticing and realizing that Grace is in her immediate surrounding was a total surprise to Sue. After all, they just barely speak during passing in the past. However, she was thankful for the assistance and let Grace know of her appreciation. I thank you for seeing me home and with the ride Sue acknowledges. Your welcome Missy but! Girl I advise you to cut back on whatever you are doing. Some of these people with truly take advantage of situation. If you know what I mean Grace says giving her unsolicited opinion. I admit lately I have been being a little carried away Sue acknowledged. For some reason, my appetite for booze now days has grown tremendously. I be having a lot on my mind, and the alcohol just seems to relieve the circumstances most of the time. Besides some men I am dealing with are full of shit. Self-center creatures, they are really starting to get on my nerves. All of them just seem to want to use me, on my back sexually, at that Sue maintains. I look at it as if I do pass out at the juke joint. George should have my back after all, I been on mine for him many times during the years, he owes me big time she communicated further. Missy, that is too much information for me, something I do not need to know about. Not my business Grace, replies as she gestures with her hand for the driver to move on. Sue, then makes her way to the porch steps, sits with both hands holding her heavy head. Stay seated watching, while the carriage rolls down the road and out of sight. During their ride away from Sue, Grace turns to look back, making sure she did not leave the woman with her face in the dirt. Everybody has a story, issues, and situation Grace says to the driver as they continue down the road.

Meanwhile the Juke Joint is starting to clear-out. It being a Sunday night most of the customer has left due to responsibility. Back to reality, work obligations and more feeding of country southern stereotypes. It been a rumor, put out years ago that colored folks are lazy. Truth be told that similarity was instigated by Rednecks to help keep job from people of color. Colored folks grow-up with the burden of hard labor on their backs. Very few knew any other way of life.

Therefore, for someone to lose a working job in the district, it hurts the reputation as a whole for the colored community. Since the Joint has just a few remaining customers. At about twelve mid-nights, the last call for alcohol is made. Because the Joint was not as busy tonight, Studd had several opportunities to re-examine present and past business encounter in his head. Mostly what he thought about was that of the fifty-five acres of property he is now trying to acquire. If any of the news about the situation with the oil is true. What properties lines have, they surveyed is a question. So far it's only rumors that have been circulating. To Studd knowledge, no monies have changed hands. However, transparency of all of the issues has to be address one by one Studd recognizes.

CHAPTER 12 . . . Spoils

The Juke Joint had a successful weekend, a profits made and no harm to any customer. The weary however, gets no rest. Or the person trying to get ahead, is Studd's belief. Have to keep it moving, being even is like being nonexistence. In the area here the game continues to change, the playing field never leveled for a man of color. Tree timber for paper and cotton is the main crops harvest around these parts of Mississippi. Meaning it is nothing but hard labor, working outdoors in the high noon sun. This manual work was back breaking and wears a man out before his time. Studd had experience this type of work previously too. Working on the farm beside his Daddy and family sharecropping, trying to operate it and make ends meet. Yet! At the end of harvest, it was the same, year after year owing the store. Continuously as Studd, passes the fields of workers, he thanks the LORD, for blessing him. For the aptitude to calculate, number. The ability has kept him out of the planting and harvest of tobacco and cotton. Studds, from time-to-time been referred to as a house Negro. Because of the service he provides to the white establishment indoors. Mainly jealous souls would bring up that characterization. Saying he was trying to act white cause of the way he dresses and talks. The fact Studd shared the knowledge he picked-up while in their presence seem not to matter.

Colored folks did not recognize how he felt. Forgetting too he was also a product of the environment. He repeatedly would have to say Sir to a teenage boy often younger than himself. Hearing many Caucasians' talking down about colored folks and that of their assumed habits did not sit well with Studd. When a man of color at any age is, call a boy by the white folks, it especially bothers Studd. Looking ahead Studd often thought, one day we will over-come these injustices. Because Studd has been giving the go-ahead power to approve or reject sudden transactions at the Warehouse. His voice in the community carries a lot more weight, even over that of some Caucasian. Most of Hunkies and Rednecks hate that part of his position. Studd has help make the Warehouse a lot of unearned income. The public does not know how the payoff from the measurements scales was calculated. Any weight under point three of a pound not counted as weight. Therefore, at the end of the day the company has profited from many unclaimed pounds. Due in part of the training Studd received years ago when his father first hired him out. Now, however Studd tries to set the records straight when there no one looking over his shoulder. For the hard-working people of Copiah County, he will give them what they deserve. A fair count for the weight the scale measures Studd want to keep his public integrity intact. Trust is express to Studd, by Mr. Charles as if it is a privilege for him to close the shop alone. Mr. Charles often recites, boy! You I trust more than I do my own kin. If it was more like you George, y'all would be running things around here. Studd did not care to hear those remarks; however, all he could do was smile as if pleased. Mr. Charles was Caucasian but from a different cultural group, Studd knew. Cause every now and again, he would hear other white folks calling Mr. Charles that Jew Boy. Studd also had figure out that's one of the reasons Jay gets alone so well with the colored community. Southern whites do not let them into their clubs or organizations.' Most of the southern Europeans whites think that the Jews are just a bit above the colored folks ranking. Therefore, the thought is they do not deserve much appreciation or respect, either. It regularly, the actions, and the vengeful attitude the whites display toward both the Colored and Jewish people. The southern Christians blame the Hebrews for the death of Jesus. There had been times known groups around these parts have burn Crosses and damaged Star of David symbols in the area to show displeasure, toward sustain individual or organizations. The largest group in the area the Ku Klux Klan has people of authority and influence running their hate sociality. Getting information about corruption is one thing. The hard part is being able to act and get justice on any issues involving colored. Whenever a person of color has dealing with the court system. They can count on jail time; due to the fact no juror of their peers is included. People of Color aren't allowed to vote, therefore aren't consider for juror duty. The systems designed to keep people of color from a voice into the local politics. With all this in mind, Studd has to be really, careful not to turn over the cart or it's his reckoning.

Meaning he will get no formal help from the white community. They would rather see the oil burn than allow colored folks to profit from its extraction. Spoil, is what some folks say about Studd, his life is easy they think. Not knowing about. his verbal abuse, he faces and hears daily. That Negro this that Negro that all day every day nothing but negativity from mostly poor Whites. As if, his presence did not matter one ounce. The North end of town is where he has been able to find comfort during his time away from the rude Whites or uneducated farm hands. In that area, there are many Colored people that tries to up lift other from their humble existence. Sharing art forms from Negro artist, literature and painted pictures capture their attention. Known as the Renaissance, Colored folks had begun liberating their mind in many forums. There even been talk of going back to Africa to form a nation by a few of the social leader. Still, even with that ideal, one would have to count on Whites to secure passage for thousands. Also help to get the commerce started to support its citizen. Studd has learned a great deal about the nature of business. Directly and indirectly from him being exposed to Mr. Charles diligence exercises of getting wealth. Not trusting of the banks, or should he say the banker. Studd refuses to place money into their establishments. Studd knew the value of his money to the banks. They used it to make large acquisition, filling up their pockets with profits and little if any proceeds or interest return to their customers. Therefore, Studd and Man used the old tunnel arrangement taught, from generation to generation of have nots. They would place valuables in some type of canister and hide them in the ground at a particular landmark site. Only, this time they may have to dig up some of the stash. Fair exchange is not robbery, happens to be Studds motto. He knew it would cost lots of cash to beat back this intrusion into their future. Studd foresees a couple of battles brewing.

He also must keep in mind, the other family member that might become involved. Poppa and Man can pretty much take care of themselves, Mama and the other little ones are a bit of concern. This matter therefore not to overwhelm the family's tranquility. A plan has to be, made that will pit one redneck white man against another. Coming up with a perfect plan will take knowledge and outstanding ability to deceive. They would have to think their swindling, outsmarting, poor old colored folks out of valuables. Studd recognizes he cannot do it alone, will need the assistance of quite a few of the others that want to settle a score. Revenge is sweet, when done with the opposition not having a clue Studd contemplates. Now to arrange a meeting place for a select group to plan this task Studd reflect on. Let them know that the complete farming region would be impact by the oil runoff situation. Therefore, a group should consist of people that have a livelihood to consider. Both White and Colored sharecropper alike will lose if the land is abandoned for the oil profits only. So much of the land would spoil. Cause by the overflow of oil contaminating the soil. For any kind of unification of the farmer to agree documentation matters. Elisabeth, her willingness would be a good contact person to reach out to the colored professional and color storeowner. Man, would handle the security and Grace, has to retrieve the important information needed to make this come together. The future starts tomorrow, it begins with a friend.

CHAPTER 13 . . . Dirty grounds

Starting the day Studd's on his way to put into motion the first step to control his future. Coming together is more than a notion. Trust is to overcome the biggest problem. It is amazing how people can work in the crop fields together, yet some still think they're better than other. Getting out the word hush-hush is the biggest challenge. Talking in code is the best way for secretive messages delivered Studd realizes. Back in the Delta, the wetlands the communication between folks was like something you never heard before. It was a blend of broken dialects Yazoo Indian, Spanish, and Dutch that they called Pig-laden. The language, the sound is that of a person more likely complaining in pain. More like sounds smother not opening their mouths to speak. Not many in the town or surrounding community could understand the tongue. Some of the old timers still remember how to talk the talk and Studd plans to use their assistance to pass message back and forth. Bloodline is important, with that being said, Studd imagines the folks he can trust. Uncle Jay, Poppa's fathers' brother is still living in them backwater marshes and a stand-up Elder in their society. Him and a few of the others, if they can be convinced to come out of the swamps for a little while. They would serve as great tools needed for covert conversations. However, before that action can take place. More assistance is needed; Poppa must be willing to enter the swamps to seek out Uncle Jay. More is needed once his location is found to complete the task. Poppa would have to be able to convince Uncle Jay it is in his best interest also in assisting. To stop the oil refineries would help keep the swamp folk's way of life from being terminated. Heaven facilitates us in that, Studd said aloud as if praying.

Back into the swamps with mosquitoes and gators away from his family and the crops. That's a lot to ask of a man that has seen the better part of his life come and gone. The last time Poppa had broken bread with Uncle Jay was at his father's memorial service from this earth. Many a moons ago, twelve to fifteen years Studd guesses thinking back. A long story short is all the swamp folks are suspicious of people from outside their world. Mostly it dates back to slavery times, when brave folks escaped from cruelty and rough handling from the white owners and field overseers. Not knowing what their future would entail but it could not be any worse than the treatment received on the plantations. Once individual has successfully escaped from the hard work and punishments of a plantation. A very few went back to rescue and liberate loved ones. They knew as well that sometimes colored bounty hunter would come into the area to recapture run-away slaves also. Ridding them of their freedom is something they think still might happen. Therefore, extreme caution today is taken. Most folks in the area once there, never investigate outside again, due to the possibility of being enslaved. So much of our family's history will never be identified Studd ponders as he continues in a hasty walk.

Before realizing it, Studd finds himself a few feet away from Elisabeth's brownstone. In arm length of the door Studd thinks and rethink. Does he want to appear eager or bold? Should he or not, knock on her door. Before his next thought is registered, her door starts to open. Once the doors open completely Elisabeth's caught by surprise looks startled herself. However, right away Elisabeth pose a question to, George, what are you doing here, did you come to visit me Elisabeth robustly inquires. All the while, a smile starts to appear on her fair complexion face. Awe, I wish I could have called first, but I did not have a telephone number. Studd continued with I hesitated, standing at your entrance that why I looked so surprise when you open the door too. But, now that we are together again, Studd goes on while clearing his throat, have you given the situation we talked about yesterday any more thought. If so, and do you plan to participate. I want to meet with you and a few other folks after I get off work this evening, Studd requested. Well, matter of fact I have thought about it a lot, and this is going to be tricky to pull-off Elisabeth replies. We will have to cover some really dirty ground dealing with those robbers in the Sheriff Department. You know Deputy Simpson is brother-in-law to the Sheriff of this here County Elisabeth said as if this was the latest news. So, Simpson thinks he can get away with murder Elisabeth interject further. Yeah, I am aware of all those facts you made, and know each being true. Which mean no mistakes can we afford to make Studd said to infuse the conversation? George, I will be available after seven pm, there's a school board meeting tonight Elisabeth informs Studd as she starts to step from her door way into the sidewalk. Studd acknowledge to Elisabeth, you sure are looking pretty this morning; have a wonderful day. Not hearing a response back right away from his remark, he asks you hear. Elisabeth acknowledged Studd vocal pleasurable comment with a wave of her hand high over her head. Studd seems to be hypnotized as he watches the swinging of Elisabeth hips as she continues her high-spirited stroll. All shake it to the east, all shake it to the west, shake for me, the one you like best Studd recite claiming something he hopes to be true in the near future.

Studd comes back to reality after being bumped by ongoing foot traffickers. Studd becomes apologetic for being in folk's way, saying excuse me to several. Now, thinking of the time Studd makes haste to get to his warehouse job. Seeing and talking to Jay before the place gets busy is his first order of business Studd rationalize. Arriving as Jay is beginning to unlock the warehouse door. Studd taps Jay on the shoulder as he calls out good morning, Jay. Recognize the voice Jay slowly turns to face Studd and replies in a harsh tone, morning George. What is the matter with you, what done crawl up your back Studd replied quickly? Arguing with my old man all night, he wants to sell the business and move up north Jay shares. That sure would put a limitation on our business venture, which is bull crap Studd said adding in his two-cent. Yeah, I know Jay agrees as he secures the opening of the steel gate with a tieback. Damm Jay, I knew today was going to be hard and that just added on weight, listen I got news I need to share with you. The County is trying to rezone the whole area, to sale land to the oil companies. That could possibly hurt our enterprise. That land purchase order with the County, did it come through or what Studd seriously asked Jay. Jay for a few seconds said nothing with just a total look of surprise shakes his head. Suddenly he breaks into a big grin, starts to jump up and down with loud laugher. What is so funny now Studd asks not seeing the humorous connection? The jackpot, George you, you have hit the main vain, the big casino, all the paperwork has been signed and notarized. There they sit in the banks safe deposit box in town. They arrived late Friday evening and I place them there for safekeeping Jay informs Studd as he sits down on a stool while holding his head in disbelieve. Studd starts to clap his hands and pat his feet as if dancing to a sound only he could hear. So happy was Studd the church came out of him as he shouts Glory, Glory, and Glory. We got it, we got it for real Studd ask to confirm what he had just heard was real. Yes, yes you are a rich man George Freeman, Jay said straight faced as he starts to stand. Holding out his hand Jay wished to congratulate Studd for his foresight with a handshake and a hug. Jay, this thing, it's not possible without you. If the rumor is true, we need to start thinking outside of the box, Studd enlightens Jay. You say your father wants to move up north, we can buy the place from him, and convert it into a general store. Your father knows something a brewing, and it is not good for the cotton or farming community. Meaning this scale room soon will be of no uses in this area. Jay, I have some saving that can be used to hire an attorney. The future I see is coming sooner than expected, are you with me Studd said as he nods his head up and down. Tomorrow morning before shift starts, we will talk more Studd informs Jay. Jay let's get this one right and live successfully we've been in rough ordeals before. Tonight, I will be meeting with Miss Elisabeth, so just stay cool and we will get through this Studd said as he walks to the scale and begin the calibration. I got your back; I know we can get this figured out in no time Jay said as if he sees into the future. You and Miss Elisabeth are spending a lot of time together, what's-up with that Jay cheerfully question Studd. I know your mama done told you to stay out of grown folks' business Studd playfully implied. Oh yeah, you got to get a belt before you can call yourself grown around here, I am told Jay said to question Studd last statement. You have been wearing the same kind of old blue denims bib overall since we were children playing in dirt. You need to man-up and get some khakis Jay said sarcastically.

This day of all days, happen to be the one many customers wanted to fuss and complain about something or another. Studd had learn at an early age to mostly listen, most just want to vent about their hardships and concerns to someone. Sometimes Studd thinks he should have been in the priesthood after listening to all the confessions. Studd so many times remind them of how it could be worst, to stay positive. Look for the unseen benefit in small blessing too. Witness how some moaners start to call Studd, Amen George after hearing his testimony. Nine times out of ten Studd, tell a story to one of his customers that he has heard from another, only the names were changed. Some are amazing, and unbelievable stories however Studd seems to satisfy them and charm the discontented down. Leaving with smiles on their faces and money in hand made all the different in the world, Studd has another satisfy customer. To the colored folks in the area Studd would always give them a little bit of advertisement. Reminding, each of them of coming attractions to the Juke Joint from near and far. Absolutely free entertainment at the Juke Joint each weekend. Something for all is Studd motto, a motto that most of the time helps attract customers. As the day ends, Jay reminds Studd of their impending rendezvous. Studd could only chuckle under his breath. It was as if Jay thinks he had forgotten about the important withdrawal. Come to think of it Studd ponders; both of them don't need to enter the bank. The banker deals only with Jay for now, for him to get the paperwork from the safe deposit box. Tomorrow and the next few days will affect the rest of our lives Studd thinks as he, sweeps up the warehouse floor. Studd brain would not stop turning, racing through thought after thought each pass. Seeing

Elisabeth in a little while will be very helpful Studd recognizes. After all, she can help him put his thoughts onto paper. With so many ideal roaming around his head, he knows he won't remember them all. He knows he is not the Griot, the keeper in the family history. The teller of tales, a family historian is not his calling, he is sure. With thoughts like that Studd categorize his shortcoming; he does not do well with short-term memory. Part of the reason he has such a hard time putting letters and sounds together to form words. Short-term memory is a problem and Elisabeth is a blessing, she has become a valued friend. LORD have mercy, Studd said aloud asking for help. He knows that these businesses they are about to gain entry into can possibly get someone hurt badly even killed. Big baller, Shot Caller often put their own twist into controlling business situations. With his associates being, a few colored folks, and a Jew align; Studd knows help from above has to be in place to succeed.

Using the church as a meeting place Studd waits for the arrival of Elisabeth. Surprise she was not there went he reach the destination Studd patience grow short. He had and wanted to share so much with Elisabeth, so much so it seems he was about to explode. Studd found himself pacing the church isles, pacing is something he usually do not do. The door begins to open and Studd turns to see who was entering the building. To his surprise it was not Elisabeth, it was Grace. What, what are you doing here Studd promptly questions Grace? His face said it all, he was not expecting this friend to be in this place. Grace, starts looking around as if this atmosphere is brand new to her. As if she had not heard him Studd again asked "what are you doing here Grace." Oh, I knew you study with Miss Elisabeth, and I had news, news I think you would want to know right away Grace answered as she continues to eyeball the place. Grace, sweetheart I want you to meet me at my place in an hour and a half. There we can discuss what news you have to give me, thanks I appreciate you, see you in a few Studd said in a military like tone. More like a command order delivered. Okay, I can do that George, Grace replies at the same time watching the church door opening. This time it is Elisabeth, Studd walks toward the door to meet her. After a swift greeting between Elisabeth and himself, he then introduces the women to each other. Both had seen the other from time to time, being a small town in which they live. Grace excuses herself after the introduction and exits the building. She left so fast I did not get a chance to invite her back for any of the church services Elisabeth proclaimed. Do you two have business or was she here to check out the place Elisabeth asks with a suspicious undertone. Well, the fact is she is the one who gave me the news about oil on the land. She has more news for me she said, I asked her to meet me after-awhile to discuss things further Studd shared. We share business she is my friend Elisabeth. I want you to know my entire friendships, want to know more about her? She is a good person to know and share information with Studd adds to enlighten Elisabeth. She is a good-looking woman; I can see why she could grab a man attention. Studd her verbal communication skills she speaks with an educated vocabulary Elisabeth notice and spoke on as well. Self-taught is my understanding Studd quotes.

Listen Elisabeth I got some more news to share, news that the land property I been trying to acquire has been finalized. I've been informed this morning that all County departments have signed-off and the papers notarized with County seals. Additionally, I will hire an attorney and the games begin Studd said as if satisfied. And you think these good old boys down here are going to allow that without a fight Elisabeth said to disrupt Georges daydreaming. The paperwork, the ownership of land will belong to an L.L.C corporation with me a silence shareholder. More of the preparation reveal after the meeting with the attorney Studd makes known. So, now that, that issue is set aside. George, what is the plan for Deputy Simpson and his activities Elisabeth questions. Not clear yet! We are still in the planning stage Studd tell his study buddy. Listen, I got a more pressing situation Studd continues, it is to read a book so more can be provided. A smile and a question follow, Elisabeth speculates her roll in any tricky combination to be dangerous.

Her question to George is how he is able to guarantee protection. Studd response came out as if the answer had been processed some time ago. Elisabeth, it seems to me that a whole lot of folks in this town know of our relationship. They know that we meet on a regular basis to study, that you're helping me to become more book wise, that reading, and writing is the help I get from you, that all the other associate and public knows, and we got to keep it that away Studd encourage his dear friend. Well, let's get busy then, what's another word, hectic; is what I 'm thinking Elisabeth said expressing her concern. Elisabeth, I have become so fond of you, trust me I would not put you in harm's way. Since Sunday, I have had folks, following Simpson twenty-four seven. He has some cracks in his armor, and when it the right time I plan to open it like a can of sardines, Studd said to assure Elisabeth. George, they have not realized yet, you are the colored man that sits and listen. The one that has developed a plan to capitalize on their loose lips Elisabeth said as if informing Studd of his own exploit. Yeah! I am the one all right; the one that does not complain and do what told Studd said adding to Elisabeth utilization statement. The need now is for that image to stay intact, let all think I an Uncle Tom catering to Mr. Charles and them. Elisabeth, let's get back to what most important to me now, right now it is that word "hectic", when would somebody use such a word Studd questions his study buddy. Hectic, is use for many reasons, to solve complicated problems that can become hectic. Repeating the same task or a busy obligation is another time the word is used Elisabeth quotes as if she a human dictionary enlightening her student. H, E, C, T, I, C, hectic Elisabeth recite to Studd giving him time to envision the word as she spells it out. Studd repeats the spelling of the word as he writes it into his notepad. Woman, please this studying is hectic Studd response to Elisabeth. You got it George; you use the word correctly in that sentence Elisabeth informs her student. Shoot! That word can be used in a lot of situations Studd said as a big grin crosses his face.

Studd and Elisabeth study for another hour or so before calling it a night.

Leaving the churches on their way to Elisabeth's place Studd volunteers to carry the notebooks. With his free hand, Studd decided to be romantic by placing his arm over Elisabeth shoulder. No, George, Elisabeth quickly replied as she brushes his arm off her shoulder. Not in public, we want folks to think of us only as friends' studying Elisabeth reminds Studd. matter fact gives me some of the books. I think that will show a different appearance Elisabeth adds. Studd agrees with Elisabeth logic let her know that he thinks her judgment is solid. While walking, a lot of small talk between the two happens, as their try to get to know one another better. Arriving at Elisabeth's doorstep a silence came over both. That's when Studd reaches out and grab Elisabeth free hand, held it tightly for a few second, smile and says good night. Elisabeth smiles as she tilts her head a tad to the left and repeat Studds words, good night. Studd watches as she climbs the stairs and enter the door. What a day Studd thinks as he moves away from Elisabeth. Beginning his walk toward home with a grin on his face he thinks of the positive in his life. At the end of the day, Studd recognize he has many open situations going-on, which he hopes to finalize. A few of the actions would secure his families future. As he continues his walk home several passer-byers speak or wave acknowledging his presence. This is one of the things, Studd likes about living in a small community. There not a whole lot of unknown, folks would usually have dialogue if it were only to say hello. Private conversations just mean not talked about folks in public, it's a code in the south. Gossip is one thing but in a quiet setting.

CHAPTER 14 . . . Get at it

As Studd turned the corner down the street, in which he lives. There stands Man, still looking sharp as a tack. It must be really important for Man to be here this time of night Studd supposes. Because they had seen each other earlier this day, they both only spoke with their eyes. Studd reaches Man with eyes wide open, Man response with an upward nod of this head, and started walking up the stair to Studds apartment. Still in silence they reach Studd's door and Studd unlocks the deadbolt. Once entering the apartment Studd without hesitation question Man about the task, he was assigned to complete. What's going-on Man you got something to tell me Studd asked? Look here that old boy Deputy Simpson he been a fox in the chicken coop. No, let me say that differently, where nothing good about him. He has been having sexual immoral acts with children that he has been taking out camping. And! This distorted bastard has been taking pictures of them too. He got his own dark room in the shack behind his house so he can develop the films himself. Studd standing there in total surprise, finally he asks can we prove this, can we provide evidence of his dreadful deeds.

George, please! Did you not ask me to handle this or what, of course I got proof? I had suspicion about him anyway; he only talks or touches women when other men are around. To test my theory, I ask Grace and Millie to make a pass at him, and he did not bite. You know something's out-of-order if he passes up on those fine ass woman. So, therefore I had questions of his manhood for sometimes. I've had people on the lookout of his where about for a while now Man informs Studd. Studd still stand quietly listening as Man continues the informative new. Man, admitted that he has knowledge of what time Simpson shift started as a Deputy. So! He decided to visit Simpson's residence Man goes on. Once I got inside the shack now, I know why he stays out in that wooded area; he has pictures of children having sex with him and each other. Look at these, I borrowed a few, see if you recognize any of the children Man tells Studd as he reaches into his back pocket and pull-out a hand full of pictures. As Studd receives the pictures handed to him, he asks, Man did you break the lock into Simpson shack? Look here younger brother, think, if I had done that, he would know someone was on to his activities. So, to answer your dumb question no I did not. But! Because the shack sits on a dirt floor, I just dug underneath the back wall. It took me some time; matter fact when I was away from the Juke Joint from time to time, I was working on that project. I dug a little at a time, covered the hole with small branches, and spread dirt on top. Each time I swept the area using weeds as brushes to smooth the landscape of footprints.

Studd lifts his head up from looking at the pictures, shaking his head in disbelief as he says to Man, you, you are something else. Do you know what can happen to Simpson if these pictures are exposed? With a smile on his, face Man starts to rub the back of his head and answers, yes, I know what those good old white folks would do to him. Yet, I have never seen a white man lynch around here before, for any reason. What you think George do you want to see something like that Man asked in a humorous voice. Suddenly there was nothing but quiet in the room as Studd continues looking through the selections of pictures, so quiet, you could only hear the sound of the clock ticking. That when Studd decided to go into the kitchen and pull out the whiskey and two cups. Here! Studd said to Man passing him a quarter cup filled with whiskey. This is something we seriously need to think about before we make a move Man, Studd suggest to his big brother. Man, did you completely cover the hole to Simpson's shack, yet Studd inquire. No, not yet I thought we might need something else out of there Man answers after taking a couple sip of whiskey. Why! What are you thinking George, Man asks in an inquisitive tone? Well. I have a few thoughts running around in my head, but we will need more pictures and some negatives for them to be successful Studd shared. The next time you go back out there I am going with you too Studd adds. Oh! No, hell no is the answer to that, you do what you do, and I do what I do Man said without hesitation. George, I thank you for your concern, but I work better alone. Not having to worry about another person is the way I like it, nothing personal. Timing is everything, George; I know you know that from your business dealings. Just tell me what else you need from there, I will get whatever, and shut the hole, Simpson will not know his place has ever been enter Man said compellingly. Man, you are the man, I thought you had hired some folks to investigate for us, but you, you had it handle yourself Studd said praising his brother's ability. Wait, wait a minute, didn't Simpson have a couple hounds he uses for hunting around there. What happen to them when you were in the area Studd questions Man. That was not a problem I just gave them some meat with some sleeping potion in it Man reveals smilingly. Fact is after a couple times of feeding them they looked for me to have their treat Man said sharing a slight laugh.

After a few minutes of sipping some more whiskey and looking at the pictures, they became silent like a baby being breast-fed. Boy! That's a shame, he would do children like that Man said speaking-up. You know George; if Simpson had not been blackmailing us, I probably would not have been in his shack anytime soon. I was not in a hurry to look into that shack; it was more about me get familiar with the dogs. Inside the house is where the goods usually kept. You know Simpson has a reputation of taking folks guns and not turning them in to the Sheriff's Department, keeping them for himself. So, I figure one day I would go into his house and explore, see if any interesting pieces showed up during my unauthorized search Man share with Studd as if he had a fool proof plan. Even if you had pull off such a thing, what would you have done with the weapons, you could not sell them around here Studd questions Man. Besides, you know if you had carried that plan out the whole-colored community would catch hell. Simpson would be on the warpath with no folks of color safe, especially the men. Well Simpson sure messed-up the plan I had Man said while folding his arms and nodding his head up and down as in discuss. Now, I guess I will abandon whose preparation Man said as he finally sat, sat down on the sofa. Now it's not necessary, our plans can be forgotten we are going to let his own folks the good old white town people castrate him. Maybe they will hang him by the neck with a rope too I hope Man envisions. These pictures are unbelievable, I understand different strokes for different folks, but this is ridiculous. Man, take your time with this I want you to be careful. If we have to pay Simpson a few times, so be it. I cannot think of anyone that would make copies of these photos right now Man, can you Studd inquires. No, cannot say that I do, wait a minute this is a long shot but the photographer for the colored weekly newspaper up in Jackson. He just might have the nerves to assist in exposing a criminal and child abusing Deputy, Man recommends. Damm, that sounds like something that just might be feasible Studd said in complete agreement. Man, listen this is what I am going to do I am going to ask Elisabeth to contact the newspaper and get the photographer's name and other information. From there I will contact him and inquire about colored folks and becoming landowner in the region. Not to worry Man, she, that is Elisabeth will only know that I want to talk to this person about our land deals, what you think about that so far Studd questions his brother. That's a start but how will you get him interested in the Deputy situation, Man asks. Like always, a little small talk first, then maybe something about if he's married, if he has children.

After that, I will direct the conversation up to the real life-size question of the many lost or abducted colored children that are missing in the area. I sure that will open up his inquisitive nature. Perhaps he will want to take picture of the completely awful mess. Man, do you support that that crazy son of a bitch fed his dogs meal from the folks he killed, Studd asked as his imagination started to think of all kinds of twisted ideals. Shoot! Aint no telling, Simpson dogs can surely hunt down colored run away from the prison chain-gang Man remind Studd of. Studd questions so, what are you going to do with the pictures, the one you got right here Man.? My thought is that since there already here right now, so let just find a place to hide them around here Man answers clearly and straightforward. Okay, somewhere around here Studd agrees, but not in the house for sure. I don't want to bump into them from time to time. Outside, under the crawl space, between the shutters, or even in a flowerpot some of the few ideal Studd propose. Look here George whatever we think of now. We won't be able to begin tonight. I am sleepy and going to lay down here on the couch and get some sleep, we will decide later okay. With that said, it seems to Studd the discussion was concluded. So, he shut-up went into his bedroom got a bedspread came back out placed it over his brother-outstretched body. Studd went back into his bedroom he closes the door and let it go for now. His thoughts were, we would get at it again tomorrow, although in bed Studd mind would not shut down. He still has business matters dancing around in his head. With many folks he has to rely on Jay, Grace and Marty and let us not forget Poppa and Uncle Jay, which was just the front, end he is thinking. After a while, Studd starts talking to himself, go to sleep man he said in a murmur as he rolled over into his side, tomorrow will take care of itself.

CHAPTER 15 . . . Something is brewing

Hearing the roosters crowing was Studds usual alarm clock, however this morning he is awake to the smell of coffee as well. Remembering Man stayed over last night he understood the brew smell. Out on the farm, most of the men in the family had completed their outhouse business, and morning wash-ups, and shaved before the fresh smell of coffee capture the house, thank you LORD. Studd thinks as he smiles exiting his bedroom door into the living quarters. Right away Studd sees Man drinking a hot brew of fresh-grounded coffee. Morning greeting were exchanges between the two as Studd heads to the bathroom. Man, do me a favor Studd asked before entering the bathroom. Will you pour some coffee in a cup for me with two sugars? Remembering he still can't drink piping hot like the rest of the family, it smells good though. Go ahead, do what you got to do, I got you "little brother' Man replies. But! If you are going to do number two, be sure to open that window all the way Man instructs with a force full voice. I remember not even being able to use the outhouse after you Man said grinning as he places coffee and sugar in a cup for George. Hey! It wasn't as bad as your snoring and being right next to you Studd shouted from the bathroom loud enough for his brother to hear clearly. I am just saying I hope you don't run me out of the apartment that all Man responds as he sat at the kitchen table.

While in the bathroom, Studd remembers he was supposed to have meant Grace here last night. Now, he is thinking what could have happen to her not to appear as planned. Right before, negative thoughts started to travel into Studd questioning mind. The sound of raps on the front door is heard. Hearing the noise, Studd called out to Man and asked him to check it out, see who that could be this time of morning. Without responding to Studd's request, Man shouts out. Yeah!

What is it you want this time of morning to the person rapping on the door? It's me, a soft gentle voice replies, its Grace. Without hesitation, Man moves from the table hearing that gentle vocally acknowledgement from outside the door. Quickly he opens the door to see a lovely looking woman. With a wide grin on his need a shave face, a greeting extended to Grace and he invites her to come in. Grace acknowledges his greeting and enters into the apartment. Man, still excited to see Grace this time of morning, seems to have forgotten his manners. He just stood there for a few seconds looking at her before offering her a seat. Recognizing she was not here to see him. He excuses himself and goes to the bathroom door to let George know that it was Grace at the door, and she wants to see him now. Oh! Okay but right now I only have on my underwear. Will you get my robe from the hook on the back of my bedroom door for me? Sure, not a problem, are you ready for it now; If not I think I can keep her company until you're ready Man assures Studd. Thanks, brother; however, I'm ready now to meet with her Studd said with a laughing tone in his voice. Man, will you let Grace know that I will be with her in a few minutes. Sure Man acknowledges, he then went to retrieve the robe for Studd. Back at the bathroom door Man, opens it a little bit to transfer the garment into Studd's hand. Taking only a few second to put on the garment, Studd exits the bathroom.

Grace woman don't scare me like that. I am looking out the window all night wondering what had happen to you, are you all right Studd inquires. Yes, I'm fine thanks for asking. Some business I had to cover last night took longer than expected. Rather than go home I thought I would let you in on the, news I've been pleased to hear. Before I start, may I have some of that delicious smelling coffee, to wet my pallet. I am sure it will help me to stay awake as well Grace continues. I will get it for you Man volunteers, cream and sugar I suppose you will need Man ask. Studd looks at Man as he walks away then to Grace and back toward Man. He had never seen Man cater to a woman like this before. Studd thinks to himself I will question that later, it's time to hear Grace's hearsay.

Grace starts to tell of the company that she had kept busy drinking last night. She tells of the four white men that talked about the plans they had for the future of this county. As she served them food and drinks it was as if she was not there. The N word and laughter was used throughout the night. However, occasionally Samuel would put his hand on her rear bottom as she passed to refill drinking glasses with Brandy. One time or another Grace had been with each of them for financial profit. Grace was a smart woman she would feed them drinks until they pass out. Place them in bed, pull down their pants and underwear. Place lubricant around their private areas and when their awake. Each believed they had had intercourse and left happy. Grace continues by telling the brothers of all the men present last night, a Commissioner a Judge the Sheriff and the Mayors brother all talking about the properties with oil below them. They plan to move all sharecroppers out of the area, by buying up the land from the owners.

The ones that don't want to sell their property will be issue a court order of intimate domain rights. A court decree that would states it's in the best interest of the community. Studd asked Grace if she knew or not, had anything been written down? Yes, Grace replied also adding that the Mayors' brother has a hard time hearing so the attendees would place notes in front of him. What was done with the notes after he read them Man questions Grace. They're put into the trash during and after the card games complete, Grace informs the brothers. Now we need to get all of them, all of the notes made Man suggest. What would that do Studd said quickly interrupting his brother. Public knowledge of the information would only put Grace in harm's way. Knowing she was the only darkie in the room and having no power. They would surely hurt her badly, probable kill her Studd includes. No, no we surely don't want anything like that to happen to Miss Grace. Man said shaking his head as if to forget that notion. However, with those notes we can share with the newspaperman, Man stops talking. He realizes he's sharing too much information. Grace being the woman with a quick wit catches the drift of what Man had said. She looked at both men, shakes her head as in discuss than respond with, you're absolutely right Man. Stop talking I didn't need to know any more detail of you guys plans. Studd and Man looks at each other for a few second before Man makes a statement. It's not a plan it was just something off the top of my head. Something I was thinking of and ran with he explains. Whatever Grace replies and starts to sip on her cup of coffee. The room becomes quiet until Grace lets them know that other conversation of interest took place at the card game too. That there was talk of George's Juke Joint place and how profitable it had become. With that, statement said Studd eyebrows rose. Another point of interest surely had elevated this conversation. Grace, you a jewel Studd shares as he walks to the coffee pot to refresh his drink. Anyone needs a cup warmer he asked as he's filling his cup. Both Man and Grace raised their hands in responds. As Studd dispenses the brew he questions Grace about the redneck's discussion. What kind of concerns in the near future should we have? All kind, anything that you can imagine, they want. Wanting what you got and are willing to do anything to accomplish that goal. So, I suggest we have our heads-up, be on the lookout in the foreseeable future Grace informs the guys. Without a doubt, you're right Studd said agreeing with Grace. Well, that all I have to share at this time, so I'll be on my way. You know a girl has to get some beauty sleep, from time-to-time Grace expresses to the brothers. As she gets-up and heads toward the door, Man, just had to give his opinion to Grace's last statement. Woman, if you got any more sleep every woman in the county would hate your guts. Because I can speak for the men, we see no flaws in your appearance. Studd nods his head in agreement, as Grace, turns the doorknob and pull open the door to exit. Thanks for the compliment, however, inter beauty in more important Grace tells.

Suddenly Studd cut into Man, what a wimp you've become, come-on man. You know you like the woman; you think she's special right? Man, just looks with a blank expression on his face. Man, just let the woman know how you feel about her Studd continues. Feeling is one thing but romance without finances doesn't happen Man said quoting an old saying. She got money, Studd introduce into the conversation. She can take care of herself, you never know. Shoot! You never know what her feelings are unless you communicate with her; she will never know about your intentions either Studd blast at Man as he throw-ups his hands as if he was surrendering. You're right George; I guess I am afraid of rejection. Look at how many suitors she has at her disposal. Many of them with long bank, I be thinking I can't compete with those fat pockets guys Man said explaining his hesitation. A close mouth doesn't get fed Studd reminds Man. Okay! Point taken; I won't be flirting with her anymore. Trust me; the next time, I talk to her, square business it will be Man proclaims. Whatever you say! You're the one that has to live with your decision Studd replies. Come on now, let us head out to the farm, we need to talk with Poppa, Studd said ending the previous chat. Wow! This is one conversation I wish we didn't have to have Man said while showing an uneasy facial expression. Each brother hurriedly gathers and put on their garments, and out the door, they went.

CHAPTER 16 . . . Retribution

While walking, out of town several vehicles passed-by without slowing down a bit. Some did; however, blow the horn as a signal for the men to get out of the way or be ran-over. Studd and Man became accustomed to this situation. More than not a disgusting racial comment would follow. Nigger and black ass boy was the words normally heard. However, the brothers never would respond to the negativity. Each would look straightforward not wanting to implement an altercation. Man, did for safety keep a pistol in his right front pocket. Studd being aware of his brothers' stash would walk on his brothers left side. Just in case, an exchange of bullets was necessary he would be out of the way. Man could then retrieve the pistol much easier and have a better chance of getting off a shot. During the walk, time to time Studd would question his brother. Try to get an ideal of Man's mind frame. In the past, a few Rednecks have mistreated Man during his adolescent years. Man has vowed he wasn't going to take any more bullshit from any of them. Man would try to stay out of their way, and he wishes them to do the same. However, the scenario Man envisions doesn't always come to be. So, in a few cases Man has had encounter with the law after confrontation and dispute with non-colored folks. Just stay alert, Man answers' Studd. You know many of these old boys are mixed-up with the Ku Klux Klan. They don't mind put a brother down for any reason Man continues. Yeah! Man, I know where we are, the good state of Mississippi where anything possible for and to people depending on color of skin Studd announce. Both men break into laughter, knowing the truth been put into the atmosphere.

After a couple more hours of walking, the brothers can see pillars of smoke in the sky. Knowing it has to be coming from the farmhouse, the brothers start to pick-up their pace. Because of the rivalry between the two, the quick pace became a race. Man being lean and long-legged breaks out in front.

Studd not wanting to be outdone reaches out with his right hand and pulls Man arm to break his momentum. Right away Man tries to shake Studds hand from his arm. It ends-up with both on the ground after their feet becomes tangled up. No harm no foul as each begin to crack up laughing. Man notices his sharp outfit was now sorted so, he tells his brother, George you got to pay for this mess. You done messed-up my best outfit, I need it cleaned, or you can buy me another one. You decide, Man said instructing his young brother of his option. Man, don't sweat me; you know Mama can take care of those spots. Man acted as he was accepting of Studd suggestion. So, without hesitating he called-out, come-on help me up George, little brother. As their hands meet Man, pull Studd to the ground and the wrestling with laugher beginning again. After a few minutes of horse play, a deep baritone voice is heard, boys, get up off the ground and act your age, it was Poppa sounding off as he sits atop his big brown stallion. Without another word said, both raise to their feet. He started it Poppa, Studd said pointing in the direction of Man. Seem like two grown men frolicking on the ground to me Poppa said. Matter of fact, what are you two doing out here anyway? I suppose you're hungry so y'all came looking to fill you bellies with some of your Mama delicious home cooking Poppa said presuming. Well, that is part of why I'm here, also I came to talk business with you Studd confesses to his father.

Poppa gets down from his horse and asked what kind of business you guys come up with that would need me to partake in. I need help from you and Uncle Jay, Studd maintains as he walks over and grabs the reins to Poppa's stallion. Poppa's eyes widen as Studd contribute more and more information about his business ventures and undesirable dilemmas. Man stands beside Studd as he deliverers the circumstance and situation of their blight. Studd with concern pleads with Poppa to get Uncle Jay to come out of the bayou and assist them with their proposal. After explaining how the plan would benefit all parties concerned, the brothers' stand quietly awaiting their father's response. Your ideals seem extremely dangerous for a many of folks. But! At the same time would be very profitable if the plan worked out without too many hitches Poppa Will deducts. Come-on lets go to the house, I need to get something to eat, and I will think on it some more, Poppa tells his sons. Can I take Gholar back to the stable Studd question his father? Then what do I do walk to the house Poppa replied with a slight frown. No, no thanks I'll ride him to the house then you can take him to the barn for me Poppa informs Studd. Off Poppa when galloping atop his stallion as Studd and Man walked and talked about the future.

Once at the house Studd duties just begins, greeting everyone and giving allowances to his siblings was mandatory. It had become a tradition to give each an allowance for their farm chores. Because of his gifts, Studd easily could delegates to others the duty of wiping down and put the stallion into the stable stall to another. After taking the two steps onto the porch, Studd greet his mother. Following the hug and kiss she asks if he is hungry. I can do with a bite or two he replied without hesitation. Go-on and help yourself, there's plenty of food on the stove and counter. George, I have to go and assist the youngsters out in the field Mama tells. Inside at the table Man and Poppa had already started eating. So, without any farther conversation Studd grab a plate and commence filling it with some of all the cooked items. Ham, potatoes and onions, eggs, and homemade biscuit with some apple butter it doesn't get any better than that Studd thought to himself. Soon he joins the others and not a word was heard only the sound of eating utensils hitting the plates to retrieve more food to fill into their mouths. A conversation starts a short while later after sitting at the table each had, had their fill. Poppa opened the talks with, in my opinion, the plans could work if all involved handle their business correctly. In the morning, I will travel to the bayous to see Uncle Jay. It will take some kind of encouragement to convince him to come out of those swamps I assure you Poppa told both brothers. Yeah, I know Uncle Jay only wants to be engaging if he can get back to his precious wetland right after he is finish with his tasks. Well, one thing about it is Jay will definitely help if he thinks harm is approaching his family that you can count on. Boys, I will see you guys when I get back. Right now, I have to pack a few things for the trip. I will leave tonight so by time I get to the swampland daylight with have arrived. I don't know the area and landmarks like Uncle Jay that's for sure. So! I'll have to give a blast from this antler horn as a signal and Uncle Jay will come fine me, Poppa said as he departed from view.

Later that night about midnight Poppa saddles-up his horse Gholar and with his travel supplies heads toward the bayou. By the crack, of dawn they were at the edge of the wetlands. Poppa dismounts Gholar, takes his supplies down from his steed turns Gholar around to face the farmhouse. He rubs Gholar head and whispering into his ear, Poppa then hits Gholar hindquarter with his hand and Gholar runs off. He watched as his favorite animal gallops away, out of view. Next thing Poppa did was rub some moist dirt onto his bear exposed skin including his face. This was to cover any oily parts of his body, hoping to keep mosquitoes away. After walking miles into the bayou it began to get dark due to all the vegetations overgrowth. Also, the stagnated water was beginning to get deeper.

Poppa also knew that when he reaches the swamps fork to take the waterway that bins to the right. All the while Poppa constantly was on the lookout for Gator's, he wasn't planning to be their next meal. If anything, it would be the other way around. Poppa has eaten Gator meat before and could use the predators hide for a profit too. Poppa walked another couple of hours then decided to sound his signaling horn. Hoping to be in hearing distance of Uncle Jay isolated hut. After several mighty blast of his signal horn Poppa waited for a reply. More than a few minutes passed without a response. So, Poppa decided to blow a few more horn blasts and wait a bit more. Being an impatient kind of guy, Poppa began walking again. However, not being foolish he began marking the trail as he travels cutting back bark from tree trunks. While wandering through the swamp, he began to notice trap markers. In his mind, it could only mean one thing, that Uncle Jay was harvesting, and he shouldn't be too far away from Jay's encampment. It seems to be a good time to signal Poppa thought, so he blew several more times. Shortly afterward a response heard. Recognizing the direction of the sound Poppa Will headed into that direction. All the while each blew short blast until they met and greeted one another. During their embrace Poppa notice a familiar foul odor and it was from his Uncle. Having not seen each other for a few years Poppa would not dare insult his relative about his smell. Nephew, you come out here to see me, it must be extremely important Uncle Jay said questioning his kinfolk. But, first let's get on some dry land. Where I have some delicious Coon slow roasting over the fire at my campsite Jay tells Will.

During Poppa Will visit with Uncle Jay, the two men talked about the past and life's current issue. It was revealed that Jay had, had a liking toward his now niece-in-law back in the day. But! Since he preferred hunting and didn't want to be a sharecropper. He never made any advances toward the fine-looking woman his nephew ended up marrying. Will listens to Uncle Jay's rattle on talking about his IF's, all the while smiling? At the same time, recognizing his good fate, of having a family to go back home to, Will, keeps the belief to himself. After reminiscing for what seemed hours Will interrupt Uncle Jay travel down memory lane. Uncle Jay, Will said in an attention-getting voice, I need your help. Silence for a few seconds, then Jay spoke. Well, I rather figured you didn't come here to socialize, what seem to be the problem. You, see my son George came up with this ideal in which we can own us some land. However, some of the White folks are trying to eliminate us from purchasing any of the black-bottom land, by intimidation. Plus, one of the Sheriff Deputies is threatening to shut down George's Juke Joint if he doesn't pay him a weekly bribe. The short of it is that we need to set them straight. Let them know not all Colored folk give in to their supremacy way of thinking.

So, Jay replied what do you have in mind for me to assist you with. To start we were thinking you could quietly sneak into several houses and leave artifacts that belong to a white neighboring farmer. We need distrust among them first, any double-crossing ideal to set into their minds. Will, you know I want to help, but before I can, I have to bring in the traps I have set out. So, give me a few days and I'll get started on the task you're describing. Great, by then we should know the name of all the rascals that are trying to derail us from our future goals Poppa Will assured Uncle Jay. With their splendid plans set and a good meal cooked, the kinfolk began to chow down not saying a word during the meal. Moonshine, Coon, Collar Green and Hot Water Cornbread was a good combination Poppa Will had to admit as he picks his teeth for meat remnant. The conversation continues after the meal with Poppa Will saying that he would stay a few days to help Uncle Jay clear his traps if he didn't mine. Nephew your company is always welcome, thanks for the consideration, Jay was swift to say. Well! That's what we do help family, selflessness is next to Godliness. Will continues to talk, saying how he has been noticing the nighttime sounds. That in these bayous it's quite a bit different from the sounds he's used to hearing while sitting on the front porch back home he shared. I suppose you're use to this, having been out here for so many years now Will presume about his Uncle. What other sound is there, this is nature at its best Jay responded as if he knew something Will didn't. I think we should get some shuteye now; at daybreak we will be booting-up to retrieve many traps. Yeah! I hear that Uncle; rest is what I need; see you in a few hours Will response. So, the last thing on Will mind is a reprisal him and his family possibly would receive. If it became known that they were the planner of a conspiracy to disrupt some white folk's harmony.

CHAPTER 17 . . . Time to ride

Back in town, right after daybreak you find Studd and Man at the Livery Stable. Each checking out the livestock the Blacksmith has for sale. Truth be spoken, Studd was acting, perpetrating as if he knew what he was looking for, in the value of a horse. The majority of his time he spent indoors at a counter. His knowledge of horses is very limited so, he uses the expertise of his brother's knowledge. Watching Man check the teeth, legs, and hoofs was a thing to behold. He was able to tell the age of the animals from his inspection. As well, he knew the value of said animal Man was smart like that. After the evaluation Man, ask the price of a big Brown Stallion and a Palomino Mare. $175 for both, the blacksmith answers without looking toward the brothers. He just continues beating the red-hot piece of metal with a ball-peen hammer. Then, Man turns to Studd and said that's a fair price, the animal is in good shape and in their prime. This is the first place we looked; don't you think we should look at another stable before we decide Studd questions Man. I bought you here because I know of the quality of the man stock. If we go to another stable these animals may not be here when we get back Man said pointing out his concern. If we leave, we might lose this good opportunity, I say let's get while the getting is good Man strongly suggest. You're the expert so I will go along with your thinking Studd replies. Blacksmith, hold the Stallion and Palomino for a couple hours, we need to get more money then return, remember I work for Mr. Charles, and my word is good. Money talks, bull-crap walks, I will be here hopefully for you the animals will too was the response the brothers received.

During their journey to fetch more money several motor vehicles pass the guys that made the brothers look at one another. It seems each had an elevation in thinking. Each began to talk at the same time about their ideal, which was their need for an automobile instead of horses. Wait a minute, I think we're about to make a big mistake Studd expressed with a forceful voice. Yeah! Your right Man said as he nodded his head in agreement. Aren't our plans for the future, so why should we ride on transportation from the past? Well said Man, I agree totally Studd concurs. Now, the fact of the matter is neither of us know how to drive a motor vehicle Studd said to no surprise to Man. Simple, we just need to fine a trainer to teach us, what about your white friend Mr. Charles son, Man questions Studd? He's hauling around lumber and building supply throughout the county, maybe we can get him to assist us with his knowledge of driving Man ask. For a small fee, I'm sure he can find the time Studd answers confidently. No more talk, of horses then, plus that dude in the stable didn't seem to be in a hurry to sell us those animals anyway Studd summarize. A pick-up truck would be the better fix for us I imagine Studd suggested. However, for me one of those big fine Buick Sedans would be more to my liking Studd continues as if testifying. Sure, your right, Man said cutting off Studd's sentence. Immediately he then began telling what kind of vehicle he would prefer. I want something heavy that will get me through the muddy roads. During the rainy season, the time we get yearly Man said informs his brother, know what I mean. Hey! That's not a bad idea, I think you got something there Studd said in agreement. I guess that will be our first purchase, let see now. Get Jay Jr. to train us to drive that shouldn't be tough. He has been one white man that has shown companion toward us Colored folks. I know his family catches a lot of flak because they are of the Hebrews persuasion. Which is a big different from the majority of the town movers and shakers Studd shares with Man. Yeah! I know what you mean, however if they aren't wearing the Star of David clothing or sitting in a Synagogue no one would know the different, Man says as if he had painted a picture. I can't debate that; you've hit the nail on the head Studd said summarizing. In a few more minutes and we will be arriving at the lumber warehouse. I hope that Jay Jr. hasn't left for his first delivery Studd inform his brother. Listen George, I'm going to cut out now. I got some responsibility at the farm I have to attend to Man tells his brother as he pats him on the back. Oh! Okay, I understand with Poppa away I am sure they need your handy man skills. Handy man, I dare you, don't you know I'm a Jack-Of-All-Trades Man said in a forceful manner. Excuse me, I most surely didn't mean anything negative about your ability, after all you the man Studd said as a slight smile came upon his face. Well! As long as you know, don't start no stuff Man replied as he tilted his head a little to the right. See you in a few hours then big brother; I will get with Junior right away. Dealing with him should be an easy transition Studd assured Man.

Upon entering, the wood chip-smelling warehouse Studd would let others know that he had arrived. He would put two fingers between his lips and exhale mightily to make a loud whistle sound. Jay, knew that could only be George entering the establishment, he would then shout back to Studd, stop that noise you smelling up the joint blowing out that foul odor. All the while Jay was smiling as his friend approached. How's it going my mellow fellow Studd say as he extends his hand to greet Jay. It's all grand my man, what's new in your world Jay cheerfully expresses all the while touching Studd's outreached hand with his. Still trying to take care of business, you know me, and with your continued support we can change, something's around here Studd shared. When you get a few spare minutes, I need to discuss a proposition with you Studd states as he lifts his shop apron from the coat hook. Sure! That's what I'm here for George, to make your life easier Jay quickly responds'. Next! Studd shouts getting right into his white folk's business personality. The visible aspect of this job seems impressive as one views and listens to the different terminology the guys throw around as they wait on customers. Particularly when only people in the lumber game could appreciate it. What Studd has to always be conscious of is that these folks he's waiting on don't think of him as equals. Outside of this establishment, he was just a Nigger with little or no value. No rights, other than to clean, pick-up or carry white folk's burden. However, this young Negro has been biting time, listening, learning as he smiles friendly while carrying out his daily shop duties. Never, has he been one to say what he wasn't going to do. Especially if it's somehow related to shop business, he saw value in all lessons. Studd heard so often, what a good boy he was from many a man, that's white man's talk as a compliment. Education, Knowledge equal Success was Studd daily quote and belief.

Once the warehouse was clear of customer, Studd was able to approach Jay and start his inquiries. Straight up, top shelf I need your assistance again Studd said cutting into Jay. Yeah! Right and what do I get out of it? Jay responds without lifting his head to look at Studd. Other than my continued friendship what else would you want; besides you don't even know what my request is, yet Studd said abruptly. You came in saying you had a thought that would change things around here. So I figured that had something to do with me as well, Jay said as he continue stocking a shelf. Matter facts give me a hand. Help me load up these boxes of nails while you tell me about our next acquisition. Damm! Jay you already know, I need some transportation, some kind of motorized transportation. Something that I can haul with Studd emphasized. I was wondering when you were going to look into a form of transportation Jay told Studd as he nodded his head up and down as if in agreement. Destined, it my destiny to be in a driver seat Studd said as to inform Jay. Slow down George, first things first, my question to you is have you ever been behind a steering wheel Jay hesitantly ask Studd. No! That where you come in Studd quickly answers. There is vehicles around here that I thought you could teach me on Studd informs Jay as he exposes across his face a big grin. I don't know what that grin is for, that ideal isn't going to happen. My father would have my hide after firing us both. If he knew I allowed you to practice driving any of the motorize vehicle. He still has to deal with them "good old boys" around here.

That means dealing with the Klan I'm sorry to say Jay reiterate. You know how jealous they are already that you're still working here, we don't need to fuse the fire. But! George,

I do have an ideal that could work in place of you training here. Okay, keep talking, what's the ideal Studd had said in questioning Jay. Out on our farm we have motorized machine, perhaps you can train on one of them. I can train you on them and you get to practice driving a motorize vehicle. Yeah! Free field hand labor at the same time Studd said to Jay as he rolls his eyes upward. Well, fair exchange not robbery Jay added to the conversation. Okay I'm in, my labor for training. I always knew it cost for schooling and this is another example Studd said to Jay as he continues milling it over in his mind. Hey, I know this can work for both of us. I show initiative to my father, and you get the training and practice you need for your vision. We just need to set-up times then we are on and popping Studd added. Our days here are long so I'm thinking Sunday Jay suggest. Sunday that's the Sabbath, Studd reminds Jay. Just another day in my belief, I work on Saturdays all the time remember Jay said pointing to his headgear. Look, do you want mine help or not, a couple hours Sundays is the best I can do, your decision. Bet! I'm there, give me a time. I appreciate you Jay and know your continued support won't be forgotten Studd assures his friend. Yeah! Yeah, yeah, a brother from a different mother I know, enough of that mushy stuff. I'm partial to the morning so let's say 8:00AM we'll meet on the south road near the fork. Now that's settled we can start cutting and milling some of these logs into planks Jay said as if instructing an employee. Let's get to it then, cause if you're waiting on me, you're backing up Studd politely answers.

CHAPTER 18 . . . Will it work out

Studd still thinking of the difficulty it will take. Of putting into place each element of shutting down Deputy Simpson. As well as the land acquisition, he has acquired from the county. Trickery and deception are the blend we have to use Studd realizes. He thinks and hopes that all of the participant he needs are accomplishing their task. To his knowledge Miss Elisabeth was busy in the city investigating, looking for newspaper accounts of children missing from the county. As well as contacting the newspapers reporter, that wrote on the cases. Man is keeping an eye on Deputy Simpson activity while he is at his cabin as much as possible. Grace is on the case, still picking the brain of that good old boy Samuel. With him its true, once with black you don't go back. Samuel runs behind Grace like a male dog chasing a bitch in heat. By now, Poppa and Uncle Jay should be out of the bayou. Both planning havoc on those that wish to deny our family fair opportunities Studd summarizes in his mind while sweeping sawdust shavings from the milling area floors. Safety is the biggest concern, if noticeable inquiries will be made it will draw unwanted attention for sure Studd knows.

Finally, the days shift end and while getting ready to leave Stuff notices that only he and Jay are at the mill to close. This absence is unusual, Mr. Charles likes to see the day's receipts before locking up for the evening. Without hesitation Studd question Jay about the senior absence. Since when had my father inform me of his agenda Jay sourly response. Well, to my recollection it's been a long time since Mr. Charles missed a closing Studd said with an emphasis on closing. He has been gone quite a while Jay admits, probably some kind of business came up that took more time than expected, I'm sure. It comes to Studd mine that a few of the regular that show up daily hadn't been seen by him today either. Well, one thing about it we know what to do in his absences Studd said to assure Jay as if everything would work out. Yeah! Let clear out Jay reply as he starts to pull stall doors close. You have heard me say many times "if you're waiting on me then you're backing up" Studd said without hesitation. George I'm going into town and grab me a cold beer, want to join me Jay asked as he locks the last gate to the warehouse. I'll have to pass this time Jay I have a date will a fine lady that I dare not keep waiting Studd replied with a grin on his face. If it's with who I think it is, I would be asking for a ride to get there early. Jay said as he nudges Studd's shoulder. Well now that you mention it and we are, going in the same direction a ride would be appreciated totally Studd implicates.

Let's mount up, the fair damsel Miss Elisabeth await the gallant Sir George, Jay says in a crummy sorry kind of British accent. What? Why are you talking like that? You been reading renaissance novels or something Studd inquires. Do you have a mighty steed for us to travel upon Studd continues asking in his British sounding drawl himself while acting as if he was riding a horse? Sir George does thou fine my tone of voice amusing Jay ask with the uncompromising speech. You're funny, Studd replies as he reaches to open the passenger door to Jay truck. Yeah Jay, she the one that can make me drool, for real. I get nervous each time I'm in her vicinity, I start to sweat, that isn't cool Studd shares. Well, in my humble opinion you have to find something you're passionate about. Why it makes you happy then tells her about it. Before you know it, you'll be done forgot all about the discomfort. Now that sounds really reasonable, when did you become such a chivalrous man Studd questions Jay. Jay starts to laugh behind hearing the word chivalrous coming out of George's mouth. Chivalrous, chivalrous that a word we don't use much around here Jay implies. How did you come up with that one, enquiring minds want to know Jay looked serious while awaiting an answer? You're not the only one that read Studd said in an assuring tone. Jay continues to look puzzled; it stayed quiet among the two for a several seconds. Then Studd decided to share, I'm trying to get into position to up lift me and the family. Between you and me Jay, I'm getting help with my reading from you know who. Oh! You mean with that fine looking Miss Elisabeth, Jay asked as a big grin overcame his face. She's has been giving me lessons, sometimes special word to master ever since I told her I wish to become a southern gentleman Studd informs his friend. Wow! That some kind of ambition you got there, now that I know that maybe I can assist you, also Jay said inviting his services. That would be magnificent Studd cheerfully express as Jay finally starts up the truck engine. Jay just couldn't help himself he began to drive off. He starts to sing, at first in a low voice. Matter- of- fact it sounds more like humming that gradually become a full blown out verse "George gotta girlfriend" "George gotta girlfriend" "George gotta girlfriend" and he's the teacher's pet, Jay sang as he drove down the road annoying Studd all the while.

During their travel into the town, the sun had just about set. A blessing they were traveling east Studd thinks. Therefore, the sun wasn't shining into the driver eyes, which would have caused Jay more difficulty, squinching his eyes. Studd had become more observant of each movement Jay made during their trip. After all, he too would soon need to know how to maneuver a vehicle. Shifting the stick and working the foot clutch. Driving seems to take feet and hand, coordination Studd surmise. Sunday isn't arriving soon enough Studd says breaking a silence. Why, why you say that Jay asks as they pull to a stop in front of the church. Why! So, I can learn to drive myself and then not hit every single pothole in the road Studd enlighten Jay as he exits the vehicle. But! I thank you for the lift it was better than a long slow walk any day, for sure Studd said as he tips his hat and closed the door. You're just not use to a chauffeur, a teamster driven wagon is what you're accustomed to. If you don't know what a chauffeur is, ask Miss Elisabeth. She should be able to enlighten you, now you have a new word to add to your vocabulary Jay shout as he pulls away from the curb. Well, one thing for sure Studd rationalizes he will be inquiring about the word Jay threw at him. Chauffeur, chauffeur Studd says aloud all the while hoping he was pronouncing it correctly.

Once inside the church Studd notice that only one corner of the buildings lit with an oil-burning lantern. Studd just stand still as Miss Elisabeth lift her head and start to smile. Before any words can come out of his mouth Studd has many visions of the future, each vision includes the woman he one day imagines being his wife, Elisabeth his dream. Good evening, George glad to see you Elisabeth said in a cheerful manner. Studd again, seen in a daze not responding to Elisabeth greeting. Are you okay George, Elisabeth question Studd after he didn't reply? Oh yeah, I'm fine, just thinking about the future Studd said as he begins to walk toward the dim lit corner and Elisabeth. Before we get started on the lesson plan, you have for me. I have a word that I would like explained Studd politely request. Sure, if I can, I'll be happy to interpret the meaning Elisabeth says as she invites Studd to sit next to her with a hand gesture. Studd as he sits his face lights up, thinking that another one he thinks to himself. The word I'm concern with, Jay threw at me as we talk stuff to each other as he drops me off here. The word, sho uf feur I hope I'm saying it right as he repeated it again to best of his ability. George, I have a question, what was you guys doing when Jay use the word Elisabeth requests as her smile became even broader. Let's see Jay was leaving driving away from the streets curve when he shouts loud that word "sho uf feur" to my recollection Studd sprout out. And! He added that a teamster could drive me. Laugher suddenly starts to fill the place and Studd begin to wonder why what's so funny. So, you're laughing cause I'm unskillful with words and their meaning Studd questions Elisabeth. George, I'm laughing because I'm proud that you trust me. Your flaws were shared and the fact that you wish to educate yourself. The word that you want me to explain is chauffeur, a chauffeur is a person employed to drive people or individually around to their destination in a vehicle, C-H-A-U-F-F-E-U-R spells chauffeur. George I'm not laughing at you, it's just the way you said the word Elisabeth assure Studd. Believe me I'm here to help but we should also be able to laugh if one another fines amusement in an action said or acted out she shares as she gently strokes Studd hand. Before he knew it, Studd frown had turn into a smile that made Elisabeth smile as well. Now that, that's settled we can get on with the lesson Studd announces, then adding thanks Jay, mockingly as his eyes lifts up toward the ceiling.

Looking straight into Elisabeth face Studd ask, can we change the subject for a few minutes Elisabeth? Sure, what's on your mind was her reply? Were you able to get any new information about the children during your visit with the reporter? Yes, I was told not only was Negro children but Whites from the bayous are unaccounted for Elisabeth shares. The Sheriff's Department still has an open investigation going on, but because of manpower and the children aren't from well-off families. Only a few hours of policing weekly are allowed for searches during work hours. Do you know if any recent disappearance has happened in the tri-county area Studd ask? I was told the Sheriff's office isn't giving much information to the Chronicle. That they didn't represent the colored folks in the area and colored didn't have an understanding of the investigation process anyway. Elisabeth, you know that's bull Studd interrupts. Yeah, right, the main investigator is Simpson, and we all know he's as quick as a turtle mentally Elisabeth expresses. Plus, he let it be known that he doesn't care about Negro. He sees us as taking away from his White superior races job bank Elisabeth says quoting Simpson's continuous rhetoric. However before I exited the newspaper office the Editor also questions me about any child missing lately. Of course, I was glad to inform him that no one has been missing of late. I also ask him to come to our area and talk with the parents of the missing and others. Want to keep the interest of discovery out there in the public view. Maybe then the law-enforcement community will follow suit Elisabeth informs Studd. I trust your judgment, if you think that'll help in the discovery, I'm all for it as well, Studd said in an assuring manner. Studd still hadn't shared with Elisabeth the unsettling news of Deputy Simpson escapades. Studd's thinking was the fewer that knew the truth the better. After all, folks around here can't seem to keep a secret more than five minutes Studd reflects. Besides, he didn't want Elisabeth to worry about something they would have no control over. Another point in Studd thinking was he wanted Simpson to continue to walk and talk as if he had no worries whatsoever. The more confident Simpson felt toward his situation, he'd talked more openly.

As the lessons moves forward, Elisabeth recognizes that her friend is really a quick study. Studd has retained all of the lessons from the previous study dates. George, you've caught on to these reading and spelling exercises. You're able to sound out most words without my help, I'm really impressed. This portion of your training is complete, we'll move to social studies next Elisabeth declare to Studd as she rubs his head congratulating him. Social Studies, what that mean Studd quickly replies. Before Elisabeth had a chance to answer the question Studd had intervened. Is it about how people, are supposed to act in sustain surrounding Studd surmised? That's absolutely, correct George, Elisabeth response then tells George that's enough studying for tonight. We'll resume tomorrow evening that is if you're available she goes on. Lady, please a cyclone wouldn't be able to keep me away. I have a passion for this knowledge. That you're so graciously providing to this little old country boy Studd politely tells his instructor. While Elisabeth packs away the lesson sheets into her book bag. Studd then advised Elisabeth that he again would like to escort her to her living quarter. I appreciate your concern and that valor which a gentleman shown Elisabeth expresses afterward. A lady shouldn't be out here alone in this darken climate Studd said ensuring his potential. We can't have anything happening to you out there, lovely lady. After all, you have all the study sheets Studd said in a chuckling humorous tone. Oh! Is that the only reason Mister, Elisabeth inquires? Just kidding, I don't know what I would do if something happened to you Elisabeth. You're special to me for more reasons than your scholarly knowledge Studd said with that didn't you know voice and facial expression. Liz, one day I want to be able to share, Studd stopped there. He stopped in his tracks reaches to grab Elisabeth hand. Looks her straight in the eyes and says, one day I want to be worthy of your admiration. Will it work out; I am counting on me and working for that to be in full effect before long Studd said courageously letting it be known. George, you are something else, you are enough man that any woman would be honored to be your significant other even wife Elisabeth said as if testifying. I have admiration for you George, just knowing you're the kind of man to achieve, to reach for better is a true statement of courage and I applaud your stance. Only a real man in my opinion isn't afraid to challenge himself she goes on, now holding Studd's hand filmier. One thing is for sure Elisabeth it's that I'm not going to work just to eat. I don't believe that I'm here just to exist after all I'm a son of the highest Studd says as he lifts his eyes toward the sky. Sure, sound right to me George, Elisabeth said as if echoing Studd's opinion.

Heading out the church door hand in hand, one would think the two definitely connected by more than fingers tips. As they walked down the road, their hands never separated. Not many words exchanged during the journey to Elisabeth's home. However, that didn't stop Studd from smile all the while. His heart rate was running a bit high due to the excitement of the company he was keeping. Studd was a bit anxious which cause him to sweat even more, this hot humid, muggy night. Studd thoughts were on how to make the woman that's walking beside him recognize. Recognize that his ambition for success wouldn't be possible or complete if she wasn't continually by his side. Still thinking to himself, Studd wonders how he can introduce Elisabeth to his way of thinking. That he wants a broader relationship between the two. A special attachment that would consist of them becoming best friend, secret keepers, confidant, lovers, and someday his baby's Mama. Suddenly Studd's thought were interrupted, Elisabeth question him about being so silent. Now, is the time to share his thoughts Studd contemplate. Oh! I guess I was thinking about the future, and I must admit a great deal of it included none other than you. I sure do hope it was pleasurable up there in that head of your Elisabeth responses in a cheerful tone. Trust me, with you in my head it has been nothing but pleasant. I was just thinking and hoping that one day we can sit down together and discuss plans for the future. As you know I have these vision and it's important to me to hear your insight. George, since I've known you, you always think before you leap. The consequence is figure out before a move made. That why, if I was a betting woman, I would bet the majority of your desires are obtain, Elisabeth had stop Studd in his tracks to express this revelation. Thanks for the praise lovely lady only thing better than those words you just said would be heard from a preacher. Not clearly understanding the comment, Elisabeth just smiles. She reaches out her hand and reconnects back with Studd hand. Slowly they continue their scroll down the avenue.

Suddenly a gentle breeze flashes across the walkway, along with that outcome the most unexpected request. Elisabeth, I want you to be my wife, will you marry me Studd abruptly confesses his desire. I know this is sudden, and if you don't want to, I understand Studd continue to nervously rattle on. George, my dear George you have a lot going on right now, are you sure, you're ready for another commitment. Marriage is a huge step, how about me becoming your girl for a while first. Let's see how that goes, let's see if we will be able to put-up with one another on a much more regular basis Elisabeth proclaim. Well at lease you didn't shut me down completely Studd replied not able to look Elisabeth straight in the face. Know this I'm not giving up on the thought of you and me becoming one, us. The vision of my future has you being the lady of many rooms. With a big comfortable living area with a front veranda and swing set. With a swing for two that will allow us to catch nice summer night breezes while socializing. I don't plan on working all day everyday believe that I'm going to arrange things so I can enjoy my family. Yearly vacations up north during the blistering summer months, I picture trip out of the country. Canada crossing from Detroit Michigan,

I've heard that a trail the Underground Railroad used for escape slaves exist Studd goes on not realizing he is walking and talking to himself. He had passed the stoop of Elisabeth house, as she stood on the step giggling. Watching as she notices George daydream into his personal thoughts. Oh! It's like that huh Studd questions Elisabeth. No, I'm with you George it's just you go into another place when you are envisioning the future Elisabeth answers. You, all of a sudden release my hand then started representing with your hand. As if you had a packed house of people listening to you every word Elisabeth tells a rather embarrassed man.

Let me tell you something about me Elisabeth, Studd announces. From the first time I saw you I have been attractive to you. As time passed, I discovered that, this feeling was more than just infatuation. It's seemed I'm consumed with vision of you and me in my head. While getting to know you as you taught me so many new things, I realize that I want to be with you continually. Elisabeth, Elisabeth, I today more than any other time in my life feels as if I can truly say I am in love with someone. You are the thought I awake to, and the smile I have as I rest my head at night. Elisabeth, you have enlightened my existence since I have known you. Today, this day I want the world to know that I am in love with the most gorgeous, sensitive lady in the world. In love with the lady that I proposal to, an offer of marriage that I sincerely hope she will one day soon except Studd tells his beloved Elisabeth. While listening and smiling as Studd spoken heartfelt words Elisabeth slowly moved closer to this man of substance. Before she knew it, her arms are wrapping around Studd body and her lips caressing his passionately. Studd a bit stunned at first quickly responds, placing his muscular arms around Elisabeth small waistline as she stood on the second step of the stoop. Out in public neither seen to give it a thought about their showing of affection toward each other. Several minutes pass before the passionate two releases their grips from each other it seemed. George, my dear George those were the most kind and caring words I have received from anyone, thank you. You, I know you are special and a gift from God. You have been a blessing to me let me tell you. It has been my pleasure to council you as you studied to improve your life skills Elisabeth expresses while holding both hands of Studd's. Still smiling like a chest cat as Elisabeth address him Studd leans forward and kisses her hand gently. This has been the best day ever, although you denied me a privilege Studd expresses. Time, time is on our side, patience is a virtue, a good or admirable quality that is Elisabeth assure Studd. Well, I don't feel totally rejected, a maybe later is better than an absolute no Studd emphasizes as he releases his betrothed hand. It's time for me to say goodnight lovely lady, I need to get home and get some rest Studd informs Elisabeth. It will be a few days before I see you again. I have several undertakings to complete, but know this, I will forever have you and our well-being on my mind he tells as he backs away with a smile upon his face. Elisabeth smiles as well, before delivering a farewell kiss and wishing him safe travel during his coming and goings. Backing away, it was a hundred feet or so before Studd turns and faces the direction toward his apartment. As Studd walks toward home many thoughts crosses his mind. Will it work, how to make his visions apparent Studd pore over. Plans are in place just stay the course is his final decision, as he pick up his pace to get to his bed.

CHAPTER 19 . . . Coming to together

A few days pass before Studd heads back to the farmhouse. He expects to meet with his parents, siblings, and Uncle. Each will then bring the others up to date with what's happening to achieve their oblige objective. Studd and them, each knows that this can be dangerous business. However, for the families' future well- being several risky schemes will come into play. Therefore, their planning has to be precise and deliberate. With the help of his family and friends, Studd likes their chances for success. Deception is the key, to have all conflicting bodies believe that their plans are still current and true.

Once arriving at the farmhouse Studd enters the front door with a greeting known to all "Peace be with you" he forcefully forwards and received a quick echo of the same message in reply. After a swift embrace from each family member Studd, grabs a seat. Usually, the family meets and departs with hugs of one another, today was no different. Breaking bread of one thing or another also was customary, so with the bacon, syrup and buttery biscuits right in front of him Studd grasps a plate and join in with the group eating and socializing. Studd marriage proposal to Elisabeth was the biggest personal news. Follow with about 20 minutes of catching up on other personal matters. However, the conversation became frantic, with all wanting to know more about the detail of the upcoming nuptial. At that point, Studd had to inform them that his desire is put on hold for now. That his future fiancé has not accepted his proposition yet that she would like his life to be more stable before she commits. Studd also shared with his family that Elisabeth has been active in his behalf. That is, helping to discredit Deputy Simpson publicly, and knows about his businesses and concerns. Silence comes over the room for a few seconds before Mama speaks. She sounds like a good sensible woman and an educated one at that. I hear, Mama said speaking in a low gentle voice. She's sure not a dummy if she is trying not to tie the knot, or jump the broom, until after some of your activities are settle. Shoot, I really don't know the woman but I think I like her already Mama, shares. Settle down there Viola, Poppa says interrupting her as he begins to infuse his opinion into the matter. I know that your son's possible marriage engagement sounds fine, but our focus has to be the solution to the problems at hand.

Let's get back to the solving our concerns, before celebrating future events. I want us all to live long happy prosperous lives. This can happen if we all pull together, and resolve this unease, let's do this and let us get it done Poppa said enthusiastically. Studd, stood and starts to applaud, realizing he was the only one standing and clapping with enthusiasm he sat himself back down. Thinking these situations was happening because of his ventures. Studd now began to speak and exposed to the group his final plans. Reaching into his rear overall pocket, he pulls out a fold piece of paper. After unraveling the note, it's placed onto the tabletop, and he begins to explain the diagrams drawing. It was more like a map with arrows and numbers indicating each order of operation. Knowing most his family members were unable to read Studd drew men and women images showing the placement for each person's route. The time of day would have to be memorize by each active participant Studd lays stress upon stress. One by one, Studd had them recite their duties and time. Wanting to be clear all knew their assignment and time to carry them out.

Okay then, it seems everyone's ready Man intervenes. Uncle Jay you're being awful quiet, how's the plan setting with you Man ask. Do you think we can carry these plans out without us getting ourselves killed Man continues questioning Uncle Jay as Poppa looked on? Then, what sounds like mumbling and babbling to the untrained ear Uncle gets out what he believes. We can get our chance done if everyone stays the course. Then Uncle Jay goes on to say that he has seen a wolf chew off a leg when trapped. Against those Crackers we have to be really careful, they would do the same to escape before allowing a colored man getting the upper hand. But I'm with you all, it's time we show them we got grit too Uncle said as he took a bite of his chewing tobacco.

Mama while listening was eyeballing Uncle Jay all the while, gone outside with that chew stuff. You ain't going to be spitting that tobacco juice up in here Mama quickly tells Uncle Jay. Without a word, Jay knew his place and starts toward the door. Here Jay, grab this jar, you can spit in it she said rushing toward the door. Jay accepts the jar and proceeds outside. Poppa seems a bit perturb, pulls Viola to the sink side of the kitchen and asks in a low voice. Why is it you seem to force Uncle out of the house? Will, Honey Baby, you know your Uncle he's not the cleanness, with him and the chew smell. Well for me, combined it's just overbearing to my nasal senses she went on. I love him, it just best if he and I socialize outdoors with air moving about. Girl! You ought to quit, he don't have no tub out there in those swamps. So why don't you do that Christian thing, draw your Uncle a bath. If you think he's in need Poppa suggest as he steps fast and hard out the door. Surely not wanting to hear Mamas reply, knowing she had words that she wasn't a shame to share either. Between parents, differences of opinion been heard several times in the past. Neither son would take sides in their disagreement. They know to stay out of those kinds of husband-and-wife discussions. So, both sons waited until the voices became silence. Then their got up from their seats kissed their mother said their byes and joined the other men outdoors.

In the shed, the two older men sat quietly, each working on a different task. Uncle Jay continues chewing and spitting while sharpening his knife with a whetstone. Poppa Will was dismantling his shotgun, cleaning, lubricating and adjusting the sight to ensure accuracy. However, once the younger brothers enter Man breaks the silence with his heavy baritone voice. Poppa, I need to talk to you, in private if you don't mine. Poppa lifts his head up from viewing the shotguns assemble.

As he gets up from his seat, he tells Man to step out the shed, after exiting he questions what is this all about son. Poppa, Mama sent me out here to ask you to send Uncle Jay back into the house in 30 minutes. WHAT! Was Poppas Will reaction, yes, I guess she changed her mind after your conversation Man informs his father. Want him in the house! For what Will insisted on knowing. Mama heard you and decided that you're right. The Christian thing to do is to help not just criticize. She's heating up a bath as we speak, so she needs you to get our Uncle to come in and see her. She said she'll do the rest from there. Poppa Will shakes his head slowly left and right before telling Man, your Mama is something else. I know she has a plan; I know it has to be a darn good one at that Will tells his son rather loudly. Well, what I saw Poppa, before George and me came out the house. Was Mama putting some of your clean clothes on the back of a chair, Man tells. Poppa interrupts, now it for me to convince our Uncle to go back into the house alone and see what your Mama wants Will said aloud talking to himself as much as Man. You have to love her, I know I do, she's a keeper for sure if you know what I mean Will recites to his son.

Will and Man go back into the shed, once inside Will tells Jay. After several minutes pass that his wife wants to speak to him. In private, I believe she wants to make amends to the way she acted earlier Will tell Jay. Uncle Jay's not in a hurry to participate, acts if nothing was being said. He continues to sharpen his blade holding his head down acting disinterested. Uncle, Uncle Jay, I know you hear what I'm saying Will said raising his voice. Will's tone catches Jay attention; surprisingly he asks what does she wants me for? She doesn't owe me an apology. It is what it is, she like thangs a certain way and I respect that Uncle Jay goes on to say with his face looking all bend out of shape. Uncle, help a man out, let me be able to sleep cozy tonight. Go inside and see what she has to say. It can't hurt you to listen, I'm sure Will said while trying to lift stubborn Jay to his feet. Yeah! Yeah! Yeah, Okay I'll go now stop pulling on me Jay replies as he knocks Will's hand from his arm. The younger brothers acting as if they were not listening nor looking rushed from the back to the shed door. Watching too as Jay enter the house slowly.

A few seconds later, a shout, of No is heard and the front door slammed shut. Hearing those unexpected piercing sounds all of the guys ran from the shed up the steps to the front window of the house. Looking in but not able to view either of them caused concern. Listening however was another matter completely. Uncle Jay's voice was loud and defiant. One could hear him saying repeatedly you're not the boss of me. Then a thunderous pistol shot rings out. No more standing around outside, to the rescue Poppa Will rushes toward the front door. Once opened he see his wife holding a pistol and has it pointing toward Uncle Jay. What the hell is happening, why the blasted gun. This is a heap of bullshit, after this word came flying out of Will's mouth; he recognized he had to defuse this whatever. Just take it easy now Viola, Will say to his beloved. In this type of situation humbleness is required Will knew for sure. Now! Uncle just got in the house Will is thinking. So how could he have cause Viola to fire off a round so fast is something he wants to know desperately? Honey Pot, put the gun down Will pleadingly ask. Sure thang! Soon as Uncle gets his rusty but into that tub of water over there, Viola said clarifying her demand. I told Uncle Jay its ducky-ducky time, but he was refusing, so then I had to show him some tough love. Maybe he needs an attitude adjustment, with the help of NOVA, I hope now he understands my position.

Honey Pot you mean to tell us, he's going to be lit-up if he doesn't obey your orders to bathe? You caught on fast, so he's not slow either, so I want to know what's the matter Viola told them as Studd, and Man watched her suspiciously. Uncle, Uncle Jay seems to me your choices are slim, and none get in the water Poppa Will says. A grin starts to come upon Will face, knowing this wasn't funny to Jay he quickly straightens his facial demeanor. Honey Pot, will you give me the weapon, before he could finish the rest of his sentence Viola, cut him off. I asked to see Uncle Jay privately, so let us finish our discussion privately husband Viola said in a calm and passive tone. But! With a gun Poppa Will responds. I got this Will, we'll be finish very shortly she said assuring her husband. Go back outdoors Sweetheart I'll call you in a few minutes she insists. Will, you can't leave me in here alone with this woman Jay pleads. She seems to have some kind of ill will toward me; I just came to help the family. Now I'm put into this real uncomfortable situation that I don't deserve. Uncle, now you're getting a feel of what I live with Will said as if giving advice, while he walks out the front door smiling.

Hey, man listen Uncle, that water ain't going to dry up no time soon. So you might as well get on behind that curtain and start to scrubbing, Mama Viola said forcefully repeating her demands. No exchanges of words are spoken for a several seconds after which. Jay finally walks behind the curtain, then suddenly dirty clothes are thrown over the curtain, you could hear them hit the floor. Soon after, the sound of splashing water is heard. Saying nothing Viola felt victorious as she bends down to retrieve, the garments. A short time later she headed out the door. Jay now seem to be enjoying the bath as he moaned as if pleasuring himself. Once on the porch Viola notice that the family had resettled into comfortable positions. So, they too had heard the going on of her and Uncle Jay's dispute. As she looks around with a small grin, she informs them that all is well. She then directs her attention to Mary, here take these clothes put them in the pot of hot water out back near the tree line. Ma, you know those things going to come apart once I start splashing them around in that hot water Mary said to her mother as if it was news. Well that just means you'll have to be really careful my darling Mama informs her daughter. Ma, ah Mama but I got other chores to complete Mary said as if testifying. The other chore can wait; they have all this time while you were listening into other folks' business Mama tells Mary. Let me know when you need some fresh water, I have some warming on the stove. It probably will need several changes Mama said as she starts to head back up the porch steps.

Mary stares at her mother's back for a few second before turning, heading to the tree line. She made some unusual sound under her breath as she begrudgingly walks quickly in order to dump the dirty garment to the awaiting tub of hot soapy water. Then Mary hears her mother shout Mary, I have something special for you when you finish. With that said it made all the different and a smile came upon Mary face as she moved the garment around in the tub. Boy! Oh boy, she thought these have to be the dirtiest clothes she ever washed in her life. It just has to be a reward for this effort; her arms were becoming really tired from swishing around the heavy garments with a wood paddle. As Mary continues her task she thinks, what it that Mama had for her is. Because, for real this wash jobs, created because Mama wants to run Uncle Jay's business whenever he comes around Mary rationalized. Mary being a few months away from her fourteenth birthday thought this was extreme training for her. She's expecting soon to have a home of her own after all, her womanly cycle had begun. Her being a woman now, it's hard for two women to be under the same roof she recognizes. Most young women of her age get married off quickly; sometimes bring wealth to the family for their matrimonial hand. Mary knows a couple bucks have been coming trying to court her, but Poppa always run them off. He calls them mustangs trying to mount a thoroughbred, but not on his watch. A young man has to come correctly to possibly escort a Freeman girl out of Will's view. Poppa wasn't looking for any field hand to hook-up with his daughters. His plans were none of his girls would be out in the fields doing backbreaking work. Not as long as he had breath in his body, he had sworn. However, Mary wasn't making it any easier; she had taken a liking to this big handsome light skin field hand name Rudy. Rudy with the big booty is what Poppa Will called him. For a man Rudy has a very unusual physique, Mary however, it seems only see's the frontal body shape of this guy that has hazel color eyes. This boy was mulatto that also had soft curly light color hair. His mother wasn't sure who his daddy is, she had been jumped on, molested and left for dead.

After awaking from months of being in a coma, she discovered she was with child. Ill legit with no name, no pot to piss in was no way for Will's ancestry to continue. Over his dead body, the bloodline of a Freeman from this day forward would not be in the sharecrop servitude of other folks. Will has a saying "say it loud I'm a Freeman and I'm Proud "that each of his children has to memorize. Every day before going out his front door each child must recite this proud pleads of Poppa aloud. Poppa himself had no schooling but he had the intelligent to have the churches Reverend write the quote on a sheet of paper for prosperity. His vision for his children is that of them being prosperous and flourishing.

About three quarter of an hour, later Uncle Jay exits the front door of the house. Clean shave with a fresh set of clothes on Uncle Jay looks like a different fellow. However, quickly he reminds us that it's the man from the swamps. While coming down the stair steps he put on that raccoon pelt hat of his and begin to talk in that Creole draw of his. Y'll laugh at me; I'm hoping y'all got pleasure. Cause that's the last one, hear me good Uncle Jay said as he pick-up his single barrel shotgun. Y'all know what though, I'm feeling real nice right about now, and I owe it to Niece Viola. I want to celebrate Will; you got any of the Corn liquor left I could sure use a swig. Uncle Jay, it's a bit early for that don't you think Poppa Will puts to a question. Will, I was asking for a drink for me, your decision is your decision. You don't have to partake because I'm gonna. Matter of fact; just tell me where the jug's at and I'll fetch it. Settle down Uncle you're welcome to the whiskey, it's out back in the storm shelter. As Will, start to walk he tell Jay to come, let's go on back there and have a few sips, I think I'll join you. Both share a hearty laugh as they marched off.

Before the tree line the storm shelter is located also. As the men approach Jay thinks, he notices some movement in the brushes. Not far from where Mary's washing clothes. Will, what kind of animals have you detect around here? Any coming beyond the tree line into the clearing Jay inquires. A few rabbits a deer every now and then, why you ask, did you see something Will, respond. Not sure, it probably nothing; the lower branches seem to be moving in one area. It has stopped now, so back to the task we came out here for. Lift up that door, let's see what you're working with Jay proposes at the same time changing the subject. Will steps into the shelter and a couple of second's later exits with a clear mason jar filled full of the spirited booze. You first said Will as he hands Jay the jug. Happy to Jay said after receiving the whiskey. Jay took a long dranks before bring it down from his mouth; he began to moan as if enjoying the taste to the utmost. Still grinning with delight Jay hands, the jug back to his Nephew. Will, tell his Uncle come on let find a shade tree that we can lean back on while we enjoy this whiskey. If you're waiting on me then you're backing up Jay said sharing his back wood humor. The men sat under that tree drinking and reminiscing, interrupted when Studd shouting out that he was leaving, heading back into town. Studd believes it's better for him to stay separated from those two when they have their drink on. He certainly didn't want to get involve in his Poppa and Uncle recollections of their shenanigan. Seeing and hearing Studd's goodbye each one of than returns the farewell with shouts and the waving of their arms and hands. Poppa wasn't much of a drinker, before he knew it his ass was knocked out, flat on his back slobbering and snoring. So! Jay decides to take advantage of the situation; he makes a decision to investigate the tree line. He had a hunch that the ruffling of the bushes was no four-leg creature. Now that Mary had completed washing his clothes and gone up front, he had his chance. No one was there to question his motive entering into the woods. With his shotgun slung over his shoulder Jay disappears.

CHAPTER 20 . . . Town folks

The next morning Studd arrives at the Warehouse nice and early. Wanting and hoping to get a chance to talk with Jay about their business proposals. As he sat on the bench at the warehouse's doors entrance Jay drove up. In a different vehicle this morning a black Ford Sedan just in time for him to hit the time clock without being late. That's right, the son of the boss has to punch-in also Studd likes that. Mr. Charles says all the time that all of them are employee to their customer. While each of them was putting on their shop aprons, Studd asked the question. Did you make any progress in any of the possible endeavors I requested? Yes, I got news, good-news Jay replies. Actually, both of the assignments you ask me to look into have come into realization. Realization, you mean they've been taken care of Studd questions Jay. No doubt, it was relatively easy when you know the right mouths to feed Jay answers. Hallelujah, hallelujah thank you Lord, Studd said just above a whisper while looking up toward the sky. He had to keep the noise down, not knowing who might be around. Studd then grabbed Jays arm, pulling him toward him asking for more details. Not now, we'll talk more during our lunch break Jay assures Studd. Smiling, Studd nods in agreement, as he, releases Jays arm. Both men walk away in different directions of the warehouse.

Studd was joyful throughout the day, greeting each customer will that fabulous smile of his as he served them. Mr. Charles notices the attitude he displayed to the customers and commends him for the way he welcomes them. He even stopped and made small talk for a few minutes. Asking Studd about his driving lessons, and if he was planning to get some motorized transportation soon. Studd was a bit surprised that Mr. Charles asked him about the driving. That was, done far away from the big house, or had Jay mention it to his father. Anyway, Studd decides to share that the training was coming along fine. That himself and his Poppa was saving and hoping to buy a used vehicle of some kind in the future. Mr. Charles without being asked gives his advice of what he considers their best bet. Telling Studd that he knew of a good used tractor that's been offered. That he could put in a word if they were looking for something in the near future. Cannot say for sure Mr. Charles when Poppa will be ready. But! I'll be sure to let him know of the kindness you're offering Sir, thank you Sir. No problem, George, you people have been good folks here in the community Mr. Charles tells Studd as he walks away. Studd, thinks, you people are what Mr. Charles thinks of them too. That smile Studd had on his face now has disappeared. What happened was, it made him more convince the working for another isn't something he want his future to consist of.

Later that evening Studd and Jay was able to hook up and discuss the land proposition. Jay assures Studd that the land has to be acquired next week. That there a lot of interest in those black bottom acres of land. Saying that a significant amount of money they'll needed at that time. Significant, what does that mean, how much is significant Studd question. Eighteen, eighteen dollars an acre was Jays respond. That's Thirty acres we are talking about is a small parcel next to what the large companies are trying to acquire. We just have to get in where we can fit in without the elephant stepping on us mice's, Jay said trying to be humorous. Studd, fining nothing funny continues looking at Jay with a straight face. Five Hundred Forty-dollar total, what kind of markers can we leave if any Studd ask. None, cash on demand is the only way this deal will work Jay shares, shaking his head. Wow! Five Hundred Forty Dollars, I surely had hopes of getting the property for a lot less, but! It is what it is. How much you got Studd faces Jay with a grin on his face. I'm going to need a loan, my friend, my brother Studd said still grinning. George, are you kidding me, I ain't got a pot to piss in.? You know the different between you and me George. Without giving Studd time to answer Jay tells, George you plan for tomorrow. I know tomorrows not guarantee so! I enjoy each day as they come. Meaning the cash, I had I spend without remorse. I know you can get a line of credit from the bank, all that money you've been saving Jay said at the same time questioning Studd. My money is in Mason jars, I don't trust those bankers. After mumbling under his breath and shaking his head Studd tells. I think I'm pretty close to those numbers, after this weekend take from the Juke Joint, I should be able to cover the cost. We can make this happen; Lord knows this is our chance. I'll get the rest of the money to cover the purchase no doubt; I know this is meant to be.

Listen I got to go now, have to meet-up with Elisabeth, Studd says. As he gets up from the bench and start to walk toward the road. He then turns and tells Jay to be sure to let them know that Tuesday you will be there to finalize the purchase. Jay stands and tell Studd okay I'll let them know I'll be there Tuesday evening. Jay then says hey George I'm heading your way I'm going into town too, so why don't you drive us. That will allow you time to get some practice on the road and in traffic. At the same time, I can analyze your driving abilities. Studd thinks for a second, a new car, never drove a car before. Oh! Okay, fine just until we get to the edge of town though Studd said while accepting Jays offer. We don't want folks thinking I'm your chauffeur now do we Studd continue as he winks at his friend. Both jumps into the automobile and next thing you hear is the start of an engine and Jay saying "Home James" much to the displeasure of Studd. You, you can cut that crap out, Studd said while starting to frown, all the while Jay laughs heartily. Lighten-up it's just, an expression of endearment Jay shares. I, I didn't just wake-up, I have heard that subservient jive being said by quite a few folks as if, they are the master over someone Studd reminds Jay. Listen George, I wasn't thinking of it as if you're subservient. I was just making a joke, not meaning to be-little you or anything. It's so much I have to remember as to not insult you "BROTHER", can I get a break. After all I got the message on saying such as "YOU PEOPLE and the N – WORD" my brother from a different mother, Jay says. Then both starts to grin and laugh as they pull away in the automobile. Okay, okay you got a pass this time brother, but that's another saying you need to add to your Quit inventory when talking to Colored folks, Studd share with Jay. Jay nods his head up and down as he said I got it, no more Home James instruction to folks of Color, just "Drive On" will be sufficient, right. Let it go now, we got an understanding Studd advises his friend. The rest of the ride to town was most pleasant; Studd's also completes his driver training, according to Jay's standards.

At the edge of town, the two switch positions in the automobile. Jay's driving is much faster even during the town traffic. As they approach the church, Studd thinks of having his own transportation. He would like to be more comfortable during a journey, with Jay's driving he held on to his seat. Once in the vicinity of the church Jay finally slowed down a bit in order to stop, however the automobile still squeal to a halt burning tire rubber. Studd quickly open the door and exits, thanked Jay for the ride said good-bye, and walked away. Studd didn't look back; he didn't want to say anything that would jeopardize the friendship of his white companion. But! To himself, that white boy drives like a bat-out-of-hell; thank God, I'm out of that automobile, Studd says under his breath. Meeting Elisabeth at the church has been constancy once his studying began; it was always something that improved his day, today was no different. Matter-of-fact getting a ride into town with Jay made him arrive at the church early. He starts to think; he'll beat Elisabeth to the place for their study date.

Only a few steps from street curd to the church door, Studd swiftly enter the building. Studd notices that the inside lighting is on, on but rather dim. To his surprise, in the shadowy he sees sitting in the corner. The person one day he will be calling his future wife, none other than Elisabeth. Elisabeth, his darling sitting there rocking back and forward. Studd hopes that the room is dim because of some romance ideals Elisabeth might have for them. Studd stands at the doorway daydreaming for a few seconds before acknowledging his presence. Good evening, Elisabeth, he says in what he thinks is a smooth sexy voice. Elisabeth head is facing down, after hearing; Studd's greeting she wipes her face with her handkerchief. After which she stands to greet Studd, good evening, how are you George she replies. I'm good but! Why are you sitting in the dark my dear, Studd ask? Oh! I didn't realize the room was that dark, my mind just happened to be somewhere else Elisabeth explains. I'll turn on some more lights, no problem she continues. After the room becomes more illuminated Studd sees that Elisabeth eyes are puffy and bloodshot red. Elisabeth, what's going-on, you are sitting in the dark crying, so tell me, hopefully I can help. She sits back down, sighs, catches a breath before speaking, George I've had a rough day. Studd reaches to hold Elisabeth hand, as she continues. I've been followed throughout the day. I notice this white dude lurking behind columns and lamppost. Each place I have visited today this same dude has been there observing my action. Fact is he got so bold, that he told me that I was looking for trouble. So! I ask him to be more pacific, asking what the problem is. That I wasn't doing anything wrong and just let me be, I not looking for trouble. This dude felt so comfortable that he grabbed my arm, shaking me. He told me; don't make him have to come back and me see him. Hearing this Studd starts to fume inside, but! He tried not to display his emotional turmoil to Elisabeth. She was up-set enough already. Studd releases her hand and gently wrap his arms around her shoulders and gives a hug. Honey, Babe, Studd whispers, and tomorrow you won't be alone. I'm going to have someone escort you to-and-from your destinations. They'll be undercover to other, but! For your comfort, they'll definitely be identifiable. Let say, have a red handkerchief in their overall chest pocket Studd assure Elisabeth.

Elisabeth, I don't want you in harm way period, this Sheriff investigation has to come to a halt. You don't recognize this dude, to me that mean, he's probably from out of the county. Probably a Redneck Klansmen member most likely from Jackson here to intimidate anybody was seeking awareness of deals. In that case, we'll just stay back for a while; let them think that he's successful. You know, I have a few

Yazoo Indian relative that will be most glad to help us out with any redneck problem we have Studd assures Elisabeth. For some reason the white folks around here seek to look over them as if their invisible Studd reminds Elisabeth. Which will help us vastly in my opinion, Chief Henry and his tribe has been friends and family with us for a couple generations. My mothers, mother was a member of the tribe. With that said, I'm sure some of them good old boys can get lost on the reservation. If you know what I mean Studd shares with Elisabeth as he smiles. Well, I surely don't want any violence to come to anyone Elisabeth stops sobbing to say. Trust me darling we'll only do what absolutely necessary for our survival Studd tries to reassure his future intended. They then sit in silence embraced for a short time, before Studd suggest calling it a night. Babe, neither of our minds is capable of getting pass this dilemma right now. So, I'm thinking, we walk you home, maybe you can take a warm bath hopefully you can relax some. And! Then I can make my way to see some old friends for assistance. How, can you do all that this evening, get around I mean Elisabeth question Studd. I'll get a ride; I know a few folks that will help a brother out when a crisis occurs. I have a person in mind, can we go now Studd says as he stands to his feet.

It didn't take long to get Elisabeth home afterwards Studd continue on to his residency. Arriving at the building, he notices most of the apartment windows had their shades drawn. To him it meant the occupant were asleep or trying to. However, this being an emergency a knock on a door was a requirement. To get to neighbor Markus apartment he had to walk to the rear of the building and up a fright of stair. Once on the second story landing, he reaches Markus's door. Studd began to knock hard on the window pane. A short time passes, and a light comes on that illuminate the inter room and a portion of the landing. Then a deep baritone voice is heard, who's that rapping on my door. What can anybody want at this hour Markus shouts? A workingman has to get some rest. Studd said nothing, just stood at the side of the door waiting.

Markus pulls back the window curtains of the door and saw it was Studd. He opens the door while standing there in his birthday suit. Undress in all of his glory he asks, George what is the matter. I know you know I'm in bed trying to get some this time of night. Sorry Markus but! It's an emergency that's why I'm here, trust me I had no choice. Markus waves in a motion for Studd to come in, what can I do to help he continues. Studd enters the apartment turns his head away from Markus as not to look at his exposure. Can you put on a robe or something while we talk Studd asks? Don't act like you haven't seen a bull before Markus said with a grin then adding what's up man! Look here Markus I got some trouble man, with some redneck, well really it my old lady that being threaten. I need to get out to the Yazoo reservation if possible Studd said as if pleading. Transportation is my problem I need your help as soon as possible. I will make it worth your while if you drive me out there tonight. Markus grunts a few times then tell Studd, okay I guess I can make an exception for you. My woman ain't going to be so happy about me leaving our love nest Markus shares with Studd. I'll make it right for you so you can bless her too Studd assures his associate. Turning and heading back toward his bedroom Markus tell Studd to make himself at home. That it will take him a few minutes to satisfy his woman before he leaves. Studd shakes his head left and right as if asking no and tell Markus that's too much information he'll wait downstairs. Out the door, Studd thinks it must be nice to have a mate to share and satisfy. A short time later, Studd could hear the sound of moans while standing near Markus's truck parked not far from the buildings second story window. Ah! Man, I don't need to hear this Studd says aloud, as he covers his ears with his hands.

About 10 minutes later Markus comes down the stair. Looks around and don't see Studd in sight. So! He calls his neighbors name, George, George lets go. No answer so he walks to the truck's driver side of his vehicle. Opening the door, he sees Studd sound asleep. Markus had to sound the alarm, George, George get-up it's time to hit the road. Hearing

Markus's, deep voice Studd awake and began wiping slob from his cheek. Okay! Okay let's go I'm ready Studd repeats a couple times. Markus jumps into the driver seat and starts the engine. However, before putting the truck into gear Markus want to make it clear. That if those lousy roads on the reservation cause damage to his truck. It would be Studd responsibility for repairs. Not a problem, this truck like a tank Studd humorously said to Markus. Then he agrees, if for any reason the truck breaks down, he'll have it repaired. Studd said, asking that Markus try to miss as many potholes as possible. Off they went into the night. A couple hours later, they reach the sign that announce their arrival to the reservation. Without incident and traveling those roads they had made it safely. Entering into their township a few dogs howled alarming the residence as they passed bye. Studd directs Markus to the biggest plywood and sheet metal house in the area. That is where his distance cousins on his mother side reside. A few feet from the front door Markus bring his truck to a stop and turns off the engine. Studd tells he'll make it known there a guess with him. Sure Markus said adding while you're in there I'm going to take a nap. It shouldn't take long Studd tells while closing the trucks door gently.

CHAPTER 21 . . . Thing is happening

Studd enter the house and is greeted cheerfully. Once the ceremonial welcoming completed. Studd starts to share with his distant cousin the reason for his late-night arrival and his current apprehension. It didn't take long before both men concerns were addressed. During their meeting, a compromise is agreed upon. Henry campaigns for several demands from his cousin for services render. Studd decides a small portion of future profit from Studd Juke Joint investments be shared for eighteen months. In return Henry and his warriors would assist in any manpower needed to persuade Studd's enemies to quit their pursuit, except murder. Also, a section of reservation land would now become available for any wish Studd may think of for the next fifteen years, a deal was struck. Studd, had become quite the negotiator himself, thanks in part to being in the service of Mr. Charles and them. In the end Cousin Henry, the Chief of Many People and Studd could see eye to eye on making the town folks pay for their many pass discretions and entitlements. They had imposed their will on folks of color for so long. Studd didn't know, until now that young girls from the reservation had been missing too. During their conversation both men admit not enough been done to find the perpetrator of these heinous crimes. And! Now it's time to do something about it. Working together, each group with their own special expertise could be able to help resolved the missing youth problem quick and, in a hurry, Studd thinks. After all each cousin knew that the town or county authority has no interest in Indian matters. White folks really didn't have any concerns with or for folks of color. Until they could lock people up to force labor in the chain-gangs. Harvest time is when they really show special attention. The local Sheriff Departments patrol officers' would fine any infraction they could to jail men of color. Then the local Judges usually farmer in the area themselves would sentence a prisoner outrageous fine amounts. Therefore, the poor individual not able to cover the court cost is confined. Maximum amount of time is given routinely to the Indian Native too. Often leaving their families alone and impoverished. That in turn continues the poverty situation. Young boys try to cover the absence of their father's income. Go out, steals get caught land-up doing time too which leads into vicious circle. Then to, Federal Marshals had jurisdiction on the Indian Reservation too. Who would seek search warrants for any suspected behavior they through the Indian might be involved in? Majority of the time Indians Tribal Police patrol themselves. They have no racial problem within. The prejudice of the white folks in these parts has been notorious for centuries.

Cousin Henry ask Studd if he would honor him by spending the night. That it was late, and they had some more catching up to do. While delivering the invitation Henry reaches into the dining rooms buffet cabinet for a jar of Corn Whiskey and glasses. Unfortunately, Studd had to decline the overnight visit, telling Henry that his neighbor has driven him out here. That he had been waiting patiently and he had to ride back with him. However, he would be willing to have a quick drink before he departed. Henry without hesitation pours liquor into the glasses. A toast for family unity and prosperity said and down the throat, the liquid pleasure went. Future invitations and farewells are exchanged as Studd departed the gracious host front door. Steps back out into the humid heavy southern heat, looking toward Markus truck Studd notice that no head was in view. After several steps, he reaches the door handle and opens the door, he sees Markus sound asleep. A grown ass man curled-up in a fetal position in the vehicles front seat. Studd, from previous experience knew not to wake folk's with shakes. He, close the door then knocked hard on the hood. It only took a few second before Markus recognized his position. He sat-up, wipes drool from his cheek and say to Studd you ready to roll. Yeah! I'm ready are you sure you're ready Studd questions the driver. If not, I'm capable to handle the wheel while you get some more sleep Studd informs his companion. Nah! I got this Markus replies as he starts-up the engine.

Down the bumpy road they go, pretty much in silence. Then it come to Markus mind to ask, George when did you master the skill of driving an automobile? Inquiring minds wants to know Markus continues while a grin appearing on his face. A few months back I had some training, I must say I think it went fairly well Studd answers. I'm quite confident in my ability today, matter of fact between you and me I plan on buying some kind of vehicle in the near future. You got any suggestions on what kind of truck is really durable Studd question the man driving this truck. Well! As you know I've had this baby for a while now, shortly after getting out of the military and it haven't given me any trouble. I try to keep the oil changed, chassis lubricated, and tires rotated. I think if that done with any make and model regularly you'll be alright Markus advises. So! How much of that maintenance can you do yourself Studd question Markus? This girl right here, Markus tells as he pats the steering wheel, I don't let anybody handle her but me. Are any of the tasks hard or take a lot of time to complete Studd asked continuing the conversation. Not anymore, I've done each several time now. I'll do one maintenance task at a time, one this month, one the next month and so on. Nothing to it but to do it, the Manufacturer Manual tells you about the interval between changes. You, you can do it too folks just have to invest in getting some specialty tool Markus enlighten his passenger. Studd starts to think, man! That could be a moneymaker, worth looking into further. The next few miles it quiet travel again between the two. Noticing it is a few hours before daylight Studd ask Markus to drop him off at the warehouse. Sure, not a problem Markus declares to Studd as he continues puffing on his cigar.

Once arriving at the warehouse before getting out of the truck Studd reach his hand into his hip pocket and bring out a stack of fold bills. After counting out several of the bills, he folds them and hand them over to Markus. Markus accepts the offing and place the bills into his overall bib pocket. Both men thank the other for their generosity as they went their separate ways. Studd watched as Markus drove off, now his plan was to get a nap in before the roosters start to crow. There's some hay in back where he can stretch-out, no need for cover hot as it is. He will be able to wash-up in the morning using the water in the trough out in the back of the shed. Cock-a-doodle-doo was the next sound heard by Studd. He lays in a still position for a couple more minute before getting up and visiting the outhouse. Once he releases his morning constitution, he notices there's no tissue available, so before pulling-up his pant, grass and leaves had to do. Next, it was off to the water trough, what better than rainwater to freshen-up in Studd thinks comforting himself after his ordeal. While washing his hands and face he continues with the thought of cleaning himself better. Once he can get into the Warehouse and get some clean cloth, Studd imagine removing the excess dunk from his behind. The water quickly dries from his face and hands; he was completely dry before he reaches the front of the Warehouse building.

Just as he turns the corner Jay, drives up and parks his sedan. Only a few seconds behind Jay, Mr. Charles parks in his private parking space. For whatever reason it took Jay sometime to get himself together, before exiting his automobile. Mr. Charles on the other hand without hesitation jumps from his Cadillac and greets Studd. Hey, George, I hope you had a restful night because I'm sure we're going to have a busy day Mr. Charles confess. How so, Studd inquires as both men walk toward the locked front door. Studd holds the steel door gate open as Mr. Charles proceed, unlocking the shutter door. Well, I bided for a large contract and won it. I found that out last night, so we have to get busy rearranging products. Jay, hearing the last of his dad's new, interrupts the conversation. But! I just restocked the shelves, they're in good shape, he boastfully declares. Studd turns to look at Jay as Mr. Charles cut into him repeating his favorite slogan "out with the old, in with the new." He continues, with we have a large contract that calls for more frontal display space. Jay's eyes widen as his mouth opens when hearing this news. Dad, will we be expanding the facility as well was asked? Yeah Son, in the near future, might even hire part-time workers Mr. Charles said informing both young men still standing in front of him. This information caused both young men to have dumbfounded look. But! Now, in the meantime we got to handle the business at hand, so let's get to work Mr. Charles states as he starts to walk away. Jay watches his father walk away. Paused a few seconds before reaching and grab Studds arm. Before Studd could make a move, he expresses he needs to share information too. George, I got a game coming up one that you too can attend. A game, you mean a card game Studd questions his friend. Yes, big-time, big-time money game with County Commissioners and big-time businessmen. They only care that your money is green, and that you have $100 to buy - in Jay assures Studd. Jay, you know I'm not the gambler; I can't afford to take chances like that with the little money I have. Yeah! I know you don't play games of chance, but I'm thinking. That brother of your William could sit in; I hear he knows his way around a card table. George listen these guys get loaded, drink non-stop, and talks a lot of shit. They will be making all kinds of mistakes. If you can talk Grace and Sue into coming that will surely distract their concentration. They both can operate as cocktail servers and entice them with their sexy voice and voluptuous figures.

Plus, they always underestimate Colored fellows anyway, they'll try to cheat and double team him not knowing I'll be working with Man. Look if for any chance we lose I will make-up half of any losses Jay said pleading with Studd. When, what nights are you talking about Studd question Jay? This weekend, Friday night I'm pretty sure was Jay comebacks. Studd still looking a bit perturbed from hearing this surprising money getting alternative tell Jay, I'll talk with Man and see what's his take is on this proposal. That's a risky plan Jay, and you seem to think the outcome can be managed Studd asked as he looks Jay in his eyes. Jay adds this plan is definitely a winner. Sue coming with Commissioner Jeff, no one will suspect her on our team. With Man, folks in the area know he's one to take a chance. So, for him to be participating would be no big deal and include me. I think that a winning combination all day long. Studd's stands quiet for a minute or so thinking as Jay looks at him waiting for an answer. Tell you what, I'll give this some more thought, talk with Man and them, and get back with you Studd said. Before he steps away from Jay, his final word said is Jay you have good day. Hearing Studd replies Jay just stood there smiling, looking, and thinking as if he had convinced his friend of a way to meet their financial needs. Okay, Jay answers then added I'll see you later too. Let's get started now Jay said communicating within his own mind. I got the transportation so we can ride out and catch-up with Man. See what his take on the ideal is; if you got the time Jay, decides to ask George. Jay, listen I'm going to think this over a bit before I ask anyone else to get involved, I just told you, so be cool. Jay starts to shake his head in discuss, and then turn and walk away himself without saying another word.

With a lot on his mind Studd, decide to sit a bit, alone the side of the building. A knee-high tree stump was just the thing; right on time was Studd thought. As he sits pondering his choices, a gust of wind blows over his body. Causing him to close his eye, during that moment, he gets a revelation. A vision of what he had to do all came into view, a panoramic picture given to him. With the disclosure, he now knows the course of action he will take. Seeing Man again is now a priority, being sure that Man would like their chances in a game of chance. He would just need to know the time and place. Then the next mission would be to get Grace and Sue committed. Studd knows if a profit in to be made, and without a bunch of strenuous activity nine times out of ten Grace is in.

After work out to the country he went, Studd that is, seeking out his brother first for his input. For this soon to be action, had to be a precision like a surgical operation he continues thinking. Now, that he's back on his feet, walking down the dirt road. Studd tried flagging down vehicles to stop. Not surprisingly to no avail did he get any travel assistance.

However, before he knew it he was back at the church steps. Prior to entering the building Studd looks around the area to see if, he notices any on-lookers. He was happy to see an Indian guy, on the lookout. He was watching the church as he sat on the stair steps next door. Studd was pleased that the deal he made with his cousins honored. Once inside the churches sanctuary he spots Elisabeth seating, reading by candlelight it appeared. With the room so dim, he wondered if the electric power was on. So, with the flick of a switch, his discovery lit-up the room and also got Elisabeth's attention. Seeing Studd, Elisabeth became all smiles; her face just seemed to glow. She rushed from her seated position, raced right into Studd arms, and delivered a passionate lip lock. Placing both arms over Studd shoulders, she went for the full embrace. Without hesitation Studd wraps both arms around her body and received her with a welcoming exchange. Then after their brief verbal greeting, they sat and traded pleasantry for a while. Follow by Studd questioning Elisabeth about her day's activities. Asking if any problems, concerns exist he should know about? No, was her answer immediately and straight to the point. No, and I didn't see that Redneck either she shared. At this time Studd chooses to tell his beloved that the Indian fellow that she may have seen. Sitting on the benches around town, nodding acting as if he was sleepy has been her security guard all along. I noticed him a couple times then I didn't see him, so I thought nothing of It, Elisabeth explains. Well, as it should be Studd, enlighten his darling.

With that being said Studd decides to convey to Elisabeth what he thinks will be their final plans of operation. Also, that he would not be staying to study this evening, but he had wished to see her and see her safely home. How thoughtful, you are toward me George, Elisabeth gratefully expresses to her main man. I have been so looking forward to seeing you this evening she goes on, while Studd facial cheeks lifts higher than ever before. With the grin Studd had you could see every tooth and the space of the missing ones. Studd suddenly stands take Elisabeth hand, blows out the candle as he helps her to her feet. He then escorts her to the door, turns the churches light switch off and into the night's humid air, they went. While walking Elisabeth home, they ran into Sue, as she was exiting the general store. Running into her, quickly changes Studds thinking on which person to communicate with. Sue, surprise to see Studd walking with Elisabeth knowing she, herself has a negative town image. Not wanting to embarrass her friend being with his lady and all, Sue spoke politely and tried to move on. However, Studd wasn't having it; he stops her and introduce his beloved to his friend Sue. Saying in the future, he hopes the two could become friends as well. Both women exchange howdy and reply that they think it possible. Studd then ask Sue if she would have time to discuss a business proposal late this evening. She replies that she's cooking dinner for Jeff, but afterward she should be free. Come on by the duplex about 9:30 pm Sue tells George, calling him by his given name in front of his woman. I can do that Studd replies then starts to tease his friend saying that ketchup soup not considered a meal. Man! Please it more to me than good looks she assures him and starts to walk away while shouting back "nice meeting you Elisabeth." Studd still has a grin on his face when he tells Elisabeth that Sue's a nice woman once you get to know her. Elisabeth notice that Sue was pretty and really has moves, the way she walks is truly an attention getter, and shared that opinion. Studd, smart enough to let that subject lie just replied, "if you think so."

Then he rejoins hands with Elisabeth, and they continue their stroll down the boulevard. Once they arrived at Elisabeth dwelling, she says, George rather than going to your apartment, stay here and get some rest. By the time, you walk home from here it will be time to get over to Sue's place. Elisabeth I appreciate your invitation however appearances matter. I in no way want the nosey neighbors spreading negative gossip, which just might affect our relationship Studd said politely declining. Look here George if you can befriend others and not worry about slander. Trust, that I too can handle any falsehood she assures Studd. Without giving Studd a chance to say another word, she starts to pull him up the stairs to her doors. Studd for some reason looks over both shoulders before entering her premise. Inside, he notices how clean and well organized her place is. Elisabeth also notices Studd just standing in one place looking around, not up-set she offers George a seat. Oh! Thanks, Studd said snapping out of his trance. Would you like a beverage, coffee, tea, and I think I'll have some chill water in the icebox too Elisabeth shares? Or maybe a bite to eat, I have some leftover meatloaf that I cook last night she when on. No, nothing for me Studd declares, as he externs his hand inviting her to come sit next to him on the sofa. Not just yet she said declining; I'm going to freshen up a bit and then walked into another room. Studd, disappointed but thrilled at the same time, starts to imagine romantic possibilities. Seeing all kind of position in his mind eye, and with his head leaned back, next thing you know Studd asleep. Studd the last 48 hours has had very little comfort in sleeping. So, when Elisabeth returns, she sees her George fast asleep, without hesitation she bends down with a smile on her face, removes his shoes, and places his legs onto the sofa. She knew her man had been quite busy trying to solve many demands.

During George's sleep, Elisabeth prepares a nourishing meal for him. Nothing extravagant by southern standards, just what's called Soul Food, sourdough biscuits, shrimps, grits, and some sweet tea? Also realizing George had made an appointment to see Sue, Elisabeth made sure she didn't allow him to oversleep. Once awaken, however Studd received a pleasant surprise. Cascading within the entire room a succulent aroma rose. His thought is how sweet it is, to be loved. Rushing from his rest area into the kitchen, he is welcomed and has a chair pull out from the table by a smiling Elisabeth. While devouring the fabulous cuisine prepared, he thanks her repeatedly for her generosity. His vision was not like this at all, but he was more than grateful that she thought of his well-being. This was one of the character traits; he had hoped would occur in the wife of his dreams. As he, sopped-up the last of his grits with the end of his biscuit Studd thinks how marvelous. A magnificent woman, which ask for nothing and looks-out for his benefit. Thank you, Lord, he said aloud causing Elisabeth to react. Sure you right George she responds to his praise, turning from the sink to face Studd. As she, starts to clear the table of the consumed meals dirty dishes.

Studd again tells her of his appreciation as he stands to his feet. While brushing bodies ever so gentle Studd, decide to take advantage. He presses his full lips, upon her soft cheek. Not resisting, Elisabeth turns her body to face his and proceeded to kiss Studd passionately mouth to mouth. Once they got started, the table was quickly clear of dishes. With one swipe of Studd's arm, discarded dishes onto the floor. Then onto the table, Elisabeth helped to position her lower torso, displaying her inner thigh. After stroking her soft smooth thigh gently for a while Studd soon began trying to remove her underwear as he continually kisses her with hungry mouth, rubbing tongues. At first, Elisabeth starts to resist, telling Studd to stop. That she didn't know what to do, that she had never been intimate with anyone. Studd assures her that he would be gentle; that making love would only hurt for a minute once he enters her. With her passionate buildup, being so strong she could not refuse the temptation. So, she joins in, helping to remove her panties and unbutton Studd's overalls. Elisabeth seeing George manhood became somewhat alarmed due to the size, not knowing if she could accommodate him. However, now with both of their private parts being exposed they soon merge into one, George was the gentleman he said he would be, and Elisabeth became at ease. A short time later moan of pleasure came over the room.

It wasn't long before Studd was pulling out of the warm wet cavity of Elisabeth's being. After his departure of them being as one, he continues looking into her lovely eyes, debating if he should reenter. He, however, stops, bent down and quickly pull-up his overall from his ankle and reconnect the shoulder straps to the chest bib. Elisabeth at the same time being confused sits-up closes her legs and looks a bit perturbed. Studd seeing her face ask if she's all right? That's it she asks, I had always expected the act to be more, more time consuming she announces. Studd, trying to comfort her replies that he doesn't want to hurt her any more than the pain that entering her had caused. Truth be told; however, he had pulled out not want to ejaculate into her vagina. Elisabeth then gets off the table while holding her head down. Studd notice the displeasured look as she closes her robe and pick-up her panties. Studd questions Elisabeth again, asking if she's alright and hears an annoying sound in Elisabeth voice. Yeah! I'm okay she expresses as she heads toward the bathroom. Not liking the sound of her response, he knew he had to address these issues right away; their future may very well depend on his immediate actions.

Knowing his time was limited, and a decision was required here now. His option was to for fill the appointment arrangement with Sue or smooth thing out here with his potential future. As Studd think of what he can say, the bathroom door opens. With a smooth restrain, voice now Elisabeth questions George with why are you still here? I know you have an appointment scheduled with Sue, go, do not be late. Studd somewhat surprised answered with I could not leave until I knew you and I are good. George, Sweetie what we just did is a beginning, now go see about our future she declares opening the front door for Studd to exit. Before leaving the doorway, Studd reaches back, plants a kiss on his Babe cheek, and said thanks for sharing. Happily, out the door he went with a smile on his face and a stay true melody song in his head. During his trip over to Sues, he notices how much construction activity goes on at night in this area of town. Midtown was becoming a real vital section of commerce, no more girls working the streets. Seeing these actions just made it more important in Studd's eyes to be victorious in the pursuit of his dreams. Also! What he notices was that no Color folks were working on any of these projects. He entertains the thought that a union put stipulation on the hiring practice so no Colors would qualify. Many groups organize into unions to keep specific nationalities from getting work in certain industries. Things will have to change Studd rationalizes.

It didn't take Studd long to reach Sues duplex. Once he knocked on the door she was there answering in no time. Sue greeted him warmly wearing only a charming red long see-through lingerie gown. Once inside she, invites him to have a seat and offered him a choice of spirited beverages to drink. Not tonight was Studd grateful decline, got to stay focus he said while looking at Sue's magnificent, curved figure. She is wearing that thin outfit under these lights, Studd thinks while trying to keep his eyes in another direction. Studd thought also, it's surprising that Jeff was still seating eating at the dining table; he had to know that he was coming over. He did not lift his head as Studd entered the premises. When Sue announces Georges, presence Jeff acts as if it was of no important. He just moaned or grunted something and kept on eating as if its, his last supper, something that Studd wouldn't have a problem with. After the acknowledgment or non-acknowledgment, Sue then closes the dining room petition door and listens to Studd devilish scheme. All in, she agrees to participate and shared with George that Jeff had already mentioned the card game earlier tonight. He had wanted her to go but she declined; now she'll have to get him to bribe her to go she tells Studd while a small grin appears on her face.

Studd let it be known to Sue that Man doesn't know of any of these new arrangements. So, if she sees him before he does let Man know what's needed, to contract him as soon as possible. With that being, said and Jeff still hanging around, surely trying to eavesdrop Studd figures. Studd tell Sue he has to get on. That it is way pass his bedtime and he'll see and talk with her more about the plans later. As Studd starts to stand from his seated position Sue tells him she'll have Jeff run him home really quick. No, don't do that, I can make it on my own Studd assures Sue. However, Sue is persistent and calls Jeff out of the dining room, get your greedy but up and come here she shouts. Sue's voice changes as Jeff still chewing food entering the sitting room. I need you to do me a favor she said in a sexy sultry tone, run George home for me and I'll do something real nice for you she alleged while winking and rubbing her hands together. You can even come back tonight if you want, she said to help persuade him to do her bidding. Jeff approaches the sofa and stands in front of them both. After a few second of rubbing and scratching his self he agrees to Sue bargaining. This with be the first and last trip I with make with this fellow Jeff declare to Sue. Don't act like that Honey she says to Jeff, you seem to forget you sit in his Juke Joint from time to time with me. That's different, we not out in public then he replies. It's after business hours, and appearances matter I can't be chauffeuring colored folks around. Studd understands, Jeff's concerns he knows how, it is in these parts. With that said Studd, jumps in with his masculine voice and tell them both that he knows how to get home and he can do it safely by his lonesome. Sues still not wanting to hear it tells Jeff to get a move on and do what I asked. Not another word to be said Jeff hurry out the door as he fastens up his clothes, while Studd watches in amazement. Woman, you're something else I tell you Studd testifies to Sue. George, you know me I just try to stay true to form, I am what I am she quotes standing near the door awaiting Studd exit. As Studd leaves the duplex he tells Sue, I'm glad we're friends and I don't have to try to get with you. What are you talking about was her response smiling? Oh! Never mind Studd said as he waves to her good-bye. So, on this clear night he hops into Jeff's sedan, both men ride in silence during the trip.

Once at his place Studd thanks Jeff for the ride, gets out of the vehicle and proceed up the steps. After bending to pick up his mail left at his doorway he enters the dwelling. Investigating the communications he sees nothing of significant therefore discards them. In no time at all, he's in front of his bed ready to disrobe and enjoy the comfort that he has truly missed. Not bothering to turn off the light switch, he dives into what he thinks will be hours of restful bliss. However, before he could adjust his body into a good resting position a thumping sound on the doors heard. Damm is

Studd's first reply hearing the second knock he moans awe shit and starts to remove himself from the bed. What, who is it knocking and why are you here Studd ask while walking toward the door. No response so Studd ask again, who's there, anybody there? Then a familiar voice is heard, Man's voice. Open the door George so we can talk, I hear you want to see me. Studd become a bit astonish hearing the sound of his brother's voice. Believing the person on the other side of the door was his brothers, he still cautiously cracks open the door. Relieved to discover it's truly was his brother. Studd quickly ask, how did you know that I want to see you. Man, rubs his forehead before answering and enter the apartment. Truth be told brother, I hesitated to come this way. It was kind of strange; while I was walking down Smith Street a sedan pulls over and slows down. So, you know me, Man said making a declaration. I started waving both of my hands openly into the air, waving them about but not over my head just about to the area of my chin. Man seeming to be acting somewhat intoxicated adds, "Not knowing who it was I asked what they were looking for". He continues, I thought somebody was looking for a date being on Smith Street and all. It shocked me discovering its Mr. Jeff the County Commissioner, Sue's old Cracker trick, once his vehicle stopped, he stuck his head out the side window. Yells at me in a commanding voice that you need to see me as soon as possible. Before I get a chance to question him, he takeoff, speeds away Man maintain, telling his story all theatrical like. Jeff he usually doesn't approach me, so I figure I better check you out, being that the message pertains to you. Now I'm here, what's happening, you alright?

After hearing Man's account of what happened to get him there Studds relieved. That's right Bro, I wanted, no I want to talk with you and I'm alright. I'm so glad that punk-ass Jeff saw you and you came through Studd says while closing the door after Man entered. Then Studd ask, did everything workout for you down on Smith Street asking with a bit of a humorous tone. All's well Man simply expresses while giving a sinister looking smile. Well I want to discuss a few things, a few changes. Plans have changes in how we're going to acquire that Black Bottom land money Studd begins. The monetary acquisitions will be made in a different manner now, one that requires your knowledge and expertise. With that being said a broad grin makes an appearance onto Mans face. Have a seat, have a seat Bro; Studd suggest directing Man to a chair. Before I share more, can I get you something Studd inquirers. Thinking his brother probably could use something to help him focus. Coffee for you Bro, or perhaps a hair of the dog shot Studd suggest as he walks into his Kitchenette area. Yeah! A little something will do nicely Man answers detailing with a hand to mouth gesture. A finger shot of liquor will do real nicely Man implies. Not a problem Studd said but decides not to bring out the bottle. In order that Man won't seem to be drinking alone Studd pours himself a glass of water.

Studd arrives back at the sitting room area. He gives Man the drink he requested and starts sharing the newest aspiration. That a card game was to take place and the participants possibly would be robbed by none other than our crew. After listening to George reverently, Man reminds George that Friday is their biggest night. That all of the employees are required needed on the Juke Joint floor. Studds a bit taken back for a few second but then made another wild suggestion. Seeming to dismiss Man's concern totally Studd said Man! Listen, listen to this, I got this ideal. Right before the Poker game breaks-up let's rob the place. Man seems to sober-up hearing that crazy comment but liked the ideal. Yeah! But they would be on the Color community like white on rice, looking for the perpetrator Man said sharing the obvious that's in his mind. Not if they didn't know it was colored folks Studd tells Man. I have an ideal of how to keep the robbers identity hidden, all robbers in black face. With additional masks to muzzles voices and each robber about the same size wearing matching clothing from head to toe. Who would know Studd said after he visualizes them in his mind? Damm! If we could pull that off, we would be like a modern-day Jessie James gang Man declares. Something to think about Studd tells Man, and too we would need several trusting folks he continues. If we rob that lily-white illegal gambling joint, they can't really make it too public. So then, only local law enforcement folks there would be investigating Studd adds while eyeballing Man. With his mind still racing Studd tells Man, if we do this stick-up, you will have to sit at the table while they are being robbed. Therefore, I would have to be the main culprit behind the face covering with the gun Studd surmise aloud. So, what are you thinking Man, Studd question his brother? I like the ideal I guess; we just have to make sure the right players are in place, no weak links Man said quoting the obvious to Studd thinking.

I'm thinking we can get a couple of those radical Indians or a few moon shining outlaws to pitch in Studd announces. I can go along with the moonshine boys Man said voicing his opinion. They don't care about robbing them rich crooked peckerwood politicians anyway. Besides their ducking the law anyhow and I know a couple of them we can count on doing right Man interjects into the discussion. What you think two or three fellows beside yourself Man questions his potential partner in crime. Two others could be a plenty Studd replies as he envisions the necessity of taking out at least one of the players. We'll need to knockout one of those white dudes, to let the other recognize this ain't no prank Studd tells his cohort. That won't be a problem at all Man said assuredly. It'll be a pleasure for somebody I know I'm down with the plan. I'll get to working on recruiting tomorrow. You just make sure you come up with a good ass alibi Man instruct his younger brother. Sure, you're right Studd said then echoed Man, a good ass alibi. Nothing more to be said right now Studd tells his brother, so I'll get with you in a couple days and let you know of any additional particular. Cool, I'm out, stay safe, when I see you again, I'll let you know which fellows are in on this with us Man whispered. Next thing you know Man out the door, Studd turns off the lights and return to his resting spot.

Before Studd could get comfortable, a knock on the doors heard again. That can only be Man, Studd thinks. Getting to the door, he discovers he's right. What, did you forget Studd questions? We didn't finish discussing the Juke Joint activity for Friday Man tells. Yeah! I know, go home Bro we'll have to come up with a foolproof plan for sure but not tonight. I need to shut this brain down for a while Studd informs Man. By the next time we meet I'll be done come up with something that will keep us in the clear, trust and believe, Studd said trying to assure his brother. Okay! Then I'll leave that up to you, goodnight Man says throwing-up his hands as he walks down the steps. Again, Studd closes the apartment door hoping that, that was the last interruption tonight.

CHAPTER 22 . . . Combination

The following day things are quite busy at the Warehouse. With customers, orders and reorganizing the stock Studd didn't have time to discuss new plans with Jay. Time alone within his head was a blessing. Time to plan and evaluate at least until after the close of business. Studd comes up with the ideal that Jay didn't need to know all the new particulars of what would happen Friday night. That it would be in the best interest of all concern. Each deed would be on the need-to-know basis. Jay didn't need to know he was to be robbed too. If he did, he just might act different than a surprise-mugging victim. After the shop closed, Jay did approach Studd with a question. George did you get a chance to talk with William about Friday night's game yet? Not want to seem too anxious, Studd lied telling Jay he hoped to talk this evening to his brother. We have to get a move on, Jay instructs Studd, and do you need a ride out to the farm he continues. Studd informs Jay that, their discussion will be taken care of. That he'll meet-up with Man a bit later. Which wasn't a lie just a stretch of the truth. Alright, we got a couple days so I ain't going to worry about it Jay expresses while heading toward his vehicle, this time not offering Studd a ride. Watching Jay as he whistles his happy ass around the building, Studd grunts a sigh of relief. Knowing now he wouldn't have to stretch the truth further to his friend. With that, part of his day over, now, he can go meet-up with his intended, Elisabeth.

During his walk toward town, Studd has many pleasant thoughts and revelations. He finds himself grinning, quite a bit mostly thinking how nice it will be driving these country roads on a brisk autumn day with Elisabeth? Ambitions he has most surely. Getting transportation under his feet is certainly doable. The child in him allows him to start making sounds of a vehicle engine running. While pretending he hears and sees automobile in the distance approaching. Studd hopes It's someone he knows, and they'll offer him a ride. But! To his surprise, for some reason the vehicle stops a few hundred yards away. Studd stops his pace too, turns and noticed that no one had exit the vehicle, it just sits. Now this action causes Studd to be suspicious. As he looks around the area, he notices it's all cleared land, no trees or brushes to hide behind, if necessary. After looking around once more, Studd decides to shout out. "Hey, do you need some assistance, hello can I help you." A few seconds later the automobile start moving again in his direction. Not knowing what to expect he reaches down and picks up a stone as he pretends to tie his shoe. One that he could conceal into his pocket as he stands up, thinking he just might need the Lords help and become the next David. If a person occupying the vehicle wants to cause him harm. The automobile finally reaches Studd as he stands still waiting to see the next action the vehicles driver might make.

The vehicle passes and Studd starts to feel some relief. However, that didn't last long, again the vehicle stops a short distance ahead. Once stopped this time the vehicles driver side door opens. Studd then get into what he thinks will be a defensive position. Getting into a baseball throwing position placing his right leg and foot behind his left and right hand with stone behind his back ready for his throw need be. Stepping out of the vehicle is a person wearing shining black boots and a long brim cowboy hat that covers most of his face. Not able to distinguish the person's identity Studd again ask if he can be of any assistance. This time the man lifts his hat from his head, and it's revealed. Its Jay grinning and shouting to Studd, George it's me Jay. Studd seeing that it was his old dumb-ass acting friend without hesitation threw the stone toward Jay. Boy! You need to quit acting a fool; I don't need that kind of anguish. I got enough on my mind; I don't need your foolishness. So! Where'd you get that vehicle from, new boots and hat Studd continues? What we got a raise I didn't know about, Studd humorously ask. You know me George, a little card playing then some shopping Jay tells. That way I make sure they don't get the money back; he maintains while smiling. And! The sedan too Studd ask, yea I won it until the end of the month Jay answers. That's when I supposed to receive my cash winning or I keep the automobile Jay boastfully replies. Good grief! The boy's sure plays for high stakes Studd tells Jay as if he didn't know already.

With them dollar signs coming into mind, Studd just knew. Knew, they would have enough money to finalize their acquisition too. Right, Studd questions Jay, right what! Is Jay's response? Oh! Just in my head that after this card game, we can finalize those properties acquisitions. Studd then became a bit puzzled, seeing Jay earlier he hadn't notice that vehicle parked anywhere near the warehouse. So, the question was where's it been hidden? Jay, where was that vehicle at during our work shift Studd inquires? Smiling, Jay replies under that shade tree out back. Didn't want the old man to know what I've been up to he continued. So, where you headed now Studd asks. Thought I go into town and wet my whistle a bit, know what I mean Jay said still smiling. Oh! All right, well I guess I'll hop in and catch a ride then Studd said while getting into the vehicle. Sure, get in I'll be your chauffeur Jay response as he reenters and starts-up the sedan. Jay, matter of fact you should sit in back and ride. Let me drive you into town Studd said volunteering his services. No, I don't think so, you're an inexperienced driver and I can't afford for anything to happen to this beauty. Remember, I'm just holding it a few days Jay said as he floored the gas pedal. With the speed, Jay was going Studd became a bit uncomfortable. He would have had white knuckles while holding tight onto his seat, if he wasn't so dark. Thankfully, that the ride duration was short, Studd was appreciative as he exits the sedan. However, he was just a bit disappointed that he wasn't allowed to practice his driving. He did however say a pleasant farewell to his friend and left Jay being grateful for the ride.

As he steps onto the walkway. Studd tries to straighten out the wrinkles from his clothing. He also rubbed his shoes on his pant legs to get off the dust as well. Now is the time to shine and put on a happy face, after all, he will be seeing his future bride shortly. Before he was able to go into the church, building an interruption occurred. At the door was a white man that he didn't recognize. At first, it came to mind for Studd to walk pass the church door. But! He knew Elisabeth was in the building, waiting for him. Cautiously Studd approached the stranger thinking he wants to be the first person talking. He would then seem to command the conversation. That he is being the questioner, would matter, as if he had authority over this white dude. Good evening, can I help you with something, do you need assistance Studd ask in a bold tone. The white dude seems surprised that Studd was questionings him. Yeah! I'm here looking for George, would you happen to be him he continues. George! That's a common name around these parts, knowing the last name would be of help Studd replies. With a smirk on his face, without answering Studd the white dude tells Studd to follow him if he didn't want any trouble. Several things crosses Studds mind as he looks confused. Uncertain of the dude motive Studd looks for anything he can use as a weapon as he follows. To Studd surprise, the walk was short the stranger unexpectedly sat. He seats himself on the bench a few feet away in front of the Five and Dime store.

Studd was quite relieved seeing this action. However, he still stood back a piece from the stranger. As the stranger start to reach into his inside coat pocket, Studd step back a bit further, watching as the stranger retrieved a handkerchief and wiped his brow. Then, the stranger speaks, George, I'm here after hearing a strange tales about missing children. Studd, starts to wonder where and how did this strange looking character get his name. You asked about a George what is your business with him Studd inquires. My name is Wesley Mason, I'm a reporter from the Jackson Register newspaper. I was told he might be of some help clearing-up some of the missing children mystery. Studd listens as Mason explains how he happen to launch his investigation. Still guarded Studd needs more validation from this white dude. Having a little knowledge of business procedure Studd asks for his newspaper credentials. Not a problem, here you go Mason hands Studd a couple pieces of paper. After reviewing the documents Studd is satisfy. Let's go into the church; we don't need any unwanted questioners asking about your interest here Studd informs Mason. I'm following you Mason said as he stood to place his credentials back into his pockets. You can leave those papers out; someone else needs to see them before George is available. Okay, whatever it takes Mason says as he continues following Studd through the church doors.

Inside the church, after the introduction of Mason to Elisabeth and the newspaper documents review Studd introduce himself as George Freeman. For a couple hours, their talk went back and forward about the missing children. Studd did leave out a few important portions of information, not giving away all of their knowledge. Studd knew he had some investigating to do himself involving Wesley Mason. As the conversation continues, Mason starts to take notes. Elisabeth asked that no names be included, only initials in case they fall into the wrong hands. Also! It was suggested that Mason make himself known in the town, especially in the white community. Let it be known that he's wishing to get into the Pulpwood business. That way he, being in the libraries and Counties record office wouldn't cause any alarms. Now with the combination of investigation going on, surely, they'll have the means to find out the truth. As well as shutting down Deputy Simpson extortion attempts on Studd's business dealings.

CHAPTER 23 . . . Waiting not sure

Several days have passed and all was quiet. Each business participant was still active in his or her assignment. Especially in getting answers to questions about Deputy Simpson activities. His committing of abusiveness has to be gotten rid of. Studd receiving information, fines it harder and harder to be patient. Now his daily routines consist of being on guard. Mainly the concern was for his beloved Elisabeth, wondering if she was safe or not. He still has to remember the quote of many before him, "no new is good news" "keep the faith, the righteous shall prevail". It's not easy trying to be secretive with so many people involved. Since Mason's arrival, the white folks seem to be even less standoffish. Meeting in large groups, they often shout and point. It seemed their conversations were direct toward the black men in their vicinity. Studd was one black man in the area most rednecks didn't bother, however. They knew of him having protection of one of the wealthiest white men in the area, Mr. Charles. Mr. Charles being a Jew would have been snubs but because of his fortune, his heritage was over-looked when doing commerce.

Also, for some reason the Deputy hadn't been around much. Usually, he would stop in the lumberyard and shoot the breeze with men of his race. Simpson would make a point of calling men of color BOY! As if he's a superior individual. Studd would sometimes play into Simpson insecurities and call him Sheriff only. Making Simpson feel as if, he had more authority over people. Simpson would every time answer back Boy! Just call me Deputy; I am not no damm, elective official. I'm a hired gun Boy! Didn't nobody vote me into this position? Simpson would talk loud while patting his service revolver. He had the nerves to put notches on the thing after his shooting of colored folks, Studd recalls. Getting rid of his racist butt will be a blessing to the Negro community for sure Studd thinks as he walks toward Jay.

After he's recognized by Jay, Studd questions him with "what you think those fellows talking about over there." You mean, them folk with the frown-up faces, it's probably bout the inquiries being made. You know that reporter from up north asking bout things. Do you think he'll need to have someone watch his back Studd ask? Hmmm! Good question, I haven't seen any of the KKK group milling around and starting commotion yet. But! I'll be on the lookout, have you heard anything about them special tasks you got everybody on, Jay continues. It's such a nice day Studd voices as Mr. Charles comes into hearing distance. Not want to share any information with others outside their circle, as Jay's view of his dad approaching was obstructed. Hey! You dudes finished itemizing that inventory yet? Before an answers received Mr. Charles continues with, because I got some other tasks, I want you guys to tackle.

Both young men looked displeased as it was close to quitting time, and each had plans of their own. What is it Sir, Studd inquires while unhappy within? Jay, however, wasn't as compromising with his facial expression or words. Dad! We've been busy all day long without breaks now something else. Come on, man give us a break Jay says under his breath. Settle down youngster this is something I'm sure you'll enjoy. I had an electric freezer shipped in from St. Louis and its here, waiting for pick-up. That where you two come into play. I want you to take a truck drive to the freight warehouse and sign for its release. Both young men look at each other with disbelief. So! Where's the enjoyment? Jay asked in a sour tone. Mr. Charles wasn't paying Jay any attention at this time. Dad, you are getting an electric something, and we don't have enough power here, Jay questions his father. Mr. Charles somehow recognized that question and belted out Oh! Didn't I mention a generator is to be picked-up also? Mr. Charles acting likes a child in a candy store as he spins around while whistling. The way I see it this is a win for us all. George, you get to practice your driving skills and Son, you'll get to see the lovely Sharon Nightingale. Ah! Dad, come on give me another incentive.

That stuck-up prude is not something I desire to get next to, period. You got a couple hours to get there before they close so, get a move on fellas Mr. Charles recites. Studd tells Jay with a straight face I'll meet you out front; get the truck I'll be there as soon as I use the outhouse.

It wasn't long before Studd was finish relieving himself and back in front of the lubber supply shop. To his surprise, there was no Jay. Therefore, he waited not sure of what to expect next. So, Studd decides to sit on the porch steps, just as he is settled down to rest his butt. Jay comes around the building showing his true colors. He was a speed demon at heart, the truck tires were shooting up gravel, all around. When the truck came to a squeaking halt Studd got up went over to the driver door and polite shoves Jeff over to the passenger seat. Jay didn't say a word just grins as Studd starts to adjust his side and rear-view mirrors. Down the road, they went passing acres of land with field hands out in the hot plantations sun laboring. Most of the field hands knew of George as being Mr. Charles so called boy. The one with special privileges the guy that none of them would call a boy to his face. Nobody wants that trouble, which would bring George Studd Freeman out for sure. Many would stop what they were doing just to see this colored man driving. Some of the folks are happy for him others jealous and had a incenses disliking of his position. Studd did feel some kind of way as he passed the many folks out toiling and sweating for minimum wages. During their travel and after passing several cotton fields being harvest Studd thought to himself, I must be doing alright driving. Because Jay had stop talking and gone to sleep. Final he gets some quite time from all of Jay's swearing.

Once arriving at the warehouse, Studd wakes Jay. Wiping slobber from his face Jay instinctively said something negative. It's about time we got here with your slow driving ass. Let the door hit you where the good Lord split you Studd replied without emotion. After climbing out of the truck Jay signal for Studd to come into the building also. Studd turns off the engine and joins Jay entering the front door. The outside of the place is spectacular care for, with all of the shrubbery and grass well landscaped. Once entering the building first thing heard was, hey stop there boy! Then another voice spoke to Jay, saying your boy he has to go around back. This came from a wooly face redneck behind a clerk desk. Ah! I don't think so he with me Jay interrupts. I trust you know who I am, and you want to continue doing business with us right. Then I strongly suggest that you shut your damm mouth bout who comes into the door with me. Now, that's settle I want to see Miss Nightingale right now boy! Jay said directing his word to the clerk. He then slowly turned and smiles hiding his face from the clerk and into Studd's view. Looking rather surprised from Jay's remarks, the clerk, just points in the direction of a back office. That a boy! I appreciate your help Jay said being sarcastic as he turns his back to the clerk.

Both Jay and Studd walked side by side down a narrow boardwalk until their reach the office door. Jay knocked twice before entering, once in Jay greeted Miss Nightingale, and sat in the chair opposite her without waiting for an invitation. Have a seat George, Jay instructed his good friend. Studd waited a few seconds to see Miss Nightingale's reaction. Because her attention went back to Jay, Studd decide to sit as instructed. During this time, Miss Nightingale seemed to start getting a bit provoked. Miss Nightingale placed both hands flat on to her big wooden desk. Speaking slowly and precise she asks what the hell! Are you doing here Jamison Charles? Jay waits a few seconds looked her eyeball to eyeball before running his fingers through his hair. Then informs Sharon that there's a generator and freezer they came to fetch. You are so mistaken; there are no items like that here for you. The only thing arriving for the Charles, you big arrogant fool is a large yellow envelope. No! That's not right; check your arrival ledger. My father doesn't make mistakes; Jay said as his face turn a pickled beet red. Not a mistake to this magnitude Jay continues. Follow me Sharon tells the two fellas as she rises-up from her desk. This is bullshit; Jay loudly expresses several times while they walk toward the receiving dock. Miss

Nightingale calls their supervisor, asking him to bring the weekly intake ledger. Once retrieved, it showed only one package arriving for the Charles. Jay's face is still red from the aggravation, snatches the ledger from the Foreman. Seeing the recordings in the book, agrees with Sharon description, Jay ordered the envelope to be, brought to him now.

Sharon receives the ledger back. Then gave the order to the foreman for the envelope, he fetches it from the mailroom. Within, no time the big yellow envelope is present and placed into Jay's hand. Jay without hesitation begins to tear open the package. Studd seeing what was happening tried to stop the impulsive Jay. Whispers asking him, are you sure, you want to do that dude. We were sent to retrieve not open anything Studd reminds Jay. But! Jay wasn't listening; his thinking was no advice is needed. He plans to investigate the suspect package, immediately. Ripping the envelope open, he discovers several written articles and two photographs. One piece was a manuscript with what looks like a couple pages torn out. Two old newspapers clipping of missing children, photograph of women handcuffed and distressed. The pictures show women undressed and in agony. Jay quickly let out a sigh, as if all the air from his lungs had fritter away. What! What you got there Studd robustly inquires? Jay, held the pictures out, offering them to Studd as he began reading an article. Sharon also takes a peek over Studd shoulder before turning in disgust.

George, give me those photos. Before one of these white men sees you with them, Sharon tells Studd. She calls herself trying to save him from harm. Knowing she's absolutely, positively looking out for him. Studd eased them to his side and back up toward Miss Nightingale. Handing-off the pictures to Sharon on the down low, he didn't want to be lynched. "In the past "a black man could be killed for just about anything when it seems inappropriate to a white man. And! Get away with it, knowing only other white men could be on a jury, Jewish men might be the exception, every blue moon. Jay's reading didn't take long; he retrieves the picture from Sharon and placed the articles back. Jay stayed silence for a minute or so then utters. Okay! So, someone sending us a message and Dad seemed to know more then he let be known. This, this here is only addressed to Charles, not a given name included. Dad wanted us George to see this for a reason! Let's go. Sharon, keep this to yourself, I don't want you to get dragged into some bull-crap Jay adamantly suggests. Don't worry 'bout me, I know for sure I ain't looking for no trouble. You fellows, y'all had better be careful she tells as she walked away, heading back toward the front of the building. Come on! Let's get out of here, we can read and view as we head down the road Jay said as if he's in charge. Studd didn't have a problem with Jay's suggestion or demeanor, follows along.

The sun was bouts to set as they travel down the road. It had to be 'bout 9 o'clock by now. Down the road a few miles, they decide to pull over in the truck to continue investigating the envelope. Studd doing the driving made sure they stop in an open area. That way the paths from every direction wouldn't be obstructing. As the two, examine the contents their realized this information was collect for a specific purpose. It appeared to be a criminal conspiracy, with Sheriff Deputy Simpson the main person involved. Now the question is why, how did Mr. Charles gain knowledge of this material? It's something about how these torturous articles appearing now. Why did he send us to fetch something he knew didn't exist? All this in order for us to retrieve this information is my guess Studd tells Jay. Tell you what George; it's late, drive yourself to your place. Then, I'll drive the truck home and give Dad the envelope. Studd nods okay, after shifting, the trucks gear into drive. He presses down hard on the gas accelerator pedal. Causing dirt and gravel to kick up from the back wheels spinning as the truck moved swiftly into the road.

Once arriving in town, Studd slows the truck down. He doesn't want his speed to be a reason for the law to stop them. It was too late to stop in on Elisabeth; Studd thinks as the passes the street she lives on. During their travel into town, both men remain quiet. Sure, that the other had on their mind the situation which occurred a short while ago. Bring the truck to a halt Studd places the gear shift into park position. Studd starts to lift the trucks door handle to exit while saying his farewell to Jay. Okay! See you in the morning Jay replies. After Jay arranges his self under the steering wheel, he pulls off in this usually fast manner. Studd shake his head in disbelief, while watching Jay flies down the main street like a bat out of hell. One thing about it Studd thinks, at least Jay hadn't been drinking tonight. Turning his body, back into the direction of his apartment Studds pace is steady. He sees Grace, wondering why, why she is sitting on his stoop. Miss Grace, you're here, Studd says, "as if she didn't know" while approaching her. Hey George, Yeah, I need to have a discussion with you a situation has come up. With an inquiring look on his face, Studd says okay let's talk and invites Grace up to his apartment. Grace nods in agreement, and then extends her arm in Studd direction for his assistance to help her rise from her sitting position.

Once up on her two feet Grace follows Studd up the stairs and into his small cramp quarters. Inside Grace's eyes start to wander; looking around she notices his place is small but neat and clean. Have a seat, can I get you a cold drink, or something Studd questions his guest as he opens the icebox. Sure, stiff two-finger of bourbon with work for me, she answers. Studd smiles before saying, I only have some Corn-mash. He reaches into his cupboard under the sink and grabs a bottle with clear liquid. Retrieving a bottle, he holds it above his head for Grace's approval turns around toward her and asks will this do? I'm a brown liquor woman, but that'll have to do for now. Studd then take hold of two Mason jar, knowing his drinking utensils where in need of an up grading yesterday. He pours two drinks; usually he doesn't drink liquor during the week. Due to unusual circumstance, he joins Grace. Extending to her a jar, she smiles and says thank you. Studd starts to sit as Grace begins sharing the information she has. Studd starts to daydream for a minute. Recognizing how good Grace is looking a fantasy came over him for a second. Quickly, he realizes he had to get his head back into the real issue at hand.

She didn't come here for any hanky-panky. Besides his future with Elisabeth matters, that the plan God willing he swiftly reflects.

Grace drank her drink down in two gulps. That wasn't bad tells Studd as she places her jar on the end table she sat next to. The news I have is that Simpsons going to be out of town for a few days. Me and my girl Ruby was over Lionel's when Simpson drove his cruiser up. Seemed as if he'd had, a couple nips by the sound of his voice Grace update Studd. I said that because the first remark that came from his mouth once stepping onto the porch was he's leaving. Studd interrupt, come-on Grace! Get to the point. Right, alright! He's leaving Wednesday won't return until the following Tuesday. He asked Lionel to look in on his place while he's away Grace notifies. Hearing that, a light came on in Studd mind. Grace, you think you can travel with Lionel and party over Simpsons, Studd suspiciously ask. It depends; I'm pretty busy this weekend. Those Log Cutting workers need someone like me to help them spend their bi-monthly wages Grace said with a grin. We don't want to interfere with your money that for sure Studd proclaims with a smile. Okay then, I'll get back with you before the weeks out if that's alright Studd question Grace. Just let me know soon as possible then, because I'll have to set up something with Lionel, Grace, answers back. Anything else, Studd questions Grace is in a seductive looking style, Studd tilts his head for her to come his way. Man! Let me outta here, I got things to do, rather than being played with by you Grace says as she lifts herself from the armchair. A bigger smile crosses Studd's face as he reaches and opens the door for Grace to exit. After she leaves, he stands on the stair step landing watching

CHAPTER 24 . . . Now is the time

While Simpson, was away from his farms property. A few of the investigating group members met there. Waiting in the tree line shadows for a hanky signal from Grace. Once that was received, they rush into the deputy's house and searched. Grace having arrived earlier with Lionel had made sure he was out for the count. She had added a couple sleeping pills to his Bourbon to make sure he'd stay unconscious while they search. Roaming through Simpson's personal stuff several articles of girl's clothing were discovered. Knowing he doesn't have children of his own, this becomes suspicious to Studd, Jay, and Grace. Once they finished with the house search. Studd orders a search of the barn and shed. Let's split up to get this done faster Jay recommends. Sure, you're right Grace said in agreement. Well! I'll take the shed, Jay you and Grace check out the barn Studd instructs. Off they went to investigate, hoping to fine even more evidence to enhance the already questionable objects found.

Studd fines nothing suspicious in the shed, however fining in the barn is amazing. Twenty minutes after starting their search, Studd's called into the barn. As he enters the barn first thing, he sees is Grace leaning over a guardrail. With her hand over her, face sobbing. Studd quickly ask what! What's the matter Grace while turning away to face Jay. Grace continues to sob as Jay informs Studd of the possible human remains found in the pigpen. Look, as if he was feeding these pigs with parts from, I'll have to say, people Jay hesitantly tells as he covers his face. Studd before another word is spoken open the gate to the pen and releases the pigs out into the open barn area. After getting a look for himself, Studd then goes over to try to comfort Grace, rubbing her shoulder while reciting he's, that Simpsons going to get his. Jay closes the pigpen gate will you Studd continue. We have to get Mason over here quick as possible Studd inject into the conversation as he walks Grace out of the barn. We'll also need to run those loose pigs out into the woods Studd shares. We can't let Lionel see them out in the field once he wakes up. You guy's can handle that I'm going to get myself a stiff drink of whatever Lionel left Grace announces. Moving away from Studds hug she repeats persisting she'd be alright; I'll be alright while fastens her pace back to Simpsons house.

After releasing the pigs from the barn and running them into the wooded area Studd asked Jay to stay with Grace while he heads back into town to seek out Mason. I don't think it's a good ideal for Lionel to see me around here when he awakes Studd goes on to explain. A Negro woman in a Deputies house is one thing but a couple of us darkie I think would really be suspect. Jay, you know what I mean, Lionel mind will be all over the place seeing me in the house with Grace. Jay nods his head in agreement and continued with, well we'll have to come up with a reason that I'm out here also Jay deduct. You'll figure it out I'm sure Studd replies. Let Grace know I'm on my way to town and I think you guys too should leave as soon as Lionel wakes. Jay waves his hand toward Studd as if to say, get out of here, that the way Studd took it anyway. As Studd walk toward the highway Jay takes a few minutes to look around. He's visually inspecting the area to see if he sees anything that's unusually out of place. With nothing catching his attention he heads into the house to assist Grace.

Inside of the house, Grace is currently knocking back her second shot of Bourbon. Jay enters and asks is there anything he can do to help, as he leans over toward Lionel. No, let me wake him Grace answers. Seeing you already is going to be a shocker to him Grace said speculating. Shaking Lionel shoulder a few times to awake him he starts to mumble something that's not understandable. Lionel, Lionel, wake up Grace, repeats until he finally opens his eyes. Trying to stand being discombobulated due to the liquor he had consumed Lionel has to sit his butt back down. Having a hangover, he tries to identify his surroundings. After a few more second of scratching his head and trying to get himself, together, he asked what's Jamison Charles doing here. Jay jumped right in with a quick answer. I saw your truck out front and wondered what's going on, if there was a problem here. Grace interrupts Jay to offer additional clarity; he just told me he was here to pay a gambling debt. Everyone knew Jay was a gambler, so that story was very believable too. Going along with Graces yarn Jay throws in, yeah! That's right. I'm here to feed Simpson's livestock too. Want to help, since you're here. Man! Don't even try it; slopping those hogs ain't my thing Lionel declares. Finally, upon his feet Lionel asks if there anything else here to drink. There still some Bourbon left Grace said as she pours a shot into a tin cup for him. After handing Lionel the drink, Grace tells, I gotta get back into town now. I have a very important appointment with the Mayor, and he doesn't like waiting, if you know what I mean she said flashing a smile as if joking. Okay! Go on I'll lock-up once I complete my shores around here Jay testify while pouring a short drink for himself. Where's my shoes, Lionel asked after finishing the last sip of his drink. They're right where you left them Grace said as she points in the direction of an armchair. Lionel starts to get up to retrieve them but with his first step, he begins to stumble. He stops, intakes a big breath of air, hoping that would help him with his balance. Then slowly walks over gets his shoes and puts them on. After which he follows Grace out the front door.

Once the others had left, Jays looking around the place noticed Lionel had left his hat. Right away he picks-up the hat and follows out the door. Shouts, Lionel you forgot your hat as he, clears the steps, and race down the path to catch up with them. Lionel reaches for his hat and thanks Jay. After a sigh, Lionel enters his sedan and closes the door, starts the engine, and drove off down the road. Jay stands there watching, waits a minute. Thinking he'll allow the others sufficient time to get down the road a bit, before he'll leave as well. However, something came over him; before he could depart Jay's curiosity gets the best of him. Therefore, he goes back into the barn, to investigate some more. Inside the barn, he picks up a pitchfork. He decides to turn over some of the hog slop on the ground that was currently stinking up the area. Being the hunter that he is, he thinks he can determine the different between human and animal remains. Using his bandana to cover his nose from the smell, he begins to sort through piles of waste. He soon discovers several bones he can't identify. He placed them together in the corner of the pen. For sure, he thinks a medical person should inspect them, a mortician at the least. Having had enough of this gruesomeness, Jay figures he'll quit the search. While exiting the barn he thinks how, do I clean the crap off these boots? Dump them in a pail of water a few times, he rationalizes.

While sitting on the porch step cleaning the crap off his boots Jay realize he's been here for several pain taking hours. Also thinking, surely his father's wondering why in the hell is it taking him so long to check in. Cleaning hog, crap from his boots should be a viable excuse he thinks in his mind's eye. As he sat contemplating, how he'll address that issue when he sees his father. While he ponders that issue, he somehow keeps getting flash backs of the hog pen. He can't get over the possibility that Simpson is doing some outlandish, immoral crap. Still with thoughts, Jay realized that it's very strange having a hog pen within a barn. The smell, the stink within the enclosed area would become overwhelming swiftly during these hot days and nights. Jay continues with his surmising that only a sinister reason would be to hide and cover up suspicious objects. With something like that being the case Simpson would have many questions to answer, either way Jay reflects. Jay finally finishes cleaning off his boots, placing them onto his feet when a large blue sedan pulls off the highway and into Simpson's front acreage. Not being familiar with the approaching auto Jay stands waiting to receive the occupants. The vehicle comes to a stop next to the company's truck and parks.

A surprising view he receives once the dwellers departed the vehicle. It was none other than George, who was riding shotgun with Mason. Jay nods facing their direction which represented his greeting. Jay questions Studd right away,

George did you stop into the Mill while you were headed to town? Before, Studd could answer the question. A second question rolls out of Jay's mouth. Did my old man inquire about my where about? No, no to answer both questions Studd responses, he didn't have a chance, I didn't go by the Mill. All shit! We're going to catch it once we get back there. I'm fucking sure of that Jay informs Studd as if he didn't know. Studd facing Jay calmly raisins both of his open hands in front of his chest then tells him. Jay, one situation at a time is how I was, taught to handle them. So, once we complete dealing with this, I'll be concentrating on how to address that issue Studd elaborates. Mason had not been paying any special attention to the guys during their discussion. He had already started toward the barn while Studd and Jay were completing their dialogue. Noticing Mason was on the move they then rushes to catch up with him. As Mason heads to the barn he thinks. What a waste of energy the two fellows were displaying. Arriving at the barn Jay shares what he had discovered and how he had stacked bones into a pile. He also declares he's not going back into that mess. In agreement with Jay's comment, Studd asks Mason if he would need any assistance before entering as well. No, I don't think so was Mason's replies. Good, I've had my fill of that stench Studd testifies. Mason before entering however, sees how mudded and slimy the barns floor looks. He decides to change out of his calfskin shoes and put on galoshes. That he retrieves from a duffle bag he carried over his shoulder along with a Kodak camera. During Masons changing, Jay shares where he had left a pitchfork. Thinking, Mason just might want to move something around.

Into the barn Mason went, while he was inside the two fellow's shares their opinions with each other of what to tell Mr. Charles about their absence. Their discussion goes on for some time without deciding a solution. Suddenly Mason lets out a squealing loud cry, not sure, if he was trying to imitate the hogs or what. Both dudes' shout into the barn, what's going on in there? Mason didn't respond right away, as he looks closer, he sees a hog giving birth; she's on her side-delivering. He now sounds relieved as he provides the guys the news. Is she in the pen or outside of it Studd ask? She's outside of the pen, on a pile of hay with what I see to be five piglets Mason reports. Well, leave her be Studd tells Mason not knowing that Mason wasn't about to venture any closer. Not a problem Mason said as he begins to stick the pitchfork back into the ground. Walking back toward the guys on his way out of the barn. He tells them that he has taken several photos of the remains and from his prospective. The bones are of human origins. That they need to rope off the area, go inform the Sheriff, so that he can assemble an investigating team. In Mason's opinion, the team needs to include the coroner for sure, because of all the suspicious looking bones in the pigpen. Wow! Damm, which one of us is going to inform the Sheriff, is the question Studd asked. Without hesitation that would be me, I suppose Jay said recognizing his responsibility. Each nods as in agreement with the statement. With nothing more to discuss on that subject, they then head back in the direction of the house.

Back at the house as Mason changes back into his shoes, suddenly the group made quiet as they look at each other. Come on! Let's make it happen Mason said enthusiastically after a few seconds trying to uplift the fellows. All the while, each of them knowing that this situation. This, here situation is more than complicated. That possibility a member of the Sheriff's Department of Copiah County maybe involved in murder. As they move toward the prospective vehicle, that each had arrived in. Mason shares that his immediate intention is to develop the photos. That he's going straight into the towns Drug Store and have them processed. As he talks, he opens the trunk of his sedan and throws his dirty galoshes in. Now, as the others were speaking Studd has a revelation. He says that he thinks Jay and himself could ride in together. That their first move should be, go to Mr. Charles. Let him know of the circumstances they have found out here. After all, he is tight with the Chamber of Commerce members. That includes the Sheriff too Studd alleged while recognizing the merit of his suggestion. Studd's suggestion so, now is the time they load into their vehicles and get on their way into town.

CHAPTER 25 . . . Hippocampus

Arriving at the Mill both young men shared important information with Mr. Charles. After hearing the troubling, the disturbing sequence of events. He orders the Mill closed and off to the Sheriff's Department is their destination. In no time, at all they had shut down the shop and loaded into the company truck. During the drive Mr. Charles, tell the guys of his thinking. Boys, let me do the talking. As he continues talking now, it's pacifically said to George, "you know you'll have to wait outside the Sheriff's office, right". Studd, being familiar with the protocol of small-town Mississippi knew what his place would be. Right Mr. Charles, Studd said answering sarcastically. Adding without hesitation, yeah! One day, before I pass away, I want to see things change down here in Copiah County, Mississippi he proclaims remorselessly while looking straight ahead. Jay recognizing Studd passionate voice and demeanor nudges Studd to get his attention. George, "Hippocampus" he whispers to Studd. That word being a signal, they used to remind the other of their memory of handling emotions. Both have short fuses when passionate about something. Feeling the nudge, Studd, sitting between the Charles, looks at his childhood friend Jay. He takes a deep breath before nodding in agreement, knowing the reason for the signal. Hearing the word signal also reminds him of his favorite girl Elisabeth. She taught him the word and meaning during their tutoring session, which he then in turn shared with Jay. Now, thinking how he was about to get started in a direction not needed at this time. After all Mr. Charles intend is for all to be on the safe side. Especially while communicating with the Sheriff's department about, what could possibly be one of the most horrendous crimes in this Counties history? One that could potentially involve a County Sheriff's Deputy would have consequences. That has the potential to cause an uprising that would affect both races communities.

Having arrived at the Sheriff's office Jay and Mr. Charles greets a couple of the Deputies before entering the building. While both of the Charles where inside Studd paces, back and forward crossing the first door entrance. As Studd, proceeded to pace one of the Deputy shouts "what you doing BOY!" as he puts his hand on the stock of his pistol. Studd hesitate in giving a answer acting, as if he didn't hear. A few seconds later, a louder command yelled requesting the same information. Studd stops turns to face the officers advise them he's waiting for his boss to come out from his meeting with the Sheriff. The Deputy trying to aggravate Studd said stop pacing it's looking suspicious. Studd trying not to be confrontational ask in a humble subservient manner "would it be alright if I sit on the step, Sir." Boy! Don't say Sir to me I'm a Deputy the officer replies. The officer goes on and tells Studd to sit his black ass on the grass. That he would be in people's way sitting on the step. Not to cause disturbance Studd sits down on the grass next to the steps. The Deputy now seen to be please with himself turns back and start talking with who Studd thinks is his partner.

Less than 10 minutes later, the Sheriff burst out the door. If he saw Studd, he didn't seem to care, while mumbling under his breath. Off, in a hurry to one of the department's sedan he went. While starting the cruiser engine he yells. Tells a couple of his Deputies who was standing next to a vehicle. You guys go, go get the Medical Examiner. I want all ya'll to come to Simpson's place. Let him know I said to drop everything and, rush, then speeds off burning rubber as the rear tire spin. Jay and his dad walk out the front door to hear the last of the Sheriffs orders. Studd notice them as they come down the building steps. Studd looking puzzled asked right away talking to them both "what's going on." They're going to investigate Mr. Charles answers with a mild-mannered voice. Studd being excided wants to hear more details of the conversation the three had during their meeting. Okay! Okay did the Sheriff act surprise, sympathetic or anything? What was his attitude like Studd wants to hear? It was as if it's no big deal, and the Sheriff gave several opinions of what I may have witnesses Jay shares. He continues with George the Sheriff said only because of who Dad is in this, here community. That he was willing to go out and take a look-see repeating word for word to Studd in a sad voice of displeasure. Let's move from in front of this building Mr. Charles directs the young men knowing this wasn't going to be a quick fix.

Its Saturday evening, ain't no sense in going back to the mill Mr. Charles announce. Surprisingly he adds I would like to see that Juke Joint establishment you two scoundrel have started that you thought I didn't know about. The young men, looks at each other all wide eyed and grins. Studd points to Jay and whisper you tell it. Jay begins to talk, tells the tale of how it got started. Mr. Charles listens mumbling under his breath from time to time as the story goes on. Well! To be honest, in my opinion you young men seemed to have started in the right direction. I suggest we go by there so I can wet my whistle he said inviting himself to the Juke Joint. Mr. Charles you sure you're up to this, it ain't like a place you've been Studd tells. Mr. Charles utters it seem to me you're implying you know where I've been. Again, the guys look at each other surprisingly. Recognizing Mr. Charles is unbending about visiting the juke joint, the guys settles on going. You're welcome to experience the Juke Joint, Jay cheerfully agrees. Hearing his son concur on the visit Mr. Charles keeps a smile on his face as he drives the truck through town.

Feeling rather proud of his two guys Mr. Charles, has just one question. This, name he didn't know the origins of, so he just belted it out. Why the name Studd's, Explosion I can understand. Suddenly the trucks cabin was filling with laugher from Studd and Jay. Seeing the guys with such a joyful reaction, he starts grinning himself. After a few seconds pass Mr. Charles, ask the question again why Studd's. Jay quiet's down to say George will have to answer that Dad. Studd sits still for a couple more seconds before answering. Sir, women are better able to answer that question They're the ones that started it and it just stuck. Sir, those women that comes to the Juke Joint is something else. Their ready to drink, dance, and have some fun after working hard out in those fields Studd said as if testifying. So, what ya'll got out there to serve Mr. Charles ask. The best Corn Liquor in the state and cold beer Studd proudly tells. However, we do have a small amount of Bourbon for brown liquor drinkers he states with a devilish grin. Well, for an hour or so I'm going to sit back with a couple of shots and enjoy you all establishment.

A short while later the truck comes to a halt across from the young men's enterprise. Before exiting the truck both young men inhaled a deep breath as they looked into each other smiling faces. Off to see the wizard, Jay said aloud as he closes the truck door after departing the vehicle. Not waiting Mr. Charles fast step his way into the shabbily build structure ahead of Studd and Jay. Once entered the sound of voices in the joint became silent. It seemed all eyes and attention became focus to the folks entering the place. Noticing the suspicious look of the crowd Jay, decided he would take the lead. The next round for the house is on me, he boastfully shouts as he directs his father to a corner seat. Right away, the sound of acceptant was with loud cheers. In no time at all the vocal chatter grew. Singing and laugher was the sound most of the patrons were distributing while consuming their spirited beverages. Mr. Charles sat quietly for a while then the drinks caught up with him. He started patting his feet them clapping his hands out of rhythm. Now, we must remember Man is on duty here at the Juke Joint and not trusting of white men. Thinking that they white men always had an agenda that wasn't beneficial toward a black man's enterprise. He tells Studd that they need to talk about the company he's keeping after his Mill shop hours. Studd then looks in the vicinity of the Charles. Seeing them smiling as if enjoying themselves he replies to his older brother, sure thing we'll talk later. The rest of the night goes smoothly, no disagreement, no fights even Sue behaved. The Juke Joint had a HIPPOCAMPUS moment.

The end of the night, cash receipts were fantastic. A total success, the brothers shared a smile. Before commencing, the discussion they both knew was in order. Man, takes a bottle of their 5-year-old Bourbon from the shelf behind the bars counter. He then selectively grabbed a couple small jars. Asks George to come over and join him at the bar. Man sits after pouring the brothers a healthy drink. Studd join Man picks up the drink and recites cheers after each down their beverage the serious conversation began. Man starts the talk with telling Studd about his contact with Uncle Jay. Uncle had spent a few nights hiding out in the wooded area of the Deputies property. He witnesses Simpson coming with a couple young females, one of each color. The thing that was bizarre was the colored one never left the house once entering. Not hearing or seeing any movement for hours after the Deputy and white female had left. Uncle cautiously made it to the window of the house, looked in hoping that the colored girl was in there, Man continues. No such luck Uncle only saw some red, colored stains on the table and floor. Studd interrupts, Man what, was it blood I'm sure Uncle knows the different. Man extends a hand motioning Studd to hold-up. Which Studd did and Man continues the red was blood and it appeared that something's been dragged into the barns Pig pen.

Now, knowing what he had seen earlier, Studd was sure a case could be brought-up on Deputy Simpson. Kidnap and Murder sounds about right Studd says aloud. Man, I didn't get a chance to tell you. What we, the Charles, and I have discovered what seems to be human bones in Simpson's pigpen earlier? That's one of the reasons I was still with the Charles's tonight when we arrived Studd tells. After hearing, what Uncle told you I can use another drink Studd says as he reaches for the bourbon? Are you joining me, or what Studd asks his brother? You having another, I'll have one too Man answers extending his jar. I hope that the Sheriff can find probable cause and arrest that son of a bitch soon, Man said loudly as if talking to the Juke Joint full of folks. With a smile upon his face, caused by Man's loud remark Studd, suggest that they close-up. Sure, right Man agrees adding, it'll be midday before I make it to the farm. Then each of the brothers finishes their drink. Turns their jars upside down and left them on the bar's counter. Out of the door Man tells Studd you know those chores at the farm will be waiting for me right. I'm sure of that too he said smiling while putting the padlock on the steel gate. After leaving the Juke Joint path and entering the Farm to Market Road, they separated wave to each other while going in different directions.

Studd has Elisabeth on his mind, thinking he'll peek into the church for a minute to say hello. Sunday late morning they should still be going strong, praising Studd thinks. A lot to talk about with Elisabeth is his notion as he begins to take longer strides to quicken his arrival to the church. During Studd's travel down the rural route the sound of vehicles horns rang in his ears. This day it was for him to move out of the way. No one pulled over to the side of the road to offer him a ride. It was nothing unusual about that, Studd rationalizes; it was all white people that passed by. After all he felt bless that no one today harassed him, while minding his own business in rural Mississippi. I'm going to see my babe yeah! yeah! He starts to sing aloud, knowing his voice is only being heard by the trees and fields.

CHAPTER 26 . . . Rapture

Arriving at the church Studd, opens the door and it seems the sermon stops and all heads turn looking in his direction. Or was that just his perception when the music stopped. No, I'm right; he thinks as the Pastor calls his name and invites him to join in. Now, he puts up a front with a half-smile as he proceeds to the front of the church where Elisabeth is sitting. Wow! She's looking lovely as ever Studd thinks as he approaches his darling. After the greeting with a hug and kiss on the cheek from Elisabeth, he thinks it was worth the notoriety. Both take a seat as the choir begins another hymn. During the hymn Studd tell Elisabeth that he can't stay long, but! He wants to talk about the Deputy situation as soon as possible. Elisabeth replies: okay Honey, go to the apartment get some rest and I'll come over early evening. While the second hymn is, being sang Studd excuses himself with that old slave mentality. Hold his arm up, hand over his head informing the Master their leaving the area. As he was leaving the Pastor, notice him departing. Brother George, he called, no need for that arm raise, we don't have to be recognize in our departure any longer. Hearing his name, Studd turns to face the Pastor after the comment he lowered his arm down. Turned back around and continued out the door. Once outdoors Studd expresses a sigh of relief as he walks onto the main town road.

Back at the farm Man has share the new of the Sheriff Deputy with his dad and Uncle. Both said that they feel some kind of way. Knowing in the pass white men never been convicted of social in justice against a person of color, not in Copiah County. Just accusing a White could get Colored folks lynched for defaming their character. Now there's a question of a Sheriff Deputy, being under suspicion. However, the different is it's another White that brings the possibility of a crime being committed to the authority. Man listens to his elders afterward express his thought. That if a White female hasn't been missing for any point of time the investigation isn't going anywhere. With that being, said Man recognizes and shares another thought. That the newspaper reporter Mason from Jackson has to get more involved. Poppa and Uncle Jay concur nodding in agreement. Once I get some of the dirt and sweat off me, I'll head into town Man gives notice. I'll fine George and hopefully we'll set something up to get Mason more engaged into the investigation. Yeah! If I remember right that sounds like, something Elisabeth is more lightly to have knowledge of Poppa contribute. Wasn't she the person that found and retrieved Mason to investigate the missing girl in the first place Poppa continued? Uncle Jay sitting on a tree slump whittling and nodding in agreement with his nephew. You're absolutely, right Poppa, Man says adding he's sure George and I would plan to include her going forward. With that being, said Man heads toward the back of the house to clean soot from his body. As Man begins his walk Uncle Jay, inform his older nephew that he'll be returning back to the bayou's day after tomorrow. It's time for him to check his traps, don't want others to think he has abandoned them. Poppa tells Uncle he understands, and it has been a pleasure to have had him around and reminiscing. We'll have to have a celebration before you leave Poppa informs Uncle Jay. The finding at the Deputies place wouldn't have happen without you Poppa told Jay. Jay replies Will it's always good seeing you, all those you stole my woman. Each began to snicker walking toward the house arm in arm.

Back at the Charles's homestead, the discussions directed toward Jay involvement in Simpsons investigation. Mr. Charles concern is for Jay not to line himself up with George so much. If the white population thought the Charles's were assisting the Negro's in purchases of land properties. It definitely, would cost them a lot of business from the landowner. Maybe even have a nightriders visit themselves. Sharecropping is the way for the power that be, to stay in control. Ownership is power mean white supremacy rules in the area. Southern whites believe keeping a knee on a Negros neck will keep them elevated and in control. Even the poor whites in Mississippi think they are better off than any Negro. Knowing all of this Mr. Charles tells Jay to watch the company he keeps, especially in the next few days. That he knows the Sheriff is mad as hell that this incident brought to the public attention. Meaning one of his own guys maybe caught up in some unscrupulous activities. Jay sits quietly as his father talks about the advantages of their heritage. In addition, for him, not to make wave, by trying to elevate his Negro friend, anyway that the way it sounded to Jay. By now Jay's mother Ms. Charles has join the inquisition, sharing her belief on what's the best way to help Negros in the community.

Jay only for so long could hold back his beliefs. He begins with reminding his parents of the Grace of God and that it should apply to all of Mankind. At their Synagogue, teaching isn't being express as if slavery is a good thing Jay quotes. That Moses led the Israelites people from bondages and isn't it time to help another group out of oppression. Both parents sat quite for a few seconds. While recognizing Jay had, absorb some of the training they tried diligently to instill into him. Listen guys I'm trying to be a warrior for God, helping those that are in stress, my friend George is my brother Jay expressed passionately. Trust, me I know there many folks that are against the up lifting of the Negro people. But! We don't have to be part of that groups thinking Jay politely state. Again, my plan is to stay out of harm's way. The Deputy Simpson has been extorting monies from George and me for months. We were already paying the Sheriff's liquor taxes. Then Simpson starts harassing our customers also on a nightly basis. So, in order for that situation to stop a give and take deal with him is established. That he gives our customers' unsolicited passage back and forth and he take a cut of our weekend receipts.

Hearing his son's dilemma Mr. Charles start to curse in English and Hebrew, as his wife tries to calm him down. That's not all Jay said there is more you should know. He continues with telling of land he acquires as an acquisition for George. That he was able to purchase Black Bottom land near the Juke

Joint. After the discovery of the County Clerk's compromising position, that he and George knew of. At the County Clerk's office, paperwork signed and notarized, sent to the state Auditor General office in the Capital. Hearing this didn't calm Mr. Charles a bit, is your name, signature on any of the documents he asks. No father Jay said as if reading his father thoughts. The land deal is George, Jay reiterates. George had other help in the acquiring of the properties. His fiancé became knowledgeable in the real-estate laws and did most of the paperwork. To make sure he could not be swindled out of it for anything, including taxes. Mr. Charles broke off Jay sentence with the waving his hand for Jay to be quiet. Then, asking if by chance some more of that land connecting to the river is still available. I believe there still a parcel adjacent Jay advice his father. Mrs. Charles listening and knowing her husband sees the veins start to pulsate in his forehead. Suggest that the conversation continue later, there will be no acquisitions obtain before Monday anyway. Jay also seeing his father's body reactions, senses he's getting over excided. Jay excuses himself leaves the room quickly to get drinking water for his father. Once returning and delivering the water to his father, he assures his parents that every precaution is being consider. That only a couple people have knowledge of how the purchase of this acquisition took place. Also that the land is currently, being managed by a property management group. So, there should be no suspicion drawn toward George or myself he declares with his positive vocal mannerisms. With that being said all I can say is "you're going to be Grandparents". Both parents get to their feet in disbelief, one day! Jay continues as he walks out of the room laughing.

Meanwhile the Sheriff is fending off newspaper reporters accusations. Each one is diving deeper into how the department handles arrests and investigations. In this County, there are more open cases of abuse involving people of color. With more lynching than many other states combined south of Mason Dixie line. The Sheriff office responds by calling the reporters agitators when inquired about unsolved cases. All the while knowing that his force, also help to oppress the folks of color throughout the County. Currently the Deputies property is off limits to all except law enforcement. Meaning the Sheriff is investigating his own department's employee which is his cousin. Because of the newspaper reporter's persistence, finally assistances from the State Police was request. The States investigating into the suspected remains began days after the discovery. The whole area had been, contaminated with foot traffic, including that of Deputy Simpson. He had continued living on the property during the Sheriff's initial inquiries. By time the State arrived the pigpen was clear of all matter that might resemble human anatomy.

The Sheriff and several Deputies stood around grinning, finding amusement as 5-gallon buckets of slime was gather and removed from the barn's pigpen. What they going to do with that slimy shit, was heard as the snickering persist by the Deputies. The States medical examiner didn't fine the situation humorous and order the Deputies to evacuate the area, 1000 yards in all direction of the barn. The sound of his vocal direction given in a tone that all knew he has authority. This quarantine would include Deputy Simpson house until further notice. Simpson protest to his supervisor because of his living arrangement to no avail, his boss had no influence here. His supervisor tells him; obey the orders and for him to hurry inside the house and pick up a few changes of clothes. Hearing about Simpson's displacement the area cleared out quickly. When Simpson exited from his house, he notices all of his pals and comrades had disappeared. Now he has a choice, try to fine accommodations in town or sleep on the back seat of the cruiser. Man! He says aloud while thinking this is bullshit. He seems to think none of this situation is his fault.

All the while, the State Police Lieutenant and his officers are searching the area thoroughly. During which the houses fireplace and other fire burning areas are examined. The investigators discovered remnants of handcrafted stone buttons. In the stoves layer of ash several appeared. Once the object of discovery was forward to the Lieutenant, he's suspicious. He had an ideal they came from a colored person's garments. He recognized the workmanship. Back in the day, his Granddaddy had a plantation with a couple dozen slave laborers. In their attempt to keep, their shabby Dunlap clothes together. The slave would manufacture buttons out of wood or flint stone. These articles found where of the type still used by some sharecroppers. Today's worker being short of capital to purchase store merchandise, used knowledge of the past to survive. Including making clothes designed from their ancestors' patterns. The State Police Lieutenant calls for the Sheriff to meet him at the Spring Water well.

It didn't take long for the gathered information of the Lieutenant to be transferred to the Sheriff. Once that news is received the Sheriff, notify all listening ears that this exploration appears to be a homicide. From here on, the Copiah Sheriff Department will be handling the investigation. He then thanks the officers of the state, for their assistance. As well as letting them know, their presence is no longer required. Now, the Sheriff is frantically looking for Simpson, whom he had forgotten left some time ago. So! He orders two of the remaining Deputies to find Simpson and escort him to headquarters immediately. During this time, the Medical Examiner is still retrieving samples from the barns area. Are you about finish here Doc, the Sheriff holler from the barn door entrance? Not getting a quick reply, he hollers again. This time he's walking toward where he thinks the Doc is. Not wanting to walk any further into the trail of slime with his Buckskin Boots he stops. From his point of view, he could see the area was empty of all investigating personnel. Now, he was thinking where that S.O.B at. After leaving the barns doorway, he notices the Examiner turning the corner coming from the side of the building. What? you making a career of this the Sheriff questions the Doctor? Listen, if you got somewhere to be I'll notify you of my fining once there completed he tells. In saying that he's hoping to have convinced the person, which seems to want to antagonize him he is doing his job. Alright, the Sheriff mumbles as he turns away from the Doctor and head toward his patrol car. Once entering the vehicle, he gets on the 2-way radio and requests the update of the Simpson search. Hearing that no one had seen or heard from Simpson the Sheriff takes off in his vehicle fast kicking up dirt as his rear wheels spin trying to get traction.

CHAPTER 27 . . . Expectation

Back at Studd's place, a gathering of uninvited guest has arrived. Each with what they think is the most important news of the day. Studd now is disappointed; his plans were to be alone with his woman. Since, the desire of his wishes hadn't come true, all he can do is be hospitable. Soon, it seemed to have become more like a party atmosphere. One of which Studd was unprepared for. Having offered all seats to guest, he finds himself standing holding up the wall. Elisabeth is now helping with the social amenities; including offering drinks, when she comes from the kitchen she approaches George. She informs him of his lack of drinking utensils. Nodding to recognize the information, he has received. Studd then tells Elisabeth okay enough of this, steps from the wall fill-up his lungs put two fingers to his mouth, then releases out a loud whistle. That stops all conversations, and he asks for their attention. You came here for a reason, and that wasn't to party. So, let's get on with what brought each of you to my humble dwelling. Right away, several folks start to talk at once. Studd has to intervene again, shutting that noise down. Studd informs his friends each of you will have a chance. That each will speak one at a time, beginning with Jay and continue in a clockwise manner. Elisabeth, standing beside Studd smiles in recognition of his handling of the situation. Put her hand upon his shoulder tenderly rubs it for a few seconds, as if approving his demeanor. Her touch is recognized and appreciated as he turns to face Elisabeth.

During their discussions, the majority of information is positive. The sharing going on for about an hour and a half finally its Studd turn to speak. After sharing about his assignments, he acknowledges the Juke Joints business will be closing for renovations. Hearing the sound of disappointment Studd assure all that it's just for a couple weekend during harvest time. It'll give them time to repair the leaking roof and fill-in some of the draft areas. That'll happen a few weeks away from now, in the meantime for each to continue with their agreed upon assignments, things are looking good. Then, Studd announce forcefully that the meetings over, that you don't have to go home, but you gotta get out of here. Most say they've been thrown out of better places, as they're going out the door. Studd however, ask his friend, partner to exit through the back. No need for town folks to see Jay coming out of colored housing. Studd and Jay both of the same mind see the request as not a problem. Elisabeth stays behind of course she has some ideals to share with her beloved.

Being alone, she identifies that Mason wasn't here to voice any opinion. Studd let her know that he and Mason had discussed several aspects of concerns. That Mason would be writing articles about the missing girls up in Jackson. He'll return with pad and pen in a couple of days for a follow-up. His article on the missing girls search should bring more awareness too Studd goes on. Trying to keep Elisabeth abreast of the Simpson's farmhouse, situation. He explains how, Mr. Charles initiated the investigation in the first place. Bring the Sheriff into the unfolding circumstance. Studd also states that more and more he knows that all white folks aren't Crackers. Elisabeth seeing multiple sides of George's personality again smiles as she walks toward him for a hug. I like this, a lot Studd say to enhance the moment. As Studd's hands begins to lower below Elisabeth waistline. She pulls away and starts to change the subject. Hey, Beloved let me cook something for you she asks in a sincere concerning voice. I'm sure you haven't had a decent meal since you were out on the farm. Before Studd could answer, she had headed into the kitchen. Studd lifts his head to the ceiling and thanks God. You know what I need Heavenly Father he says aloud and proceed to the kitchen. Once into the kitchen area he stands near the back window quietly observing. George, go in the other room and have a seat I got this Elisabeth orders as she begins to pull pots and pans from the cabinets. So, Studd hesitantly follows her orders, goes into the living room area turns on the radio to listen to some Chitterling Circuit music. The expectations are high, now that most plans have been formalize. Each participant has completed or just about finish with their task.

Walking down the low lit street Man is seeing Sue in a different light. While walking together Man strikes-up a conversation involving properties. That soon he's expecting to be able to purchase some for room rental in town with numerous bedrooms and uses as a Green Book stop destination. Sue cuts in; it ain't that many colored folks around here that looking for an overnight stay. Man, tell her he's been informed from one of the Red Cap train porters. About needed safety housing for Negro. Those destinations in booklets will come out soon for traveler wanting to spend a night in an environment not detrimental. I am meeting with Mr. Green to establish our towns as a safe house environment stop. Now I will need a hostess for the boarding house. Man, now realizes he has Sue's attention. She knows her looks are only going to carry her so far. Sue tells Man, after you get all the acquisitions together for this adventurous endeavor let me know. I would like to participate in what seems and sound like a profitable and adventurous venture. If you need cash revenue, I might be one to invest; she said trying to become a limited partner. Man, grins tell her he's looking for a partner for life; does she think she might be interested in something like that? Slow your roll big boy, Sue said as she takes a step back away from Man. You know for some time now; you've shown interest in Grace; Sue says to silence Man advance.

Sue, I thought everyone knew that was just flirtation between her and me Man said hoping to convince her of his current request. Sue takes a breath then delivers, Man, you know I have a reputation so let's just keep it business like, she acknowledges. Now realizing he has her full attention, Man moves back in. Sue, we've known each other all our lives. We have checkered past that's questionable to some, think about it and let's discuss it again soon. I want to give you time to consider a future prospective as me being your husband. Man, then reaches out his hand to help her from the street back onto the sidewalk path. Really, Sue, I don't know what came over me to become such a visionary. While we've been together walking, now we seem natural to me. Awe! Sue expresses as she comes back onto the walkway, that's a whole lot, she vividly states. Once beside Man, Sue has a request, come closer Man let me smell your breath. Wondering if you've had some mind-altering chemicals Sue informs. I didn't see you consuming any alcoholic beverages while we were at Georges spot. Man has no problem moves in with a straight face while obliging her. The rest of the evening stroll went very well, it seen for both participants. Sue became so infatuated with their conversation, not wanting it to end. She invited Man up to her place for a nightcap.

Back at the Sheriffs headquarters, sitting at his desk the Sheriff ponders the reason for stone buttons being in Simpson's fire pit. Considering the amount retrieved, more than a single garment has to have been burned. He's looking at his watch it seems every couple of minutes, now becoming irritated the Sheriff start to pace. Pacing, and thinking how this will affect his department. Also, thinking about the number of unsolved investigation in the County. Plus, knowing election time isn't far off either he thinks to himself. Because of him picking his lips his mouth has started to get dry. He walks over to opens his office door on his way to retrieve a cold beverage from the ice cooler. As the Sheriff pick out an Orange Faygo soft drink. The sound of human voices echoes in from the hallway area. Through the doors window he sees the two Officers, he assigned to fetch Simpson first. Without the sighting of Simpson, he starts to hyperventilated. Recognizing his condition, he reaches into his breast shirt pocket for heart medicine. Quickly he pops one of the pills under his tongue, waits for the influence of the lifesaving drug. A few seconds' passes he gets relief and Simpson enters into the building hallway too. Hey Boss, Simpson said greeting the Sheriff as if it's just business as usual. Feeling relieved a bit now, the Sheriff without hesitation orders Simpson into his office. Simpson looking dumbfounded after hearing the tone of the instruction given to him. He follows orders and enters the Sheriff's office. The Sheriff also enters the office without retrieving his drink.

Once the doors shut, the sound of raised voices throughout the first floor gets everyone's attention. Stopping what they were doing as they tried to listen to the vibrant discussion between the Sheriff and Simpson. The Sheriff wasn't receiving any of the explanation his Deputy was trying to make viable. Nothing that Simpson states during the Sheriffs interrogation sound rational. The only relevant statement given by Simpson is he gave hitchhikes rides. From time to time, he changes order of events. His current description of events circumstance definitely now comes into question. Truth be, told if anyone other than the cousin Sheriff was interrogating Simpson. He would have been hearing the sound of the Miranda Act. This is a procedure that Law Officers recite to person in custody. Anything said can and will be, used against them. However, this is a case of someone trying to help cover-up a suspicious looking incident on the down low. Simpson not known for being one of the sharper knives in the drawer did not seem to catch the Sheriff's drift in helping him out of this situation. The Sheriff's day overall; has become frustrating, after several hours of question and answers. He tells Simpson to get out and not to talk to anyone about his whereabouts, past or future. The Sheriff also placed Simpson on leave of absence; it's to keep him out of position for questioning. He informs Simpson he will receive a stipend while off active duty. Simpsons shows disappointment in the Sheriffs decision. Voicing, however a concern of not having access to the departments' vehicle while away. The Sheriff did stay true to Departmental policy on this matter. Letting Simpson know he's on his own in that regard. Also, he's to turn in his badge, weapon, and keys to all department storage lockers. Simpson did request use of a vehicle until day's end that he hadn't found a place to stay yet. Permission granted the Sheriff said as he collects the articles Simpson placed onto his desk. Simpson thanks his boss and departs the office. The Sheriff blows his breath into the air, thinking what a tragedy.

Now that the State is involved in this investigation, he wasn't sure if he has power to facilitate a justifiable outcome to satisfy his essential basis. This situation at the Simpson's farmhouse, it will stir up such a big concern in the area. Even if Simpsons placed under arrest, and a jury trial is convened no white jurors would convict him. Certainly not for the disappearance of some colored girls, the Sheriff recollects. After those thoughts pass through his mind, he sits back at his desk, inclines in the chair, and lights up a cigar. However having a white girl testimony, now that's a different matter.

Now, Grace and Lionel are getting their heads together. To make sure that their part of this conspiracy isn't discovered. Lionel has been a colored folk sympathizer for as long as he can remember. As a child, his father had him witness a lynching. This happened because of a white woman lying about a man of color whistling at her. Later, it's discovered that's how the colored man would call his Hound dog to his side. Even to this day, once that case had been determined being false the hangmen showed no remorse. It seems the whole lynching atmosphere was that of a picnic event, in Lionel's mind. The celebration of a colored men life was that of no avail to most white southerners. During this time, it was less than seeing a hog slaughtered and placed into a smokehouse. Colored folk's bodies were left where hung, others afraid to retrieve them for days. Lionel's folks never owned slaves they were Rednecks themselves. Many times working right beside the folks of color and sharing with each other. There, seemingly sharing go nowhere fast conditions while growing up made Lionel head strong. Head strong in the mindset of letting his mind work for him not his back. Lionel liked the success of working the pulp paper business but not the side of the dirty timber cutting. Being a quick learner as a youth, during his schooling Lionel ran to school daily envisioning himself becoming a well-dressed with clean hands individual. Lionel ran away from home as a teenager, going to sea and returning. He came back to Copiah County after several years with means to succeed. With promissory notes from well-known east coast banks, he started a freight delivery company with two mules and wagons never looking back. Lionel also began paying colored folks equal to their white counter parts unbeknown to all. Lionel has a sympathetic heart knowing hardship happen to good folks of any race, having been in those positions a few times.

Grace knew about Lionel's younger days in the county, that's why she put up with him collectively. Meaning she collects and he leaves after a few hours together. But! Working with George, she needs to keep Lionel close. For some reason his past haunts, him and he'll drink in excess. To the point of talking during what's called a black out. He would tell of situation not knowing of the content after his awaking. Grace recognizes this could become dangerous knowing what he knows. Becoming public knowledge about any of their concealment would get them all killed this Grace is familiar with. A white man in her surrounding isn't strange, abnormal is her being alone. Several time there been a couple white men at her residents at the same time, leaving neighboring folks to opinionate that Lionel's is her pimp too. Grace being a person of positivity believes a wealthy episode in her future will come into fruition in a few more weeks. The celebration would also include her leaving this mug hole. She imagines being able to afford greener pastures with an annual income coming from investments that George facilitated. It has to be, any place larger than this small town she envisions. She waiting to share her plans for her departure, she anticipates telling George once all deals have verification evidence. In the meantime, knowing loose lips sink ships so, silence has to be practiced. So! After a quick review of the current situations both agree they've done all they can in contributing for this cause. Praying now for a joyful life for all involved.

CHAPTER 28 . . . The beat goes on

Mason comes back into the town with news that wreaks havoc. He heads to the offices of the County first. After, a short conference with the Counties department heads, Sheriff, Medical Examiner, and Prosecutor. A warrant issued for the arrest of Simpson. It takes a couple days before the warrant serviced. After all Simpson has a lot of closet information on many of the powers that be, in the county. Including Judges pass undercover dealing. Hearing of his pending warrant and being assure of this being a public formality only, Simpson turns himself in for arrangement. With no eye witnesses to any, possible crime Simpsons released on his own word that he would reappear when summoned. Many of his fellow officers, attends his arrangement, showing support. After the arrangement and no bail bond set a cheers heard, they begin to celebrate as if victorious. Simpson still without access to a vehicle needs to hitch a ride to his place. With his troop of Deputies, a ride to the general store and home wasn't a problem. Picking up some Beer and Bourbon on the way to the farmhouse,

He's now able to gladly return to his house. Once arriving they find the door wide open. His Sheriff Deputy friends draw their weapons at the door of the premises. A strong stench could be smell before entering. Upon entry, Simpson could see what appear as if critters had invaded his property. With animal feces all over the place, it was no place to entertain. Those animals had used the facility as if they had a new home and toilet to call their own. Recognizing the situation, Simpson offers the guy's bench seating away from the house. Out from the stench under a shade tree would be the best place for their refreshments he thinks. He had also decided to grab a sleeping bag before exiting the house. That he would camp in front of the house until he can get it cleaned out. He then asks the guys if any knew of a cleaning person to come clean-up this mess-up. After a few thrown out suggestions Simpson replies that he seems to be in need of more than one cleaning person. After consuming several shots of Bourbon with Beer chasers, Simpson lips get loose. While shooting the breeze with the fellows, Simpson exposes his fascination about those big butt Nigger gals. How they do good cleaning jobs with their soft lips and high butts voicing his unsolicited opinion. As he shares the information, he places his hand between his legs in the area of his private, saying to the fellows, "know what I mean". Now, that opens the conversation to if he has ever had any colored gals here before. Simpson catches himself, declaring I don't kiss and tell, I'm just saying that they can clean knobs really well, beginning a robust laugh. During the group's conversation Simpsons asked where had he been staying? I have friends and family member down in the bayou he proclaims. You know out in the bayou swamp area they speak a different dialect, Creole a mixture of Portuguese, French, English, and African. He goes on to criticize the living conditions and their personal hygiene. Simpson did however give good review on the cooked food. Telling tales of their primitive life style and mating habits. Down there he said their throw lines into the water and catch catfish and trap crawfish all morning confessing to his pass whereabouts.

Simpson braggadocios comments become suspicious to one of the Deputies. So, he tells the group he has to go to the outhouse, workout a few things, be back in a few. All the while thinking about the times, he has heard of Simpson behavior toward Negro women. That Simpson has a reputation of taking them into the woods after stopping them for some minor infraction. It's said he gives them a choice disrobe, submit to him physically or jail. Quite often the women have report to family no option, are giving. He, Simpson would drive them to the wood and attack them sexually. Deputy Ironwood is rather new to the department, coming from North Carolina. Being a city guy Ironwood didn't relate to colored folks in the same manner as most country whites. Because he was educated at a Police academy his sense of investigation was more progressive.

After turning the corner of the farmhouse, he walks a narrow path to the outhouse. A hissing sounds heard, being one to investigate he did just that. With his weapon drawn again he walks several cautious yards beyond the tree line. When an unexpected undernourished woman dressed in dirty shabby ripped clothing, he comes upon. Not sure of how to approach her, The Deputy he hesitates a few seconds. Then decides to holster his pistol drop to his knees still a few yards away and begin to whistle a well-liked tune. Hoping this action will show he means her no harm. While whistling softly to her he reaches into his shirt chest pocket and retrieves a stick of peppermint gum. Still whistling he slowly unwrap the gum from the packaging and extends it with his hand to her. Ironwood, knows it's a female that's in distress. What race at this period in time unknown, until he can get closer? Closer to determine or she turns her head he thinks. The girl recognizes the song and begins to sing along, turns her head and it revealed. She's a white girl covered in dirt. At the same time, a man's voice heard coming from behind Ironwood. Easy, easy now I mean you no harm Ironwood heard as he reaches, now putting his hand back on his holstered pistol. No need for that the voice suggests in a Creole dialect as Ironwood turns to face the sounding of the voice. Seeing this big burley looking colored man Ironwood stands to his feet. What! What the hell's going on here he said demanding to know. This girl has been lost in the wood for I don't know how long Uncle Jay tells the Deputy. As he speaks Ironwood, sees this colored man is dressed in animal skins but much cleaner than the woman looks. Who are you Ironwood ask as he continues to look toward Uncle Jay suspiciously. I'm Will Freeman's Uncle; thinking that notoriety may make a different. Continuing Jay explains I noticed her out in the bayou by herself while I was out checking my traps informing Ironwood. Standing a distance apart both men talked about her as if she can't comprehend. She begins to rise to her feet when Ironwood noticed she had shackles on her ankles. Now the Deputy begins to recollect that some time ago female prisoners had escaped from a farm detail a couple weeks ago. She had to be one not captured, but! Was the swamp better than prison life Ironwood question within his mind? Hell! Never thought I would be glad to see a Damm Cop she said in an accent hard to describe. Madam are you able to walk, I am Deputy Ironwood he says as he approaches to give her a hand. Yes! Eyes all right this Nigger here been trying to help me out these here woods I reckon. Uncle Jay interrupts, Deputy that's not all that out here that you need to witness. There is a burial site with expose human body part showing Jay expresses. Deputy Ironwood then has a remorseful look on his face. Ironwood tells Jay we have to come back to that I must get her some assistance; these shackles have worn through to the bone. Amaze she still walking at all, wait here with her I'll go get some help he continue giving instructions. That nigger been putting some kind of sap like, stuff on my ankles and I ain't felt a thing she tells the Deputy. Both men look at one another, recognizing that she's not appreciative or aware of the foot saving remedy he'd applied. Rather than leave, Ironwood withdrew his weapon from his holster and fires a single shot into the air. This will bring the officers to them, he said sharing his vision.

A very short time later several white men with weapons drawn appear. Most in Deputy, uniforms see the woman in shackles their quickly recognize who she is. Congratulations began coming Ironwood way before their even knew what the whole situation consist of. However, what did seem to be their biggest concern was why this Negro was standing before them with a rifle in his hand. With a shackled white woman beside him, them being alone in this wood area. Fortunately, for Jay, Ironwood was there and began sharing. What he knows of the situation and asks for their assistance in getting the women to the hospital. Simpson in a stumbling run is the last to show-up, with a stack barrel shotgun in hand. Finally made his way to see what the commotion was. Once in the sight of the woman he's stopped in his track, and she starts to scream. Keep him away; keep him away she repeats continually with a look of fear across her face, while other looks on astonished. Ironwood notices her distress steps between the two trying to relief the women of any concerns. Simpson backs away as he tries to get his thoughts together to answer any for coming questions. Easy, settle down it alright we're all here to make sure you get back safely where you belong Ironwood said attending to calm her. He, he hurt me before she said pointing toward Simpson. That statement got the attention of each officer presence. With that account, being made Simpson start to retreat, walking backward, and shaking his head as if denying her accusation. Eventually turning and running back toward the farmhouse.

The officers looking back and forward toward the woman and following Simpson's abrupt exit. In disbelief Simpsons associates not knowing the circumstance of her raging anger. They began to question her about the problem she has with Simpson. As she's being escorted to a Deputies patrol vehicle, she informs them of her ordeal with Deputy Simpson. It hard to believe the ordeal she describes, from kidnap, rape, torture to witnessing murder. This information comes from a witness that's a convicted felon. With perhaps a get even agenda toward law enforcement. While this news of Simpson is, being passes along Jay is paying close attention. He had stepped back, yet in hearing distance. Knowing the Deputies would isolate him from this sequence of events, especially about one of their own. Knowing how this is news worthy, this is deadly; Jay starts easing away from the area. Unfortunately, Ironwood wasn't one of the Deputies to take the woman prisoner to the hospital. He's still on the case, seeking out Jay.

A short while later Ironwood sees Jay heading down the path toward the swamp; he calls him by name Jay. Jay hesitates a second then turns and answers, what can I do for you Deputy? Jay, you mention an unmarked gravesite earlier I want you to show me it. Show me, the area with the exposed body parts. I need to confirm it before I report to my superiors. Before a first steps taken Ironwood question Jay did the survey part or parts look to you as if currently placed? Deputy, the grave is shallow and because of scavenging rodents, a lot of the soil been pushed away Jay shares. From what I seen exposed I would say the site is less than a month old Jay continues giving his opinion. I didn't touch anything; thought I leave the probing to you guys that get paid. The professionals, with the tools to use, Jay said in a sarcastic manner, as he said he'll lead the way. Okay the Deputy replies, thinking he was prepared Ironwood heard many strange sounds in the marshland, this kind of journey is unfamiliar territory to him. He finds himself looking around constantly. Jay notice Ironwood reactions to the different sounds and assure him he's in good hands, that his safety is important to both of them. Ironwood is a brave trooper for sure recognizes this Jay character has pick-up the pace to get them through the swamp marsh.

Once arriving at the site Jay excuses himself telling Ironwood, he has to go take a dump. Go; go do what you gotta do Ironwood said acknowledging Jay's reason for leaving the area. At the site it appears to be human remain surfacing Ironwood determines. After an hour or so, Ironwood realizes he'll have to make it back on his own. Being no one fool, Ironwood marked areas in which, they had passed during their excursion. As well as bring appreciative for a compass. On his journey back to solid ground, He realizes that Jay too had left marker on several tree trunks. Now his duty is to inform the Sheriff of the situation. Meaning he'll be returning, with others to retrieve specimens. Come back out in this mosquito - infested location to investigate more. Jiminy Cricket! Ironwood confess to himself knowing his thoughts are more than accurate than he wishes them to be. Wet, from sweat and stagnated swamp water he finally arrives back to the farmhouse. So, glad that he'd previously placed a change of clothing into his County Patrol vehicle. He observes no one else is around; therefore, he got a pale filled it with well water. Disrobed and cleaned every inch of his contaminated body.

While driving well above the speed limit back into town Deputy Ironwood notice a colored man driving one of the Charles Milling Co. trucks in the opposite direction. Never having seen this scenario before, he turns his patrol car around. In pursuit with lights and sirens on, he catches the driven truck and pull over the driver. Exiting his vehicle, he quickly draws this pistol from this holster. Advances to the truck's driver side with pistol aimed toward for a head shot. Ironwood, knowing he had seen a colored driving, forcefully orders step out of the vehicle. To his dismay, it was George Freeman driving along with Jamison Charles. Is there a problem officer, George question? As Deputy Ironwood now begins to place his pistol back into his holster. Not answering George's question that he seems to dismiss. Ironwood turns his attention to Jay, are you okay Sir, Ironwood ask the passenger. Jay being himself acts in an indifferent way before snickering and answers. Deputy Ironwood didn't find Jay attitude humorous replying with his own smart remark. You snicker and a nigger riding along, a side by side. Are you holding hands too as you roll along Ironwood said retaliating to Jay's unwanted sly? Sir, I'm an officer of the law here to protest and serve. In doing my duty I look out for the public and their properties. Its unusual seeing a colored driving one of the milling companies trucks that why I stop you Ironwood tells Jay. Perhaps it would be better for them if you Milling Company inform the Sheriff's Department that you all allowing colored to drive their vehicles Ironwood said as if it's more than a strong suggestion. Now, Jay being just as arrogant as the Sheriff' Deputy tells Ironwood. You, work, patrol in this county, we pay you to protest and serve. Currently I don't need either of those, so thank you very much for your concern, Jay continues. Deputy, are we now free to continue our delivery? Jay persists in questioning the now red-faced Deputy. You're Jamison Charles right, Ironwood says making the remark sound annoying. You have a good day Sir and yes, you can be on your way, drive safely now hear. Ironwood knows that Jay's daddy has some clout, in the county. That he wasn't looking to ruffles any powerful man feathers.

Ironwood turns and takes a few steps away from the truck as Jay and George grins at each other. But! Ironwood turns back around toward the truck just as fast, and hollers back. Wait, driver let me see your drivers' identification. Those smiles quickly disappear from both former participants faces. Each man seated, knew that no such paperwork currently exists. Well Sir, I have no identification of that kind with me Studd tells Ironwood. Jay jumps in giving his two-cent, Deputy this is a training exercise he submits as if he has authority. Okay! But a permit is still a requirement if that's the case; Ironwood says as he opens the driver side door of the truck. Step out and place your hands behind your back he orders Studd. You need me to protest and serve the public right Mr. Charles, George here ain't complying with the law, Ironwood responds to Jay's comment. Come-on Deputy don't do that, that's not necessary I need George to help unload this delivery Jay said voicing his opinion hope for some sympathy. Protect and serve, I can't be derelict of my duty Sir, Ironwood utter while placing George into the back seat of his Patrol vehicle. Damm! You, Ironwood, Jay blasts out in rage. Continuing, his outraged with a few select curse words, then declare I'll be down to the jail just as soon as I get this load deliver, addressing the statement to both men. With nothing else to discuss in his judgment, Deputy Ironwood steps back into his vehicle, starts up his engine, reserves his vehicle direction and down the road, he goes with his prisoner. During their travel to the County Jail, Studd has many unsolicited thoughts. Recognizing, he'll now have tickets and court cost fees to pay. He knows he could have used these monies better in some other acquisition. But! He's thankful he has some cash available, and that his incarceration shouldn't last long.

The Copiah Counties Jail is in a small rural town too, were news travel fast. Within two hours of George's arrest, Elisabeth has arrived dressed to the nine and at the front desk. There to post bail for her man, however she's told the courthouse cashier office closed for the day. There no amount set for his release either. Asking if she's able to see George the abrupt answer is, no, only a wife or lawyer has that privilege before his arrangement. Elisabeth being concerned asks if it's possible for her to leave anything, she gets another resounding no. Next question from Elisabeth is what time, is Georges scheduled court appearance. The desk Sergeant, answers no set time, court opens at 9:00 a.m. turning his back and walks away. Elisabeth, a bit disappointed stands at the desk counter for a minute to get her thoughts together. As she turns to leave, Mason appears entering through the front door. Which bring a small smile onto her face, seeing him gave her some relief. Mason has more experience in dealing with law officials being he an investigating reporter, she thinks. After a short greeting toward each other, Mason proceeds to the front desk. The desk Sergeant notices Mason this well-groomed colored man as he places his satchel onto the counter. The Sergeant knows this ain't one of their regular colored approaching the counter. The Sergeant than questions Mason, what can, I do for you. Before answering Mason thinks, this Deputy looks so unprofessional. He's in wrinkle shirt, unshaved, and has bad breath. Mason holds his breath as he replies to his question. That is, he wishes to see George Freeman and where can their have a consultation. The Sergeant now looks dumbfounded not expecting to hear this from a colored man. You're, and you are who the Sergeant asks, all the while Mason had anticipated this reply. Readily hands his state's attorney license paperwork toward the Sergeant. Elisabeth, surprise also is relieved after the Sergeant returns the paperwork and tells Mason he'll have George with him in a few minutes. You're full of surprises Elisabeth says to Mason being more relieved as they smile toward each other, as they walk toward a bench to wait. During their wait, Mason assures Elisabeth that this infraction is minor. That George released should be on his own recognizance. Being he had no outstanding warrant, holding down a tax-paying job a reputable man in the community. Elisabeth's concern is for him being release today. She knows how colored men for time to time gets lost in the system here in Copiah County, Mississippi. An overnight stay can turn into several months of hard labor before a court appearance. Mason pledges to Elisabeth that won't be the case even if he has to spend the night on the bench too.

It's discovered that a States practicing attorney can sign out a minor offender prisoner. Elisabeth is pleased in hearing this revelation. Released Studd says a prayer of thankfulness, he knows all too well the possibilities of what could have happened. While in custody, Studd heard Deputies sharing about the new slant in the ongoing missing girl investigation. That someone has come up to identify Deputy Simpson as a person of interest. He shares with Mason and Elisabeth while their travel to his apartment It seems their suspicion about Simpson is valid. The fact that a white woman has accused Simpson carry a whole lot more weight. Her giving information of others it has happen too as well. The good old boys believe those white women word before anything. They think their tongues never lied if it's not about them personally. This is the ongoing premise in this county that colored folk recognize. It would appear the Sheriff and Prosecutor would have no choice but do the right thing. Meaning arresting Simpson that sap sucking, redneck wants to be cracker. Prosecute him to the fullness' extent of the law. If that happen it would be a relief to Studd's' business and the colored community in general him being a total asshole toward the men especially. It would be very nice if that situations resolution concludes quickly. Studd now thinks one business issue seeming to be clearing up; monies won't continually be going down an unplugged drain. With Simpson currently on the run, his hand isn't stretched out for payments. The other business concern still going to take a few days Studd thinks as he tries to shut his mind down. He knows that traffic issues are minor and shortly will be resolved with a few dollars out of pocket.

Still on the run Simpson, travels back into the bayou. He finds himself without a good defense for the accusations thrust against him. He decides to go out, into the wetland wanting to regroup, trying to figure out defend scenarios while isolating him-self. Not knowing his way around the bayous swamp area very well, hours later he finds himself in unfamiliar territories.

Simpson finds he's wading in chest deep water on foot after sinking his canoe. Due to his reckless firearm discharge while discombobulated. Caused from the alcoholic beverage drinking he had been consuming. As he, paddle down the marshes streams he begins hearing and seeing things that wasn't there. Frightfully he shot off his gun into the canoe causing it to sink. He's unable to repair it in his current surrounding, no dry land, losing the few supplies he has quickly gathered. He thinks fortunately, for him the water in this area is shallow.

With the sun setting and no land in sight, while wandering for hours. He gets himself stuck as he stumbles into one of Uncle Jay's traps. He released a yell, so loud because of the excruciating pain, birds nearby took to the air. He had totally forgotten the rules of swamp foot travel in shallow water. That one should drag one foot after another, so not to accidently step upon an unmarked trap. Hunters set traps in area their suspects are corridor of various pray. This medium size trap was set off on one of his ankles, clamping down with such force it breaks it. Blood starts to gush from his body, which he knows will draw swamp predators. Frantically he tries to get his leg entrapped recognizing his dilemma. Realizing it's an impasse as gators approach. An impossible situation he doesn't think he will survive. Firing his weapons until out of ammunition, he tries to beat off the gators with the butt of his rifle. He continues to fight with knife in hand until he's overcome by the many feeding gators pulling him apart. There is too many of them for him to prevail as the gators had submerged him. He knew he wouldn't be able to keep these swamp creatures at bay for long, not going to happen. The thrashing stops as gators with body parts in their mouths go out in different directions. Leaving only the sight of blood, remains in the stagnated waters. Alligator's will eat their own too, being they are cannibals by nature.

CHAPTER 29 . . . Moving direction

Days after the disappearance of Simpson, the investigation at the farmhouse suddenly stopped. The white women prisoner founded shackled in the bayou wandering gave testimony. After her horrendous abduction, and her testimonial she's released for prison custody for time served. It's discovered Simpson wasn't alone in those scandalous activities. His partner in crime was a prison guard that worked within the female prison system. Evidence proved the women prisoner hadn't escaped she was delivered to Simpson's farmhouse by the guard for the guard's sexual pleasure. That he the guard also had helped in kidnapping-colored females. Girls and women whom they would have their way with them disposed of. They got rid of the body by feeding their chopped-up body parts. Distributing, various parts to bayous alligators' pits or to the barns hog pen. If time allowed in inhumane cruelty, they would have sport with some of the colored females. Disposing of them alive in alligator patches watching as, they scream as their torn apart. Being caught the guard shares in an unremorseful matter their exploits. Often during his sharing, he acts as if pleased of their outrageous behavior. He was tried by his peers' a group of twelve white men for the kidnapping of a single white female prisoner. The guard is, convicted after a lengthy deliberation, the verdicts agreed upon, and he's sentence to hard labor, natural life in prison. No evident from any colored females were permitted. Giving personal accounts of past misbehavior by the defendant were inadmissible the judge orders. During the trial of the former prison guard several mysteriously fire occurred. Fires that burned down Simpson's and the prisons guard constructive properties. Because of the kidnapping accusations of both men, no attempt to extinguish the blazes by locate fire department occurs. Also noted during these trying times in Copiah County, no people of colors were engaged in any locate county law enforcement harassment.

On the surface it appears all is good in the area. However, that was not the case, particularly with the area's good old boys. Some of them becomes agitated and began to rebel rouse. They had gotten the news of a Copiah County land purchase, and that its buyer is unbeknown to them. This event is causing a big racket especially seeing colored folk putting up structures. Building brick formations, which aren't easy to erect or dismantle. The audacity heard throughout the reign, some powers in the county tried to shut the devolvement down. Lawyers were trying to get court ordered wits to stop the actions. To no avail, the highest court authorities in the land sanctioned it. The developers were able to show cause of how this project would benefit commerce. Bring tax dollars to an unstable economy. The Klu Klux Klan's Grand Knight in Copiah County, agreed after seeing building plans. He too sees the marketing and commerce value; this construction will bring into the community. The Grand Knight gives the local project his supreme blessing. Letting, everyone known that it is to be without incident.

Studd's coalition of family and friends had foreseen many of the obstacles in their path. They proceed in getting all necessary state and local paperwork done properly and in timely fashion. The greasing of hands is converted when absolutely, unequivocally necessary quietly, when it had to come into play. The dreamed plans didn't come true easily, and Jay Charles was such an important part of it happening. Such apart that Studd secretly is having his friend's handprint placed on a corner stone of the main structure. Putting his full name on a structure would endanger him and his family. For years to come Studd again, speculate. Studd's coalition having sworn to secrecy continues, most realize how this action enchants their case. Personally, financially, all in the group sees a brighter future in their community. Even so, the Good Old Boys are still feeling some kind of way. Seeing colored men making wages their figure could be theirs. Labor Unions recognized masonry as skilled labor. Colored men ain't allowed in Skilled Trade shops unless working as laborers. Colored men can only carry bricks sacking them throughout the worksite locations, not manually placing them together with mortar. How Studd and the coalition was able to get around this unfair practice was to bring in a couple out of town Journeyman. Ones that would supervise colored workers fairly. Men that participated in the project sympathize with the current plight of colored folks. They're allowed to oversee, while colored men brick and mortared the structure. Constantly a group of disgruntled white men would cause disruptive delays. To the point the flow of building materials, many days didn't arrive. The Sheriff Department eventually had to start escorting trucks to worksites until private security in place.

Most don't have a clue that the Sheriff and a lot of other hands that are being fed monetarily while this construction is happening. Many of the areas white folks suspect the construction is being instigated by Northerners. Or a group other than locals, with deep financial pocket due to the fact, the property is developed right on the Pearl River, a prime piece of real-estate in the county. Currently the sites transformation into a shipping pier for industrial trade is taking place. George "Studd" Freeman has received a line of credit from a bank. A national known and owned bank in another nearby state, which speculated the opportunity value, sees the possibilities for financial growth. Because of a strong business plan and collateral, his team put together. In addition, to the purchase of the black bottomland, and river front access Studd's now have securities. That he used too received the largest credit line for a colored man in the Tri-State area's history. The banker sees it as a no-lose situation, so they invested heavily in Studd's endeavors. Speculation is a word Studd familiarizes himself with devoting time for study routinely.

During the days of the Simpson commotion, Studd was able to put together a strong coalition. With Elisabeth's continued help, he familiarizes himself with the art of acquisition. Mr. Charlie and reporter Mason's knowledge helped tremendously in securing permit documents. Studd knows the important of having knowledgeable associates. Studd holds onto Elisabeth hand tightly as they continually watch some of his dreams come together. That, now on a regular basis they attends church together. Leaving it to no one imagination, in public they showed compassion toward one another. Times had changed so much in Studd life. So much so, that he's given new responsibilities in the running of Mr. Charlie mill operation too. No longer is he just the laborer he now assigns tasks to men of both color alike. Studd management skills seem natural, knowing how to address situation. He would start the daily mill operations with short meeting of his crews. Each man knew of his responsibilities, often Studd would assist in task he had assigned. This action has built up worker morale knowing that any job assign is something the boss has done too. Because of the productivity, the men displayed Studd requested and received permission to started giving production bonus. Studd attire during work hours has changed too, he out of the worn bib overall. Long sleeve collar shirt with creased trousers is his boss's attire.

Locally Studd's management position has become accepted, yet he's still talked negatively about. Mr. Charlie, a man of some influence had also paid attention; he witnesses the drivers' license situation Studd had. So, on payday in Studd's envelope along with his wages, a paper driver's license with the name George Freeman appeared. One, not short for words, Studd let it be known how grateful he is to and for Mr. Charlie. Visions now dance in his head of purchasing a vehicle. Before his thought is finalize, Mr. Charlie gets his attention again, calling George. As Studd lifts his head to respond he see Mr. Charlie extending his right arm toward Studd dangling several keys in his hand. Still overcome with the emotions of the licenses gift, Studd just replied yes Sir. Here take the truck and drive yourself home after the shift Mr. Charlie said as in ordering while joyful. Jay too has a smile on his face seeing his childhood friend so elated. Sir, Sir I thank you and appreciate all the support you've shown me throughout my life. Mr. Charlie smiling tells him and Jay to close-up the mill and walks out the door. Jay elated himself jumps for joy as he hurries to complete the inventory, ask George what you going to do now, go pick-up Elisabeth. Studd still standing in a trance, has no word for a change. Finally, thank you Lord, thank you Father comes out of his mouth. Jay now has made his way to George; put his arm around Studd's shoulder. He then begins to rock George back and forward a few times before leading his friend of friends out the front door. Both men said their so longs and departed the parking lot, each driving in a different direction.

Once into town Studd, observe there's, church activities happening, so he decides to stop in. Entering the building he quietly sits in the back of the sanctuary; he then witnesses a couple activities he didn't recognize. Only a few people were in attended, with one giving instruction to the others. After being noticed by the group they signal George to join them. Studd's attendance and endowment to the church had begun to be notice by the deacons. To the point, this board insists he join the advisory committee. Studd not eager to wear that hat, informs the committee he wouldn't have time for the dedication the position requires. He said I would strongly suggest you pick Miss Elisabeth as an addition she's very capable. Also, it would be in the churches best interest to have a woman join the ranks of authority. That he would however be willing to continue to contribute toward whatever the board initiates. Having a quick informal discussion the committee's members without hesitation, votes Elisabeth into a position without her acknowledgement or acceptant. The move was very informative to Studd he now recognizes he had crossed over to a man with a form of materialistic power. Studd thanks the committee for their indulgent, insight and excuse himself. Out the church door with a broad smile, he's now headed to see Elisabeth. Hope he hasn't put his foot in his mouth he contemplates. Rationalizing he says aloud, she's at the church all the time anyway. It shouldn't be displeasing to her having a churches decision-making title. Most church parishioners would treasure an opportunity of this caliber.

Knowing Elisabeth's visiting her parents, Studd decides to drive over, hoping he'd get a positive reception. Arriving at Elisabeth families place, Studd sits quietly in the truck for a minute or so to gather his thoughts. Studd exit the truck, walks up the path to the families front door. Before knocking on the door, he checks his attire, including smelling under his arms. After all, he had worked in them all day. All is good he, surmise no, unpleasant odor and only a few wrinkles on his clothing. Breath checked, now into the scholars' domain he thinks as he raps on the outer screen door. He's aware that both of Elisabeth's parents are educated folks City College of Agriculture and Mechanical graduates. He hopes that just his entrepreneurship won't be looked down upon. That his interest in their daughter isn't below they're standards. He has met them a couple times, entering, or exiting the church only. This action, visiting of his girl Elisabeth at their uptown home is surely unsolicited. A bit bold Studd himself recognizes; he also understands that this action will informs the parents he's not afraid of controversy. That he can stand on his own merits, mentally and financially if an assessment is required.

After a second rap on the door, an illuminated light come on in the front room. Seconds later Elisabeth's father arrive, yes can I help you Sir was his responds once the doors completely opened. Studd quickly introduced himself as George Freeman, son of Will and Viola Freeman. That he would like to schedule an appointment with him for the very near future. An appointment to discuss a matter of importance Sir that I truly believe would benefit both families' future opportunities. Mister Freeman, I recognize you from church, but I don't know what it is that we possibly can have to discuss that an appointment is necessary. Studd not fazed by the disconnection, interrupts. Sir, please meet with me at Betties café on East Robert E. Lee Street; day after tomorrow at 6:00 pm it will be worth your while. During our talk, we can have some of Bettie's famous desserts. If you are not sure or apprehensive about me, Sir, please ask around the business community, my name again is Freeman, George Freeman hoping to see you there. I'm sorry to have interrupted your evening Sir, however I do look forward to a mutually beneficial discussion Sir, and Studd said apologizing while turning from the door and stepping off the stoop. Now this unexpected visitor comments have left Elisabeth's father discombobulated. He watches Studd get into the Charlie Milling Company truck and take off down the road before closing his door.

Once back into the living quarters of their home, Elisabeth's mother questions her husband about the visitor at the door. He informs his family that a young man name George Freeman had requests an appointment with him for day after tomorrow. Hearing Georges name Elisabeth starts to celebrate, jumps into her father's face questioning him if the meeting might be about her. Settle down girl, you weren't even mentioned Elisabeth's father informs her. Matter of fact what is it you know of this confident rather arrogant young man Elisabeth's father asks her? I've known him awhile and have helped him accomplished several entrepreneur projects in the past. He's a real enterprising person if you will, I believe his future is only looking brighter Elisabeth shares will her parents. As Elisabeth explains her view toward George, her parent catches each other eye. Without saying a word to each other, they know Elisabeth has a fancy for this young man George her enthusiasm is obvious. Well, I'll have to do some more investigating before I decide to meet or not with him Elisabeth's father shares with his family. Father, you have to meet with him I'm sure it's an opportunity that's beneficial. He's a young man that's coming up, a black man that you and he can use each other's expertise. Remember we are our brother's keeper Elisabeth's mother interjects into the conversation. You women have already made up my mind for me; I see Elisabeth's father tells the women as he leaves the room. After his exit, both women start discussing George and what it could possibly be he want to meet and talk about. Elisabeth finally breaks and reveals her secret, that she and George have been seeing each other in a romantic nature. So, is this George the young man that you've been studying with at the church on a regular basis too, Elisabeth's mother questions?

Yeah! That's right Mother and since we've gotten to know each other. He has revealed how very important family orientation is into his future. Thing is, we've been talking often about a life of matrimony. Several times George has expressed to me his interest in that kind of a situation. One that he said would definitely benefit us both, Elisabeth said while blushing. What! Girl, have you really been considering a proposal from this man, Elisabeth's mother asks? As Mother moves closer to sit next to her daughter, she grabs her arm all the while a cheerful tear starts to roll down her cheek. Mother, it only been discussed, the likelihood of me marring anyone soon is so far-fetched its funny Elisabeth said rationalizing to her mother. Honey! If this man is the enterprising person you'll describe, I foresee him questioning your father about more than just commerce business. Mother then let go of Elisabeth hand, lifts herself from her seat, while continuing talking aloud while dancing to music in her own mind. She suggests they start formulating a plan for the impending nuptial that she's proclaiming.

A couple days has passed since Studd's conversation with Elisabeth's father. He hadn't seen his possible betrothed either. His plan is the next time he sees Elisabeth alone he'll be getting on one knee and propose. Now however Studd knows that visual images and well-spoken expressions will matter, with Elisabeth's father. Studd dresses as if on a date going to a Sunday after church affair. For the meeting he's wearing fresh pressed shirt and trousers, shoes shined so bright you could see your reflection in them. Studd arrives 15 minutes before the schedule appointment with his possible future father-in-law. He rehearses a few lines of a conversation he's anticipating having also. Being a bit nervous, he orders a Whiskey shot and down it as fast as it's delivered, chasing it with water. Also, he's aware that eating peanuts will cover the smell of alcohol he began shelling and consumes them. Still thinking of the proper etiquette for a formal meeting Studd contemplate if he should rise from his seat or not when greeting Elisabeth's father as he arrives. Looking around Studd recognize the place isn't formal, so he decides to stay seated when he does appear. Studd's paying close attention to the doors entrance to see went Elisabeth's father enter the dining establishment. Studd notices this well-groomed gentleman (in Black Bowler Hat, Gray Double Breast Long Coat and Black Shallow Stripe Trousers) stand at the doorway for a few seconds. Looking about as if investigating his surroundings, finally he notices Studd and began walking toward the table. Studd does rise from his seat as his visitor advances, and each reach out their hand to greet the other.

Both men trade pleasantries, once seated Studd offers to purchase appetizers and drinks. A Sweet Tea with Lemon was the only request Studd's visitor ordered before questioning about his appearance there. Sir, I'm grateful for you taking the time to meet with me in these surrounding. Let me assure you that all intentions that I'll mention are true and honorable. I wish to share with you a business plan as well as a bank line of credit I have. Please Sir, once I display these plans of information to you, which isn't to be broadcast. It's not for public conversation, can I have your word Sir. Our conversations can't become public knowledge at this time. As Studd start to open the folder for review, Elisabeth's father stops him. Placing his hand over the folder before any, visible words are exposed. Mr. Freeman, you've requested my presence here, but! I'm not sure what or if anything you're about to share has to do with me. Sir, my proposition is two things; let me not beat around the bush. Number 1 is I'm here to ask you for the hand of your daughter for marriage. The second is for us to broaden our relationships and become business partner as well. Studd express his intentions without hesitation as Elisabeth's father sat in silence. After Studd finish his deliverance, both men sat silence with straight face for a minute or so. Next question asked was from Elisabeth's father, do you love my daughter Mr. Freeman. With the quickness

Studd answers, with all my being Sir, I've loved her from a far for years. As I've gotten to know her more, it has become easier daily to love her. Sir, believe me knowing she's an educated and Christian woman I knew I would have to be able to offer a future. Before entertaining the possibility of us becoming one in marriage. A financial stability had to be a reality to move forward Studd said while continuing to move the open folder back toward his invited visitors' hand.

Let me get this right Elisabeth's father questioned Studd. Mr. Freeman, so, you have plans for yourself and my daughter's future, do she have an ideal of what you're contemplating? As he awaits an answer, he runs his finger over the first few paragraphs of Studds document. Sir, please address me as George, Mr. Freeman is my father, Sir. To answer your question Sir, I'm in the mindset that Elisabeth and I are of the same accord. With that said Elisabeth's father, ask George, to give him a few more minutes to review the documents. A few minutes pass before Elisabeth's father lifts up his head from reading several articles the business plan. I think you have a magnificent plan here that will enhance families for generations in this community. You have my word that it won't be shared, my word is bond.. A few more of them, "that a boy" are expressed to Studd while their sipped Cola's before they decided to call it a night. Both men leave with smiles on their faces depart the building and went their separate ways driving..

CHAPTER 30 . . . Build to Succeed

Getting the approval for marriage to the fairest woman in the land, Studd institutes a plan for his proposal. Not knowing anything about purchasing the appropriate rings, he seeks out Jay for advice. Upon meeting with Jay in front of the Mill before work, Studd tells Jay of his marriage proposal intention. Once being told about the situation Jay being the friend that he is, began to tease his old buddy. Busting out loud Jay says sarcastically "Oh! So now Studd's the man, is ready to be neuter, are you ready for George to be on full time lockdown. While laughing so hard he has to hold his stomach not to bust a gut. Studd stands in silence and waits for Jay to recover from his tantrum. Okay! Okay Jay says as he tries to catch his breath. Finally sensible words come out of Jay's mouth, to Studd's thinking "so you got the go ahead" Jay said congratulating his friend. Of course, you know how I do, Studd replies with a look of confidence on his face. Elisabeth's father came around to my thinking; I gave him insight to our future. She's worth keeping for sure, if the community would not have mind. I would have made a move that way myself Jay informs his closest and oldest friend. Jay, you're not her flavor Studd said with a smile as if he was reminding his crony of something new. George, you're my dude for sure I'll make arrangement for the jewelry store to remain open, and then we can see what selections they have. What day do you want to do this Jay inquire? You make it happen I'll be ready whenever Studd said assuring Jay. Done deal, Jay said as he come within reach of Studd, grabbed his friends head he shake it gently as the agreement finalized. Being released from the friendly head embrace, both men walk into the Mill with smile on their faces. During the rest of the workday, many of the area customers' start to congratulated Studd for his future nuptials. Now! Studd knows Jay had to have been running his mouth sharing the plan nuptials prematurely. It's all good though Jay has been a brother since their short pants, bare foot days. He's talking as if bragging, very boastful, happy for what about to happen.

Now that Elisabeth's home has an open door, policy to her intended. Studd's time and presence there talking with her father often precedes time with Elisabeth. The two men fine that their mind set has so much in common. Being a 32-degree Free Mason himself, Elisabeth's father suggests Studd enter the organization. That it would open door of fellowship and many other business opportunities around the state. Studd found the suggestion interesting; however, saying he has to learn more about the structure of the organization. He knew yearly dues are required to participate but! Really how would this benefit him? Studd assures Elisabeth's father that there would be more discussion once he gets more insight. Being a businessperson, himself Studd know to investigate himself not to just go by another prospective. A concern Studd has is; if he joins a Mason's Lodge is family members allowed to participate as well. To change the subject Studd requests a cold drink. For that, Elisabeth's summoned from the kitchen. Once, Elisabeth arrived in front of the two men. The request for some cold lemonade is ask for by her father. She gives him the turn-up mouth look, afterward saying you called me in here why you didn't ask for the drink while I was in the kitchen. Your intended wants the drink; I called for him, her father replies. Studd smiles at them both then says thank you baby as he looks into Elisabeth's gorgeous face. I'll come with you Elisabeth Studd informs her as he gets up from his seat and follow her into the kitchen. Elisabeth's father now retrieves the newspaper from the end table and begins to read the business section. In the kitchen, Studd stops Elisabeth as she reaches for a glass. Turn her to face him pulls her close and proceeded to kiss her soft full lips. It didn't last long before Elisabeth pulls away. Stop she says now is not the time. I like that too much to begin and. you know what I mean George. Okay! Okay it's just hard seeing you looking all domesticated and me not able to touch you Studd said as he takes a couple steps back to look at Elisabeth full voluptuous silhouette. As Elisabeth retrieves the drink for Studd, he seats himself down at the table. Once Elisabeth joins him, they share with each other some of their day's activities.

With their wedding date set, the whole county became aware. Of the courtship of the most admirable and prosperous black, couple ever. Elisabeth and her mother have tried to include all members of both families to participate in this nuptial celebration. It's as if money is no problem in their planning, lot of business will benefit in this ceremony. The catering and flowers alone will cost a fortune even to a wealth couple. While most of the arrangements are, finalized Studd is staying busy with the construction of their future domains, which includes home and business. His time has become limited so much so that he has to delegate several duties to his special associate. His two main men remain loyal partners' brother Man and lifetime friend Jay, continually by his side. They had been Ride or Die from the beginning, now a new partner will be included, Elisabeth. Can things get any better Studd thinks to himself; rich bottomland with river access had been purchased. Purchase land with also the possibility of oil extraction. The Juke Joint being ran without any hiccups for the present. The future looks very promising for the newly form LIBERTY GROUP Studd foresees. By-and-by Studd's prosperity continues to come to fruition with him having gain legal jurisdiction of acres and acres of surrounding land.

In the early afternoon on the third Saturday of May, the 24th day of 1913 George "Studd" Freeman and Elisabeth Connie Smith in front of God and hundreds of witnesses' pledge their love for better or worse. Becoming man and wife, until death do us part. The couple asked that monetary gifts instead of presence be donated to the building fund of the newly formed Negro County Hospital committee in their names. People of all walks of life attend the ceremony. Many famous and some infamous characters attended as well as. City, County and State Officials came. Entertainment of that day, was that of who's, who on the southern Chitterling Circuit. Betsy Smith, Jellyroll Morton and Louis Armstrong just to name a few entertained their guests. Joyful noise lasted throughout the evening and well past midnight. However, before the night was over Studd and his lovely bride had disappeared, through a small back panel of the reception tent while the dance floor was packed with celebrators. It was unbelievable; maybe even a first for the area. All races danced on the same floor at the same time, HALLELUJAH. No racial incidence throughout the festivities.

Studd and Elisabeth did not just ride into the sunset after their nuptial. Once returning from their northern, Detroit, Michigan honeymoon. They further enhance their arising with the help of the local International Mason's brothers and the NAACP organization helping in the advancing of many of Studd's and Elisabeth's initiatives. Soon, the area of folks grew in numbers, so much so that a town's charter is written having a population of 1,029 people, GEORGETOWN came into existence. The name selection was due to the large number of men named Georges. Allowing each to think the town was giving homage to them. Georgetown became a traffic light town with a general store, a gas station, a café, also had a beauty and barbershop. Man established a hotel for color folks passing through. The Georgetown Hotel named in the Green Book for a safe haven for colored travelers. Helping grow the surrounding was many famous colored entertainers staying nights. Folks either traveling south to Biloxi MS or to New Orleans LA. The lively vibrant neighborhood grew into several dozen row houses. First used for migrant worker, later families settled permanently with the Mills expanding and more laborers needed.

Commerce began to pick up in the small town, a Bank and Post Office came, occupying new structures. Elisabeth recognizes that a place of worships needs to be in the community. She starts to pursuit funds for a church building. At the same time a search for an administrative Pastor is seek out. Elisabeth not being shy about expressing herself often would talk famous entertainers into doing charity fundraiser event to benefit the church building fund. She always had a persuasive way to get sympathetic involvement from local or visiting dignitaries. Even request traveling Preachers that are passing through to preach a service before their left town. A temporary pitched tent at the end of town stood with a tall wooden cross, visible for all to see. That was the starting point of Elisabeth church sanctuary initiative. Most women loved the ideal of Sunday service; they would put on their finest attire including hats. The bigger the better soon they became known as Sunday Church Hats. Milliners stay busy in the surrounding area. Men and women alike wore fashionable hats during this period.

For now, living is good for colored folks in Copiah County. Thanks in a great part to the vision of the Freeman family. Studd's Juke Joint enterprise being embezzled from Simpson had come to an end, after his strange disappearance. Colored residence hope's its permanent. Studd actually was able to purchase Simpsons plot of land for back taxes under his Limited Liability Company name. Knowledge is power; and continually improving for social awareness for the colored folks in the area. Schooling is extremely necessary for the community to succeed. A seed's planted for it to flourish; that includes visionaries to build and develop. George and Elisabeth Freeman what a partnership - team. That special relationship goes on and on as the couple now gets ready to discover parenthood God willing. Build to succeed in the future; is their additional motto going forward. It's all relevant, remember the card game robbery. It was successful, after the fact; Jay was informed of the robberies ad-liv action. No one was seriously injured; all the perpetrators got away free and clear. Caucasian in the area, believes only some other whites could come up with such an elaborate plan and execution, after being knocked out with inhalable sedatives.

About The Author

Jerry J. Powell is the third child of Willie and Rosie Powell, the middle child. Having two older brothers and two younger sisters to share with. Blessed to have never been homeless or without a meal to eat. Proud to have been a child raised by two caring, encouraging, and challenging southern parents. Whom often reminds one that anything is possible when having your mind focus on a vision. This requires study and diligently working toward the goal.

Primary education was in the Detroit, Michigan school system, with technological training at Focus: Hope C.A.T, and Lawrence Technical University. Automotive manufacturing management ended after over 25 years of service. Happily, retired and being constructive, trying his hand at using his imaginations to pen words to paper. Hoping that reading this story will be enjoyable to others.

www.ingramcontent.com/pod-product-compliance
Lightning Source LLC
Chambersburg PA
CBHW030517020726
47494CB00004B/1129
9781736638750